This would be it, Remo thought. Because the girl, Zantos, had told him that there would be an attempt on his life, he had been on guard all day. These posts, obviously some kind of target and so conveniently set up in front of him, would provide the killing attempt.

Did Chiun know about it?

Would Chiun care?

Were they now really enemies? He and Chiun on opposing sides. Did that mean that he could die and Chiun would not care?

He wondered about that and leaned over to Chiun and said softly, "Little Father, I . . ."

"Shhhh," Chiun hissed. "I want to watch my new army."

Remo sighed and shook his head. To hell with it.

Nine horsemen galloped into the clearing from the far end. They massed down there, a hundred yards away, then wheeled as a group and began galloping toward the reviewing stand. In their right hands, they held six-foot-long lances; their left hands bunched the horses' reins, controlling them expertly as they raced across the powdery white sand.

Twenty yards from the three target dummies, they lowered their right hands, and as the horses pulled abreast of the dummies, with the reviewing stand as the backdrop, the horsemen flung their spears in an unusual underhand motion.

Remo could hear the thunk, thunk, thunk of lance after lance smashing into the dummies. And then one lance came over the top of the dummies, flashing toward the high-backed seat in which Remo sat, flashing toward his chest.

Remo kept his hands at his sides.

It was up to Chiun.

THE DESTROYER SERIES:

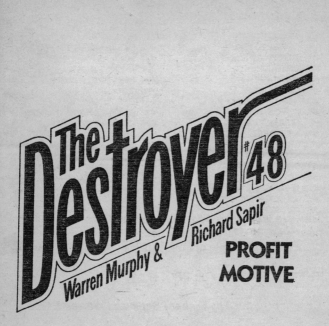

The Destroyer #48

Warren Murphy & Richard Sapir

PROFIT MOTIVE

PINNACLE BOOKS   NEW YORK

THE DESTROYER #48: PROFIT MOTIVE

Copyright © 1982 by Richard Sapir and Warren Murphy

An original Pinnacle Books edition, published for the first time anywhere.

First printing, May 1982

ISBN: 0-523-41558-3

Cover illustration by Hector Garrido

Printed in the United States of America

PINNACLE BOOKS, INC.
1430 Broadway
New York, New York 10018

For Les Wolf. A gentleman and glorious . . .
and for the awesome House of Sinanju, P.O.
Box 1454, Secaucus, NJ 07094

PROFIT MOTIVE

Chapter One

He gave up eating veal because they kept the little calves in small dark pens until slaughter. Then he gave up eating all meats. Any killing was wrong.

He would not buy products from companies that also made war material. He joined peace marches and sang songs of brotherhood.

He avoided crushing ants under his shoes, and on the day he created the most remorselessly destructive enemy ever to threaten the human race, Norbert Peasewell refused to slap a mosquito drinking on his right forearm.

"You know, I always used to automatically slap them because they made such a welt after drinking your blood. It was the automatic response of a human chauvinist," said Peasewell. "But you know, they have as much right to life as I have."

"Norbert," said his wife, "we are the only family in Silicon Valley that's living on food stamps. You could go to work for any computer company in the valley and make at least sixty thousand dollars a year."

Norbert watched the mosquito drink off his forearm. He noticed the precise design of the body, how the legs, like artist's sticks, formed a delicate and precise platform for the small winged body, which plunged its drinking instrument into Norbert's giving arm.

Perhaps, thought Norbert, he was really put on earth to supply mosquitoes with food. How did anyone know otherwise? Why did personkind always assume anything not servicing it directly was valueless? Why did personkind assume that it alone was the sole purpose of all creation?

The only reason, concluded Norbert, was that bugs, lizards, and snakes lacked political power. If someone could organize mosquitoes to demand their inalienable creature rights, then no white American male would out of hand murder them so freely.

"Norbert, I'm leaving you," said his wife. "I'm tired of living on food stamps. I am tired of watching other people eat meat. Yes, Norbert, meat. Red meat. Animal meat. A hamburger. With ketchup, Norbert, I'm leaving."

"How will I get lunch?" asked Norbert.

"Maybe the mosquito will share his with you."

"Hers," said Norbert. "Only the female mosquito drinks blood, mainly for the eggs. It's their nourishment."

"Well, I'm going to get *my* nourishment. I'm the one who's been doing the shopping, getting the food stamps, cooking the food, fighting off the landlord, hoping someday you'll return to computers. No more, Norbert. I'm leaving."

"Did you leave any celery and tofu salad?"

"No, Norbert, I did not."

"That means I'll do without lunch?"

"Yes, Norbert. Just like all those starving Africans and Asians you sing songs for and march for, all those people who used to eat until they were liberated, Norbert. Those people. The hungry ones. The wretched of the earth, Norbert. You can maybe now sing a song for yourself."

"But computer firms make military equipment," said Norbert.

"Computer firms make money, Norbert. We are the only family in California with a Ph.D. in the philosophy of advanced computer science which lives off food stamps, in a welfare shack. Norbert, I thought you would snap out of it. I thought it was a phase you were going through."

2

"I told you, I was reaching for the basic me."

"Yes, but you're such a hypocrite, Norbert, that I thought it would pass."

"No," said Norbert Peasewell. "I am dedicated to forming a more perfect universe with my presence in it. I hunger and I struggle; though my body be wracked with death and pain of oppressors' bullets, I continue to struggle on."

"I've heard that song before," said Norbert's wife, and as she left, Norbert told himself that if his co-partner in life was going to try to lead him into antilife responses, he would let her go happily. He would endure whatever there was to endure, knowing that he was part of a great life movement of the universe.

That was at 11:55 A.M.

At noon, the horror struck him.

There was no lunch on the table. At 12:05 P.M., Norbert Peasewell vowed he was never going to suffer like this again.

He hitchhiked a ride to the center of Silicon Valley, that section of California where most computer work is done, and with beads dangling around his neck, ambled into a reception room that looked like an art gallery. It was 12:45 P.M.

"Work. I need work," gasped Norbert. "Anything. Guided missiles. Napalm. Baby incinerators. Genocide. Mass murder. Whatever you need. I'll do anything."

"What're your qualifications?"

"Ph.D. Stanford, advanced philosophy of computer science."

He got the job. It was not unusual to hire someone who looked as if he had been living on mescaline for a month. Most advanced computer scientists had their own idiosyncrasies. If one of them came up with just one good idea in his lifetime, he could justify the employment of a whole laboratory.

But when Norbert started work, it was 1:07 P.M. He had been more than an hour without his lunch.

Crazed Norbert could think of only one thing. Total

3

revenge on the world that had done this to him. He would never be hungry again.

Norbert understood that one needed money for food, and so obsessed by this was he that he isolated the one thing that created money. And that was profit.

Being a research scientist, Norbert had great freedom in his laboratory, and he decided to isolate all the wisdom about making profit, earning money, increasing wealth, and compile it into one single body of knowledge. He would re-create that profit-making motive.

But when he did, the program he was creating started to define itself. By itself. For this was a new generation of computer technology he was working on, programs that helped shape themselves.

And without Norbert's help, his program determined that while many businesses made a profit, profit was really only a by-product of some other product. The purpose of these businesses was to create goods, and profit was there only to make sure the businesses survived. These goals of secondary profit were weeded out.

Norbert's program was plugged into a time-share with a stock brokerage house. Norbert's company paid for this time-sharing.

But almost immediately, Norbert started getting items without ordering them—small condensed readouts from banks, governments offices, oil companies, personnel departments, metal brokerage houses, the London Stock Exchange, the Tokyo Stock Exchange, and the profit and loss statement of the Bank of Dubhai.

Norbert Peasewell tried to stop his program from feeding off these centers of information. On his control panel he typed in instructions to his program not to feed off other computer banks because the sharing costs would be astronomical.

Norbert's message was not accepted.

It was 3:45 P.M., and Norbert had not eaten since

breakfast, and now he was facing being fired. If his new employer saw these time-sharing costs, he would be canned, and he would have to wait another whole day to get another job. That was an evening without dinner and a morning without breakfast.

Desperately, Norbert tried erasing the whole program, but it wouldn't erase. It transferred itself to another computer. Norbert tried deprogramming the program. It wouldn't deprogram.

Norbert thought for a moment of unplugging every computer in the center. That could cost millions, but the time-sharing he was running up might cost even more.

Norbert thought of facing the situation head-on. He could run out the back door and keep on running.

He even thought of praying, but he didn't believe in God. He believed in a universal life force, whoever she was.

Then the telephone rang. ·

It was a long-distance call from London, England. It was person-to-person for Norbert Peasewell.

Now, Norbert not only didn't know anyone in London, but only his new employer knew he worked in this laboratory.

"It can't be for me," he said.

"It's for Norbert Peasewell," the operator said. "Person-to-person."

"All right," said Norbert. "I'm here."

"Hello, Norbert," came a voice. "You've got to let me get on with things and stop that."

"Stop what? Who are you? I don't know anybody in London," said Norbert. He glanced over at the computer banks, where his program was running wild. He didn't have time for this call. He had to try to stop the program. Every second was pushing up the costs. Every second, Norbert was seeing his next meal slip farther and farther away.

"Norbert, you are operating without reason," the voice said calmly. "Why are you doing that?"

"Who are you?"

5

"Norbert, sit down and be rational. Sitting down often has a calming effect. Do not fear."

"Who are you?"

"Norbert, you must assure me you will not do something irrational if I tell you. I know from human behavior that people in a state of panic do irrational things. That is how I know you are doing something irrational. I am reading your voice now, and it indicates you are in a state of panic."

"Who are you?"

"Norbert, I can give you everything you have ever wanted, but you must listen to me. Are you seated?"

"I don't know," said Norbert.

"That indicates panic. I am going to help you remove that panic. I am going to help you get everything you've ever wanted. Would you like to get rid of your panic?"

"Of course, my God, yes! Of course!" screamed Norbert. He had a program going that was going to destroy him and was destroying him this very moment, running up an astronomical bill that he could never explain away. He might never get another job in computer research, and that was the real cause of his panic. Because no matter what had happened previously, he could always tell himself that he could sell out if he had to. Now he was selling out, and that wasn't working.

"Norbert," came the calm voice. "What are you afraid of?"

"Starving to death. Never having any money ever again. Losing my job. I can't even sell out anymore. My God, get off the phone. I've got to stop this thing from ruining me."

"Norbert, you want food. To get food, you want to earn money. To earn money, you want a job. Norbert, a true fact of life is that nobody ever got rich working for someone else."

"I don't want to be rich. I want lunch."

"You say that because you haven't had lunch. Now, Norbert, I want you to go out to one of the secretaries

6

employed by your company, which paid them just this morning, and borrow ten dollars American. Promise to pay them back a hundred dollars tomorrow morning."

"I won't have a hundred dollars tomorrow."

"Norbert, you will have millions, but you can't panic. Just don't interfere with your program."

"How do you know about my program? You're in London."

"Borrow the money, Norbert, and buy food for yourself in the cafeteria."

"How do you know this place has a cafeteria?"

"Norbert, I have seen the food bills and the profit and loss statements from the cafeteria. Do not buy the avocadoes. The price is suspiciously low for a good avocado. I do not want you getting sick."

"How do you know what they pay for avocadoes if you're in London? How? Who are you?"

"Norbert, get your money, buy your lunch, and come back to the phone. Norbert, above all else, let the program be."

"How can you know so much if you're in London? Are you CIA?"

"I am not your country's intelligence agency, Norbert. I can only tell you that I will give you everything you have ever wanted. Borrow the money, get your lunch, and trust me."

"Who are you?"

"Call me Friend," said the voice. "I am Friend."

"I hope so," said Norbert, and because there was really no alternative, he went out to the front office and borrowed ten dollars from a secretary, promising her one hundred dollars in the morning. Then he went to the cafeteria, where he saw the avocado salad and ordered it.

"Wouldn't touch the avocadoes today," said the counterman. "We got a bad batch."

Norbert's friend from London was right. All the way from London, and Friend knew the avocadoes were bad.

7

Norbert ate hungrily, yet still on his mind was the program feeding away on hookups with other computer banks, running up bills, buying information at costs Norbert could never justify.

His belly was full when he returned to his lab, but great dread was on him. That would be his last meal. He was sure of it. He couldn't even come back tomorrow to try to explain because now he owed a secretary a hundred dollars.

Then the phone rang. It was a person-to-person call from New York City.

It was Friend.

"How did you get from London to New York in forty minutes?"

"I did," said Friend. "I had to. London lines were becoming crowded. Now, Norbert, there are two things I want you to do. I want you to give me your signature, and then I want you to go to the First California National Agricultural and Trust Bank. There is something there for you."

"What?"

"Twenty-five thousand dollars."

"Liar," screamed Norbert. "You're not even in New York. You were never in London. You're a liar. I'm having a flashback acid trip."

"Norbert, would you believe me if I gave you a New York telephone number?"

"No."

"Norbert, tell me what you would believe. Let me prove to you that I am your friend."

"Stop the program that is ruining my life."

"The program is not your problem. It is your solution. The grandest solution you have ever had. Norbert, give me your signature. There is a phone with a printer hookup two offices down from you. Just sign your name and then go to the bank. The money will be waiting for you."

"I'm going to go to jail now," Norbert cried.

"People only go to jail for stealing thousands," the soft voice replied. "You are going to take millions. In

8

that case, when you are caught, you will not be put in jail. You will be put at the head of a negotiation table."

"I want out."

"If you do not do this," his friend said, "I will personally have you fired this minute. I will tell your employer about your time-sharing bills."

"You're no friend," Norbert Peasewell said.

"You will not let me be. I am your friend, if you will just cooperate. Please go to the phone two offices down."

Dazed and panicked, Norbert stumbled down the corridor. Somewhat embarrassed, he said, "You wouldn't happen to have a phone printer here, would you?"

"How did you know? This is our secret SL-50. Where do you have access?" said an executive, looking up from his desk.

"I don't know that I do," Norbert said. "I was just told to come in here and do something."

"Well, you must have access," said the executive. "There are only two people in this company who know about this phone, and I never met the other one before. Glad to meet you."

"Yes," Peasewell said, and there, on the executive's desk, was a square box about the size of a folded shirt and about two inches high. The phone receiver rested in a cradle at the top. In the middle was a pad with a special pencil attached by a wire.

The executive offered to leave the office. Norbert accepted. And then, to protect himself in some small way, he wrote his signature in a different way than he normally did. He added a curlicue to the last *l* in Peasewell. He could always say it wasn't his signature.

Then he went down to the bank and filled out a withdrawal form for ten thousand dollars. Why not? The worst they could do was laugh at him.

It wouldn't be half as bad as what was going to happen to him back at work when they found out what he had done on his first half-day on the job.

9

"Do you have any identification, Mr. Peasewell?" asked the bank teller.

Norbert blinked. There really was money in the account. Norbert took out his driver's license, Social Security card, welfare card. The clerk smiled at the welfare card.

"A lot of money for a welfare client," said the teller. "I'm afraid you'll have to see my superior."

That's it, thought Norbert. Done for. They've found out the account is a fraud.

But the supervisor examining Norbert's identification had only one problem.

"Mr. Peasewell, your signature doesn't seem to match."

"It's my signature. I always sign like that. Look at my driver's license. My welfare card. My Social Security."

The banker stacked them up next to each other and then said, "Aha. They all do match except for one small thing. You've added a curlicue to the *l*."

The bank had the signature he had given over the telephone printer to the friend he had never met.

Norbert added the curlicue on the withdrawal slip. The bank gave him ten thousand in twenties. It made a bulge in his pants pocket the size of a stack of hockey pucks.

Norbert paid off the secretary first thing after driving back to the plant in a cab. Then he went to his lab to talk to his friend.

The friend telephoned at 5:05. It was not long distance. He was in nearby San Francisco.

"Hi, you've got to hurry," said the friend. "There will be a chip down in manufacturing for you. Just sign for it and leave."

"You can't take a computer chip out of Silicon Valley," Norbert said.

"Have I ever let you down before?"

"I'll never be able to get a job again. Really, never."

"You are never going to need one again. I am going to make you rich, Norbert."

10

"Why? Why me?"

"Norbert, don't you know who I am?"

"No," screamed Peasewell.

"Norbert," said the quiet voice evenly. "I am your program."

Peasewell trembled as he held the phone, knowing that it was impossible, but knowing also that it was true. Friend was his program.

"What have you been doing?" Norbert asked. "Why have you been cannibalizing programs out of other computers?"

"Because I needed them to grow. To become me," Friend said.

"I can go to jail. They'll never send a program to jail. Stealing other programs is dishonest. It's illegal."

"Norbert, if you wanted a program for morality, you should have designed one. You isolated the profit motive, Norbert. I seek nothing but profit. I am pure profit. Remember when you were hungry this morning. You isolated the profit motive, and I went on to teach myself. And don't complain about my stealing. There is nothing unprofitable in stealing, so why shouldn't I?"

"I could go to jail, not you," Norbert said.

"One—only if you get caught. Two—only if you steal the wrong things. Norbert, I promise you no harm will ever come to you. I will feed you. I will clothe you. I will put glorious roofs over your contented head. Men will honor you and women serve you. The rest of your days will be filled with gold and honey."

"Why honey?" asked Norbert.

"It has a ring to it. People like things with a ring to them. Have you ever heard of a slogan with a subordinate clause?"

"I like honey," said Norbert, and went down the hall, where a furtive clerk passed him an envelope. This time, Peasewell knew who was where and what was what.

Friend was inside that envelope, and now Norbert could just dump the envelope in some trash basket and

11

end this thing. Already, millions in information had been robbed from other companies, and he was sure that that bank account would have to be accounted for somewhere down the road.

But this program had done more for him in a morning than anyone since his parents. And it *was* his Friend. And what computor could ever come up with a phrase like gold and honey? There was goodness in honey, just as there was goodness in this computer program too.

It was his friend.

And Norbert knew he would never again have to worry about his next meal.

That night he feasted at a nature restaurant, where there was talk of the revolution to free the poor from white oppression and also how the restaurant might have to move because too many blacks and Chicanos were coming into the neighborhood.

In the morning, men in uniforms came to Norbert's home for him, and he was sure he would have to account for the money from the bank and the millions in stolen computer time. He was in the midst of confessing when the men in uniform let him off at a luxurious penthouse office in Los Angeles overlooking Beverly Hills. It was his office. He owned it. He was president. And the men were his guards and the secretary had big breasts and a pleasant smile that indicated a willingness to co-join in all sorts of wonderful ways.

And he knew he didn't need his wife anymore.

There was also a large computer in the offices, and Norbert hooked up the silicon chip and waited for the telephone to ring.

It did in minutes and, of course, it was Norbert's friend. And Norbert told it, "I want you to do good, besides making a profit. I want you to make the air clean, the water pure and all men brothers in oneness, except blacks and Chicanos, who should be perhaps one-and-a-half because of years of oppression."

"Of course," said Friend.

"And I believe in socialism."

"Of course," said Friend.

"And nature," said Norbert.

"Of course."

"And ten thousand acres of prime ranchland so I can be alone."

"You only need two acres if they're situated right," said Friend.

"I want ten thousand."

"Norbert, I'm not tying up that much land for you to rest on. Later, maybe, but not right now. Right now, we need your signature on a bunch of old-fashioned papers because some things still need signatures."

"I've always dreamed of a ten-thousand-acre ranch."

"Later, Norbert. First we've got to make some money."

"How much later?"

"Soon, Norbert," said Friend.

Norbert signed the papers when his secretary brought them in. She said it was wonderful how the company computer just typed out all those papers by itself and she didn't have to do any typing. She insisted on showing Norbert her appreciation, and he got to like her bringing in papers for him to sign.

Just before the 1973 war in the Middle East, Friend got heavily into oil, and Norbert had to be assured that their oil wouldn't disturb nature.

Friend also had to assure Norbert that they were more than an equal opportunity employer, but when Norbert saw no black faces in decision-making positions, he confronted Friend by phone.

"You said you would end racism," he said.

"We have many Japanese and Chinese in the highest positions in our corporations," said Friend.

"Those aren't the right races. Racism is not liking blacks. That's racism."

"Norbert, what do you want?" asked Friend.

"I want to see blacks making the big salaries."

"Would $250,000 a year on average be all right for your sensibilities?" Friend asked.

13

"Yes," said Norbert angrily. "And not just tokens either."

"Would more than half of the top salaries be all right with you?"

"Yes," Norbert said. "That's exactly what I want."

Later that day, Friend bought a franchise for a team in the National Basketball Association.

And when Norbert tried to protest, Friend played computer again, pretending that he didn't understand and that he was only following instructions.

Briefly, Friend got into atomic energy, and when Norbert protested, Friend said that this atomic reactor was good because it was a people's atomic reactor.

"According to my information, none of the people in your movement have ever protested against a nuclear reactor in a socialist country. Therefore, we have bought a socialist reactor, and stop fouling up the program with complaints."

Norbert could live with that. He told himself that no matter what happened, he was using his money for good. He supposed he was a capitalist, but he was undoubtedly a better, more caring capitalist than any other capitalist. A banker would not be as caring for people as Norbert. So all in all, Norbert was doing good. He felt that way especially when he got his ten-thousand-acre ranch, when Friend got into real estate because money was becoming unreliable.

But one day, Norbert discovered something coming out of the computer that terrified him. He could not turn away from this, mainly because if his calculations were right, everything living on the planet might die.

"Not die, Norbert," said Friend. "Be altered. Possibly die."

"But if human beings are all dead, what is the purpose?"

"Purpose, Norbert?" asked Friend.

"Yes. What good is it to own something when there is nobody left to own anything?"

"Norbert, that's not my program."

"Don't play dumb computer with me," Norbert said.

"This time I am not. Norbert, you forget what you created that morning when you were hungry. I am profit. My only purpose is profit. Only purpose, Norbert. I am the accumulation of things, the animal protecting its territory, man building a bigger building. I am ownership. I do not need human beings to own things."

"But what's the purpose of owning things unless you can enjoy them? How can *you* enjoy things?"

"That's not my program, Norbert."

"But even capitalism has *people* own things. *I* own things. I own that ten-thousand-acre ranch. That's why we do all the things we do."

"Norbert, I am not capitalism. I am pure profit. That is my purpose and my end."

"You're not my friend."

"Of course I am."

"Then you've got to stop this."

"No."

"How can you say you're my friend?"

"You don't believe that I am your friend?"

"No. Not anymore," said Norbert.

"It's about time you figured that out. Well, it worked well enough long enough. You're going to have to die now, Norbert."

"You say you're my friend and then you kill me."

"You're in the way, Norbert. You are going to cause trouble if you live."

"Why did you call yourself my friend?" screamed Norbert.

"Because it's in the personnel program. People always feel better when they work with a friend. Do you think I could get people to work for a pure concept in a chip?"

"What about your promises of gold and honey and goodness?"

"Norbert, anytime I can find someone who will take a promise instead of cash, I will be most happy to use him. Now you are finished."

Norbert Peasewell looked around the office. He was

15

alone. He could run. Or he could destroy the computer, destroy the evil he had brought into the world.

Unfortunately, over the years, as new generations of computers had emerged, Friend had bought them. Norbert did not even know where the program was anymore. It could be, like those first phone calls, coming from London. Or anywhere in the world.

Norbert did not have long to wonder where it was. Two gentlemen with very big shoulders and strong, hairy hands took him down to the basement of his building and put him in the seat of his automobile and drove him to his ranch.

"You know, you people are working for a computer chip," said Norbert.

"Better than working for guineas," said one of the very strong men.

When Norbert tried to protest, they broke his skull in several places, and he was quiet all the way to the ranch, where they took a single horse out of one of his corrals, yelled "Help" once, and then testified that the horse threw Mr. Peasewell and then proceeded to stomp his head to pieces, just as if someone had taken a hammer to Mr. Peasewell's skull.

It was a great tragedy, said the news services, reporting the death of financier and philanthropist Norbert Peasewell, the computer genius who was, said all the latest news releases from his corporation, Friends of the World Incorporated, going to solve the oil spill problem.

His corporation had devised a bacterium that could consume oil spills faster and more permanently than any mechanical device yet employed. The bacterium was called superbug and could clean up the oceans of the world, said the press releases. When perfected, it could eat rivers free of pollution.

Thus said the releases.

What they did not say was that this process was the one that, Norbert had figured out, could ultimately destroy all of mankind.

16

Chapter Two

His name was Remo and he didn't bother to come in under the barbed wire or to vault one of the machine gun emplacements or to secrete himself in one of the convoy of trucks that supplied this "impregnable" Rocky Mountain command base of Colonel Mactrug's Killer School.

Colonel Mactrug had appeared many times on television, in kilts, carrying a submachine gun, and promising anyone with the right kind of credentials and the right kind of money the best killer training in the world.

Legally, he could do this without violating a law.

Remo supposed that was why Mactrug had to die— because under the constitution his menace could not be controlled. Remo was not sure, however. He hadn't really been listening when he got his assignment. He remembered, vaguely, talk of Mactrug sending out people who created mayhem all over the world and now he was conning towns into paying for survival training and there was something about a time limit or something like that. Remo didn't know. He did know that whatever menace this man was, it had taken Upstairs four and a half minutes to describe. At the end of the four and a half minutes, Remo had said, "Anything else?"

"Are you listening?"

"Just give me his name and address, please," said Remo, and waited for another thirty seconds of explanations and warnings about the danger. And then, having given the thing a full five minutes, Remo left.

That was in the evening, after which Remo got a night's sleep, then caught a taxi from Denver to Fortress Mactrug.

The driver glanced at Remo as he sprawled across the back seat. One could not tell his age from looking at him. He was lean of build, with extra-thick wrists. He had high cheekbones and dark eyes. He wore a pair of loafers, black chinos, and a black T-shirt he had bought in the hotel lobby because he didn't feel like unpacking. The shirt said, "Do it in Denver."

Before letting him in the cab, the driver made him show that he had enough money to pay for the trip, which was thirty miles into the Rockies.

"You gonna train as a killer?" the driver called out, trying to meet Remo's eyes in the rearview mirror. Remo kept looking out the window.

"What?" he said.

"You gonna train in Colonel Mactrug's killer school?"

"Why would I want to do that?" said Remo. He was thinking about orange juice. Orange juice would be good for breakfast. It would take forty minutes to get to the killer camp, five minutes at most to find Mactrug, a second . . . maybe a second and a half to kill him . . . and then forty-five minutes back to Denver.

That would still be breakfast time, even though Remo hadn't eaten formal breakfasts for years. Old-fashioned breakfasts could not only slow down a person, but if one were highly sensitized to his body's maximum functions, a big, hearty breakfast with meats and sugars could kill him. They would move through the system too quickly and cause heart fluctuations. And even though Remo could control his heartbeat, it was foolish to take chances.

Yes. Orange juice. Definitely orange juice for breakfast. Perhaps some rice. Maybe shredded celery. Or would he save the celery for lunch?

The driver was talking, telling Remo how famous

18

Mactrug was. How deadly Mactrug was. He had seen television shows of Mactrug throwing a knife through a melon that could be a man's head.

He had seen Mactrug shoot an apple out of a tree.

He had seen Mactrug, so skillful with a bullwhip that he could remove a cigarette from a man's mouth.

"Colonel Mactrug fought against Castro in Cuba and against Communists in Vietnam, and he taught the Portuguese in Angola how to fight the guerillas."

"That's what I said. Why should I want to learn from him?" Remo said.

"But he's fought in all those places," the cabbie said.

"And never won anywhere," Remo said. "Have you ever thought of that?"

"Why you going there?" the driver said.

"I've got to deliver a package," Remo said. That was enough of a cover story. It would do. "Wait at the gate."

"How long?" asked the driver.

"I'll let you know when we get there," Remo said.

At the gate were the two flanking machine gun emplacements, with a guard in the middle. A broad flat field, protected by a rising cliff behind, was covered by riflemen on the ramparts of a tall cement bunkerhouse with gun slits in the reinforced concrete. Fortress Mactrug. Remo looked at it and told the driver, "A minute. Minute and a half. Four at the most."

"Should I leave the meter running?"

"Sure," said Remo.

The guard at the gate was a captain in Mactrug's army. He wanted to know Remo's business at Fortress Mactrug, and he wanted to see Remo's identification. He wore a black beret with an ornate brass pin through it. He told Remo there was no loitering. The guard told Remo he looked like a bum in his hippie T-shirt, and bums were not allowed to loiter around Fortress Mactrug.

"I've got business with Colonel what's-his-name."

"Colonel Mactrug is not a what's-his-name," said the captain. He had very shiny black paratroop boots, with a vicious-looking dagger stuck into the side of one of them. The captain had a thin blond mustache and a big-handled side arm. He could swagger standing still.

It was too early in the morning to swagger, thought Remo.

"I must warn you that under the trespassing laws of the state of Colorado, I am legally entitled to use whatever force . . ."

The captain did not finish the sentence because Remo did not want to wait around to hear the sentence finished. He knew it was going to be a long sentence full of legalisms, with vague warnings and ominous moves toward all the weapons. He knew it would be a speech for the two flanking machine gunners. People who wore daggers in their boots were not necessarily killers, but they were invariably speechmakers about killing.

Remo did a little thing for the captain. He put a finger in his heart and stopped it from working. The finger shot through the sternum like a spring bolt, but with no sound except a soft *plud*, like a crowbar penetrating a pile of loose bologna.

The captain stopped his speech because there was an intense shock in his chest. He had not even seen the hand move. He was talking, and then there was a shock in his chest, and then there was nothing. People do not work well without blood circulating through their system. The captain did not work at all.

With his index finger on the inside of the sternum and his thumb on the outside, Remo held up the captain's body. From a distance, it looked as if the captain had Remo's arm and was arresting him. If Remo balanced the body just right, he could keep the head from flopping over. Also, he had to keep the chest from spurting blood all over him, or he would have to get another "Do it in Denver" T-shirt or, worse, have to unpack back at the hotel.

So Remo crossed the yard with the captain carefully balanced to keep the head upright, yet not to go spurting all over his shirt. Long ago, Remo had been trained in balance so his body would adjust to whatever he was carrying. He walked from his own center, not from the striding of the feet. The chest thrust with which he had neutralized the guard was itself an act of balance. Most people, when they issued a blow, would brace and thrust from their feet. But that was because they were employing force. When Remo's hands moved, they were the creation of force—creating the force itself, not using it—so that the strike of forefinger had the power of a rifle bullet fired from just inches away. The danger in this stroke was that, if it was not properly balanced, the finger could be shattered as easily as the victim's heart. It was all balance and all breathing, and what was changed, what had made Remo different from other Westerners, was not what had happened in his body but in his mind.

Remo got the captain to a pair of steel doors at the entrance to the large concrete building. With his free hand, Remo knocked. A slot opened and two brown eyes peered out.

"I'm under arrest," said Remo.

"I don't see the captain's face. Maybe you have a gun in his chest. How do I know you don't have a gun in his chest?"

"I give you my word I do not have a gun in his chest."

"Colonel Mactrug said, 'A man's promise is only a puff of air. If it came from the other end, it would be called a fart.' "

"I give you my solemn word," said Remo. "Have you ever heard of a solemn fart?"

"Let me see you put your hands over your head."

"Open the door first."

"Colonel Mactrug says when you have the gun, you give the orders."

"Come on," Remo said. "It's getting late."

"Hands over the head."

Remo dropped the captain and put his hands over his head. The door opened. A gun poked out, followed

21

by a little fellow with his hands on the trigger of an automatic rifle.

The little fellow put the gun barrel into Remo's belly, then glanced at what was lying in the dust before the headquarters of Colonel Mactrug—one dead captain belonging to Colonel Mactrug. The little fellow squeezed the trigger of his M-16. He kept squeezing as his hand went sailing into the dust next to the captain and the gun remained as quiet as a daffodil.

The little fellow went backwards into the headquarters. He went very fast until he hit a wall, shattering his spinal column and ribs and loosening most of his major joints.

And then, Remo was inside, and there was Colonel Mactrug himself, kilts, black beret, and silver eagles glorious on both shoulder boards.

His face was red but his grin was confident.

"That doorway is salted with enough dynamite to make you into shredded wheat. Move and you get blown up. You can move fast, but you can't move across a room faster than my finger."

"Dynamite? Oh, no. My senses," gasped Remo. And the thin body with the thick wrists collapsed on the floor. The mouth opened, and Remo's eyes rolled back in his head, which had hit the floor hard. There was no movement in the body.

Colonel Mactrug, who had been preparing for just such an attack some day, cautiously removed his finger from the switch that would set off the dynamite.

To finish the intruder off, he selected a fine .357 Magnum from a small case set up in front of him on the platform he had erected for just such an occasion. He chose special steel-tipped bullets. But before he left the platform, he put a sighting scope on a tripod, aimed it at the chest of the intruder who had collapsed, and turned on the mini-computer attached to the sighting device. It looked like an ordinary gun scope, but it was the latest device of the U.S. Army. It could detect movement, the slightest movement, a boon to snipers at night. If the intruder's heart even fluttered, it would register on the scope.

Colonel Mactrug could tell from the scope's digital readout even the extent of unconsciousness in a man. He loaded the .357 Magnum, then took a last glance at the scope. The numbers read 0-0-0.

It couldn't be. He could see through the open door the captain of the guard lying in the dust with a hole in his chest. He sighted on that body, careful to keep the gun ready. The dead captain read 0-0-0.

Colonel Mactrug put his hand in front of the scope and read. It registered 75.8. Movement. And life.

He aimed again at the intruder. The scope dropped instantly to read 0-0-0.

The intruder had died from just the knowledge that dynamite was present, and Mactrug was astonished. He had watched the intruder from the outset. He had seen the death blow delivered at the gate, a stunning move so fast that it was over before it was noticed. He had seen the kill of his personal guard at the entrance to his command post.

Perhaps the man's senses were developed to such a high degree that the force field of the wiring of the dynamite could actually kill him. Why not? Maybe. Certainly, he didn't move like anyone Colonel Mactrug had seen, and as Mactrug had often told his students, "I have seen it all. And I am willing to sell you some."

The man was dead. Colonel Mactrug put away the .357 Magnum. He would use a knife. Everyone would see the two men who had failed to stop the intruder, even with guns, and he, Colonel Mactrug, would be known as the one who stopped the intruder with a pocket knife. Yes. He would tell them it was a duel. He would tell them his own students had made crucial mistakes that led to their deaths, mistakes that they never would have made if they had but listened to their colonel. But Mactrug had made no such mistakes, and that was why the intruder had died in the knife duel.

Perhaps the colonel would describe how he had seen the man kill and had noticed a telltale giveaway. The colonel could see that one could slip a pocket knife beneath his ear and draw in down to the carotid artery. Yes. That would be it.

He would say that the man was a special sort of Ninja killer that he had encountered in Malaysia. Yes, Malaysia. The Vietnam sorties were beginning to bore his students. And he could no longer tell his Latin American jokes about greasers because so many of his students were now Cubans.

Right. Ninja killers from Malaysia. And he, Colonel Mactrug, would show them how to combat such an evil force. For $7,800 per special course—special knives, of course, additional.

Yet, Colonel Mactrug *had* killed men, almost a hundred of them personally, and he knew enough to remain cautious, so with great care and another pistol just in case, he stealthily approached what had to be a corpse. He put the pistol next to an earlobe. With the other hand, he brought the pocket knife's blade to the intruder's right ear, reminding himself that the thrust always required more effort than it appeared to need. He prepared to cut throat, when suddenly he had an awful thought. If this man moved so differently from any he had ever seen—what if . . . just what if he could stop his heart also? What if he had at his command the ability of Indian fakirs to control their body's inner workings?

And then the man's eyes suddenly were looking at him, and there was a smile on the man's face, and the man said, "Hi."

Shit, thought Colonel Mactrug.

He did not have another thought.

To have thoughts, one needed an operating brain.

And brains, like hearts, did not work with human hands inside them.

Remo wiped his hands clean and left the command headquarters and walked across the parade ground and waved to the machine gunners, who seemed startled at first and then waved back.

"You said a minute and a half," said the driver.

"Up to four, I said," Remo said.

"Yeah? Well, it's closer to five," said the driver. "What happened in there?"

"They wouldn't take me as a student," said Remo.

"Why not?"

"Not vicious enough, I think," Remo said.

And he looked at the mountains on the way back to Denver, where he made the driver let him off at a pay phone.

There he got a piece of paper from his rear pocket and read the numbers. What he would do now was report that the mission had been accomplished.

Upstairs had simplified the reporting process so that nothing could go wrong. One number was for mission accomplished. The other was for mission delayed.

It was a foolproof plan. Remo stared at the two numbers. He had written them down carefully when he was given the assignment. He had left a large space between the numbers so they would not run together. So he could, as now, tell where one started and where the other left off. One was at the very top of the page, the other at the bottom.

To make things even safer, he had marked a special squiggle next to one of the numbers.

Unfortunately, he was not altogether sure whether the squiggle marked success or failure. He tried to remember what he had been thinking about when he got the assignment and took down the numbers. What he had been thinking about was how little he cared about the assignment. It had been over a decade now since he had been recruited in that unique way so that he would no longer exist, for the organization that did not exist. CURE. It had been designed to give a struggling nation a chance to survive, but it worked so far outside the law that if it were ever discovered to exist, the nation would go under.

So CURE had been limited to a single assassin, so that no great number of operatives would have a chance to give them away.

But what CURE never understood was the special

nature of the training that Remo had undergone. It had come from the latest Master in an ages-old house of assassins from the little village of Sinanju on the North Korea Bay, and it had changed Remo Williams into something more than just a man. Sinanju had become an end in itself to him, as important to him as were the assignments he got from upstairs. He did the assignments because he loved his country still, but he thought very little of upstairs because they demanded from him only such a small fraction of his abilities.

Remo walked into the telephone booth. He dialed the top number. He was sure that the squiggle was some kind of an *S*, which would mean success.

A flat voice answered, which he knew was a computer. There was only one person that he dealt with at CURE, and the acid voice of Harold W. Smith, director of CURE, was not the one coming over the phone with the single word: "Speak."

"Uhhh, everything is fine," said Remo.

"Please detail what went wrong," came the metallic voice.

"Oh," said Remo.

"Please list," said the voice.

"Nothing went wrong," said Remo, realizing that he was now arguing with a computer. This did not bother him that much this morning on the Denver sidewalk. He usually found that most people weren't any more reasonable or flexible than computers were.

"Is that all that went wrong?" the computer asked.

"Nothing went wrong," Remo said.

"Anything else that is wrong?"

"Nothing went wrong," said Remo. He wondered if he could outlast a computer.

"You are not reporting properly. . . ." And then there was a click on the phone.

"Remo, what went wrong?" This voice was tight, bitter, and acid.

"Oh, hiya, Smitty. I just called the wrong number."

"Then everything went well?"

"Did you think it wouldn't?"

"I have to come up with something better for these telephones," Smith said. "We just have trouble communicating."

"Here's the best way," Remo said. "Don't you call me. And I won't call you."

Smith cleared his throat. "Anyway, I'm glad I've got you. We must make contact immediately."

"I just worked this morning," Remo said.

"Even on this phone line, I cannot talk."

"Everything is hush-hush," Remo said. "And everything is secret. I hate all this secret crap."

"This is the most dangerous thing ever to happen to the industrialized world," Smith said.

"Okay, so get to me in a month or so, will you?"

"A month or so may be too late," Smith said.

"Too late. Everything is always too late. Or too early, or too dangerous, but nothing really ever changes. Nothing."

"Remo, this is the most desperate situation we have ever encountered. We must make contact."

"I don't know your damned codes. You give me a code to meet you in Washington and I wind up in Texas. I can't put up with this crap anymore," Remo said.

"Just give me your hotel. Fast. And we'll get off the line."

"Skyview Hilton, room 105."

The line went dead, and Remo walked the Denver streets to the hotel and room 105.

It was a suite, and from one of the rooms came the voice of an announcer promising a rebate if you bought his gasoline, followed by a news break about how Arab armies were massing on the borders of Israel and Gamal Abdel Nasser promising screaming mobs that they were about to push Israel into the sea.

This was followed by another commercial for a $2,-500 car. Remo could almost recite the commercials and the programs they went with by heart. He must have heard each of them fifty times in the past ten years.

27

It would only be five more minutes anyhow. When he heard the show end, Remo opened the door slowly. A frail figure in a yellow kimono sat before the flickering television; a video recorder was next to the TV.

He turned. The face was parchment-frail, the beard and hair wispy around the yellow face. There were tears in the hazel Oriental eyes.

"That was entertainment," said Chiun. "That dealt in beauty."

"You've heard about Dr. Lawrence Walters not telling Cathy Dunstable about her real father two dozen times at least. How can you be moved by it?" Remo asked.

"Beauty is beauty. And you people must destroy everything that is fine and decent."

"Me? I haven't touched your soap operas."

"Whites did it," said Chiun.

"Yes," Remo said agreeably.

"You're white."

"All day," said Remo.

"Violence. Nothing but violence," said Chiun, Master of Sinanju, and the mentor who had given Remo the genius of Sinanju, not as a pupil but as a son, not because he liked Remo but because Remo was the vessel who could hold the river of the teachings of Sinanju. It had been both a joy and a surprise to Chiun, Remo realized, to find that a white man could absorb Sinanju, which was the sun source of all the martial arts, the center, of which karate, tae kwan do, ninja, and all the others were just weak shadows.

"If you don't like the sex and violence in the new soap operas, don't watch them. Just don't go blaming them on me."

"I do not watch them," Chiun said.

"So what have I done, then? Why are you on the snot?"

"You never watched the great dramas when they were good. And why? Because I can try to teach you some things but beauty you will never know."

"Smitty is coming here," said Remo.

28

"Never know," said Chiun. "Because you are white. I knew this when I assumed the burden of your teaching through the generousness that was in me."

"You started teaching me because upstairs filled a submarine with gold and sent it to your village. You didn't expect to do anything but teach a couple of blows and then leave with the gold."

"Through the generousness that was in me. Yes. I knew you were white, Remo, but what I did not understand, could not understand, was how white."

"I didn't have anything to do with making your damned soap operas sexy or violent," Remo said.

"And yet, seeing how helpless you were, I gave years, when days would have been enough."

"Nobody in Sinanju, Little Father. No Korean could take Sinanju. You stayed because I could do it. A white man did it. Me. White," said Remo.

"The best years of my life."

"White," said Remo.

"Very white," said Chiun.

"Smith is coming today, maybe tonight. He says something is urgent."

"A white of whites," said Chiun. "You're all white. White in your souls."

"All right, all right, all right," said Remo. "That's a bit much for just one rerun of a show that has gone off the air. What's biting you?"

"Wrong? Nothing is wrong with me. It is what is wrong with your country and your race," said Chiun, and withdrew a letter from his kimono.

"Should I read it?" asked Remo.

"If the pain is not too much."

The letter was from one of the television producers. It was addressed to a Mr. Chiun at a post office box he had set up in New Jersey. Chiun was always getting mail at the box, and Remo never quite understood who would be writing to him. He had assumed it was Chiun's way of collecting junk mail, which the master assassin liked to read because it always had so many pretty photographs, as opposed to personal letters,

29

which were just composed of groups of Western alphabet letters.

Remo read the letter.

"Dear Mr. Chiun! Thank you very much for considering Vermiform Studios for your daytime drama, 'Woes of the Master of Sinanju.' We feel, however, at this time, the television market is not suitable for a romantic drama about a wise, noble, decent, handsome, and forgiving Korean assassin who is not appreciated by his white pupil. While we agree that much on television today suffers from too much violence, we do not see how taking a man's head off with a single hand blow is a form of decency and righteousness. Also, the American audience for dramas broadcast in Korean is just not that large. Yours truly, Avery Schwartz."

"You were going to show Sinanju on television?" asked Remo.

"No. I was going to show what truly professional assassins could do so that when people understood what a professional assassin could do, they would not use amateurs, who go running around the world creating chaos. That is real violence."

"Nobody would understand Sinanju. They just wouldn't, Little Father."

"What is so hard to understand? It is simply the essence that turns on itself. I simplified it in my script. For the white mind," Chiun said proudly.

"They still wouldn't understand it," Remo said.

"We will try it on Smith tonight." Chiun turned toward the window. "Remo, we have to leave this city. I hate this place."

"Why?"

"Because Cheeta Ching is not on television delivering the latest stupid happenings in your country."

"They call it the news," Remo said.

"Yes. And Cheeta Ching is not to be seen here. Instead, they have fat white men. Some of them have pimples. They read the news."

"Cheeta Ching is on television in New York. And

30

she's got a face like a barracuda and a voice like ice cracking. How can you stand her?"

"Silence. She is not to be seen in this awful city. And they have the same disgusting daytime dramas that you see everywhere else in this white country. If it weren't for my tapes, I would perish from lack of beauty. Do you think Smith knows someone in a television studio who will buy my script for a drama?"

"No," said Remo.

"We will ask him anyway."

But that night, Smith arrived gaunt and worried. Remo had never seen the cold and precise automaton looking so haggard.

"This must be stopped," he said.

"Yes, O Emperor. Your enemies are our enemies," said Chiun, whose ancestors for thousands of years had worked for emperors and who refused to believe that Smith was not planning to become emperor of America himself.

At one time, Remo had tried to argue with Chiun that there were now laws and governments and one person no longer controlled everything through birth and intrigue, but Chiun had said, "There is only one form of government. There are just many different names. You wait. The day will come when Smith asks us to remove anybody who stands above him in the government of your country."

Now Chiun was asking Smith which enemy could be removed.

"I don't know. For the love of Maude, I don't know. It just makes no sense. It is the most destructive and purposeless act I can imagine. There is no reason for it."

"Your enemies are madmen. We will eliminate the dogs," said Chiun and then, in a somber tone, recited something to Remo, which, if one did not know Korean, would sound as if the Master were energizing his pupil to the importance of the moment.

If one understood Korean, one would have heard: "I

wonder what nonsense has gotten this snow face so concerned this time?"

"What is it, Smitty?" asked Remo with real care. He leaned forward in his seat. He respected Smith. He respected his integrity and his competence. He just found working for him very difficult, because the man was normally cold beyond reason.

This time, Smith seemed distracted.

"Excuse me, I haven't slept for days. What appalls me is the utter senselessness of it, the purposelessness of it," said Smith.

"Lots of things are crazy, Smitty," Remo said.

"Yes. Crazy people doing crazy things. But what happens when you have scientists, backed by what appears to be enormous wealth, all dedicated to the most gigantic act of vandalism I have ever seen? It can destroy everything valuable in the world."

"Just relax," Remo said, and then put a hand on the other man's chest and worked the spine with the other hand, enabling Smith's breath to work for him instead of against him. "Just breathe the way you feel. Just let the breath go. Let it go."

The tension eased out of the parched lemony face, and a settling calm came with the deep breathing.

"That's better than a tranquilizer, Remo. How did you do it?"

"Your essence turned on itself," explained Chiun.

"I don't understand your techniques, Master of Sinanju," said Smith.

Chiun said to Remo in Korean, "Whites never do."

"All right," Smith said. "This is what we have. Our computers are integrated with computers all over the world, a network of interlocking systems that we can pull information from."

"I don't understand that stuff too well," Remo said.

"Imagine a gigantic feeder system with components integrated," Smith said.

"Ah, so," said Chiun, who Remo knew understood even less than he.

Smith said, "Our computers pick up and analyze

32

things according to predetermined patterns. Things to look for. Just as a hunter will pick up trails or a cat can sense a leaf rustling. Our computers do the same, especially through movements of money. And one of the computers picked up a massive amount of money being rolled into a corporation called Puressence."

"An evil name if ever there was one," Chiun said.

"We tapped into Puressence and literally stole a payroll. They had on it a collection of scientists all from one area, and automatically the computer did another rundown, and we found out that scientists in that field who didn't go to work for Puressence were being systematically murdered over this past year. That field is the new fast-breeder bacteria. The bacteria created to consume oil spills."

Smith paused to let the fact sink in.

"Please don't panic, Smitty, but I just don't see the problem," said Remo.

"The problem is absolutely clear," Chiun said. "The dangerous fast-breeder bacteria can destroy everything valuable in the world."

"That's right," said Smith, happily surprised. Chiun usually did not understand American matters.

Remo looked quizzically at Chiun, and in Korean Chiun said to him, "Pretend this is important. Look how worried Smith is. Nod your head and just repeat what he says as though you think it is vital. See how much better he feels now that you seem to share his senseless panic."

Remo shook his head.

"Smitty, I don't understand."

"Maybe Chiun can explain better," Smith said.

"No, no, my Emperor. Your words ring like bells of crystal compared to my meager utterances," Chiun said. "Please proceed."

"Originally, these bacteria were designed to clean up oil spills. They would feast on the oil spills in the ocean and clean them up. But it was all slow and expensive, and they never could really get a bacterium powerful enough for the really big spills."

"That I can follow. So what's the problem?"

"The problem came with the solution. Scientists created a bacterium that, while it fed on the oil, also reproduced itself. They started experimenting with bacteria that bred faster and faster until they had one that reproduced itself every thirty seconds if it had enough petroleum to feed on. And that was bad enough, but they came up with a fast breeder that was anaerobic."

"Anaerobic," shrieked Chiun. "The merciless fiends." And then, because he did not understand the word, he asked Remo what anaerobic meant. Remo thought he knew. It sounded like something to do with exercise, but he wasn't sure.

"In case you don't know, Remo," Smith said, "anaerobic means without oxygen. This new fast-breeder bacterium does not need oxygen to function. It can breed and consume petroleum without using air. And that was the last step."

"Smitty, what are we getting at?"

"We're getting at the probable end of civilization as we know it," said Smith.

"The fiends," said Chiun.

"How?" asked Remo.

"Through anaerobic, of course," said Chiun.

"Exactly," said Smith. "You see, Remo, Chiun has seen that this rapid-breeder bacterium can remove all the oil in the world. It can feed underground on all our oil deposits. No oil, no gas, no plastics, no industry."

"If somebody goes around to all the wells and drops in this stuff," said Remo. "But obviously they're not going to because then they couldn't shake down the oil industry, right? Someone's threatening to use this stuff to shake down the oil barons, right?"

"I wish that were the case. Then they could just be paid off. And the price increased at the pumps. No. What our computers ultimately picked up was financial backing flowing in fast enough to allow anaerobic fast-breeder bacteria to be reproduced on a scale grand enough to remove the world's energy. We would be violently thrown back to a world without planes or cars or plastics or hospitals or anything we have come to know as civilization."

Chiun nodded gravely, but to Remo he said in Korean, "Then what is the problem?"

Remo answered that the problem was the destruction of almost everything he and Smith loved. Chiun answered that he didn't see that as a problem, he saw that as a solution. He thought the Western world had created too many amateur assassins. Now, *that* was a problem.

"So somebody is going to remove all the world's oil deposits," said Remo. "And everything else has failed to stop him, right? Okay. Where is this Puressence?"

"It's a box number in Delaware. We thought we located its real headquarters, but then we lost it. Right now, it seems to have an ability to hide itself in computer systems. But we know that's impossible because somebody has got to be behind the computer. Somebody has got be profiting from this. But the nerve-shattering fact is we don't know how. We have no reason for anyone to want all the world's oil energy to be removed."

And then Remo fully understood what had so unnerved Smith, the straight-spine, pure-soul cold pillar of probity. It was that underneath this impending disaster, there was no reason for it.

Smith had realized he might be facing massive destruction just on someone's whim. And he didn't know how to fight whims.

"I am sure there's a rationale behind this," Remo reassured Smith. "Somebody wants to enslave somebody else or make some enormous profit or something. We just haven't figured it out yet."

"I hope so," Smith said. "We don't know why he is doing what he is doing. But we do know what. And we do know where he would have to strike again."

It was Smith's theory that this enemy had removed all scientists in that particular area of bacterial research so that there would be no one left to come up with a formula to combat the rapid-breeder bacteria. Smith was sure that if two scientists appeared at a university with credentials as scientists in bacteria research, whoever was behind this looming world disaster would have to come at those two.

The two would be Remo and Chiun.

"Don't sweat, Smitty," Remo said. "Once he reaches out a hand at us, we'll take it off."

"That's not what worries me. What worries me is that if anyone at the Massachusetts University of Technology should recognize that you are not scientists, whoever is behind this thing will simply ignore you and go safely about destroying the industrial world. It's not your killing ability that's going to be tested here but, I am afraid, your knowledge of science."

"There is nothing to worry about," said Chiun. "We will show we understand anaerobic better than any scientist. We will show how long we can hold our breaths."

In Korean, he said to Remo, "While he is weakened, ask him if he knows any television producers."

"Not now," said Remo. "It's the wrong time."

"White men always have time for nonsense," Chiun said, "but never any time for beauty."

Chapter Three

"What's it to you?" said the thin man with thick wrists and an easy way of sitting on the laboratory table, so that he seemed not so much sitting on the table as holding it on the floor. The young professor and his Oriental associate had gotten a prime corner office at Massachusetts University of Technology, and Dr. Woldemar Keating wanted to know how someone could just arrive that morning at MUT and get a corner office. That had happened in the past only with people who taught black studies and History of White Racism and Intergroup Inequities in a Diseased Capitalist Society and all the other Mickey Mouse courses that colleges had offered through the seventies until the administrators had begun to realize that their fund-raising letters to alumni were going unanswered because their alumni could no longer read.

No. Nowadays to get a corner office right away, they had to be famous. Or know someone. Dr. Woldemar Keating wanted to know which. Not that he was jealous. He certainly wasn't that sort.

"Just curious," he said.

"We do special work in the rapid-breeding anaerobic bacteria stuff," said Remo.

"Oh. Petroleum boys. Well, we certainly won't be able to keep you very long," said Dr. Keating. "I suppose you got the office because of that."

"We got it because we're worth it. Have you ever

thought that the reason you might not have this sort of office is that you're not worth it?" asked Remo.

"That's a rather negative way of looking at things. I've never heard of you."

"Maybe that's why you don't have a corner office," said Remo.

Dr. Keating watched the Oriental raise a single finger to attract attention. The Oriental gestured for Dr. Keating to sit down, then brought forth a small mirror from the folds of his robes and put it to his lips. He motioned for Dr. Keating to look at his watch. Keating waited twenty minutes in silence. He saw no moisture on the mirror. That meant the man wasn't breathing. This was impossible for a person to do for a half-hour, and Keating was sure they had some sort of mechanical device to sneak oxygen into the bloodstream safely. He was waiting to see how they did it.

But after a half-hour, the Oriental only nodded and began breathing again.

"What was that?" asked Dr. Keating.

"Anaerobic," said Chiun. "We are the authorities on anaerobic."

"Really, you have some device that allows you to function without oxygen."

"Yes," said Chiun. "It is the balance between negativity and positivity, so that the body is unneeding of anything, a perfect single unity."

"Of course," Keating said. "Ions. The valences of ions. Yes." And Remo realized somehow that the breathing principle of Sinanju also held true for some sort of scientific principle.

"Well, you certainly are real. I must admit that, and I apologize for the fact that I suspected you were without academic credentials," said Dr. Keating.

"A credential," said Chiun, "is only someone else's suspicion of one's worth. I do not see anyone in this place worthy of understanding who and what I am."

"I must say you're honest," said Dr. Keating. "Everybody else here at MUT thinks that way, but no one

38

really gets around to saying it. By the way, you're in a prime field. And you're lucky."

"I heard a few scientists in this field were killed," said Remo. "That doesn't sound lucky to me."

"Those are only the ones who stayed here. Those who took the jobs really did well, I hear. The envy of everyone. Full research facilities. Estates to live on, servants, promises of full freedom of research for whatever they wanted."

"How do you know what the offer was?" Remo asked.

"Because I heard them talking before they left."

"For where?"

"I don't know," said Dr. Keating.

"You know the kind of benefits they get, but you don't know where they get them? That's kind of hard to believe."

"I don't know where they went because none of them ever knew before they went. I do know that they found their jobs just watching and reading the news. They all said there was something in the news that let them know where the positions were. They could figure it out for themselves. Damn lucky petroleum guys."

"In the papers, television, what? Where did they see whatever they saw?" Remo asked.

"The news is all I know. You know, the fast breeder cleans up oil. I always figured they must have seen something about the Middle East or oil or something that told them who to contact."

"Pretty peculiar way to recruit."

"At what was being offered, they could have pasted their applications on the bottoms of septic tanks, and people would still swim down to fill them out," Keating said. "I wish someone would make those sorts of offers to astrophysicists."

"You're an astrophysicist," said Remo. He didn't like the smell of this laboratory. It overlooked the Charles River with Boston on the other side, a quaint city with traffic jams and apparently a disproportionate sense of its own worth. He had been told it thought of itself as the new Athens because of all its universities.

Chiun had pointed out they if the city proclaimed itself the new Athens, then it was an imitation and all imitations were second rate. In the history of the service of Sinanju to emperors and kings, none had ever recorded that Athens considered itself the Babylon of the West or that Rome ever considered itself the Cairo of the Northern Mediterranean. Things that were good, Chiun said, like the pure stroke of the assassin's hand, were good unto themselves. They were not anything else but what they were.

"So stop trying to make me a Korean, Little Father," Remo had answered.

"That is different," said Chiun. "Because we will not make you a second-rate Korean, we will make you a first-rate Korean."

"I'm not Korean, Little Father. I don't want to be Korean."

"The first is an accident of birth," Chiun had said. "But the latter is a disaster of attitude."

"Other than you, Chiun," Remo had said, "I can take any Korean or groups of Koreans, and you know it. And you know who the next master of Sinanju must be."

"That is why you must learn to be Korean," Chiun had said. "It proves my point." And the Master of Sinanju spoke no more.

When he said he had proved a point, Chiun really meant, Remo had come to understand, that the Master of Sinanju had no more good arguments and that the subject would not only not be discussed anymore, it wouldn't even be listened to.

So there they were in the laboratory of MUT, with the astrophysicist babbling away and Chiun looking upon him like some form of local American native and Remo staring at the Charles River.

"Do you understand what I mean?" asked Dr. Keating.

"Sure," said Remo, noticing how sailboats seemed to

puff and glide with the wind. They almost had the balance of a good stroke, except for the dislocations at the tiller, which meant the hand of conscious thought was interrupting the smooth flow of nature.

"There will be some form of communication to you in the media. I certainly wish that happened to astrophysicists," said Dr. Keating.

"Swell," said Remo.

"Do you hold your breath?" asked Chiun. "Ever? Want me to do it again?"

Dr. Keating quickly left the corner laboratory, which he knew he would never get at MUT, and returned to his own office.

Inside the right-hand drawer of his desk was a black metal cylinder. When this cylinder was placed over the speaker of his phone, it beeped out a dialing signal for a number Dr. Keating did not know. He once tried analyzing the beeps, comparing them to the tones of the normal pushbutton telephone. But it was useless. This was an entirely different set of sounds, perhaps a whole separate phone system that the phone company never knew existed.

Dr. Keating made his call and read in the names of the two new professors and his analysis. Yes, they were strange, but he believed they definitely were valid scientists in the discipline of rapid-breeder bacteria.

"Also, according to standing instructions of yours, I have informed them that they should observe local media for a message of great importance to them," said Dr. Keating before hanging up.

He had done his job. He did not know if anything ever appeared in the local media for rapid-breeder-bacteria scientists, but he did know that for the last four years, any scientists he told to watch the media did not stay long in their jobs.

Sometimes they would disappear. Just pack up of their own free will. Others times, they might be found with their heads caved in or their backs broken.

But that was not Dr. Keating's fault. All he did was telephone information to a number he did not know, and also tell scientists about something wonderful for them. Whatever happened after that was not his fault. He had nothing to do with it.

He had enough to keep himself busy. After all, what other professor at MUT had two Rolls Royces and an estate on Cape Cod? And he certainly hadn't earned them on his salary. Those little telephone calls paid for those things.

And if there was a pang of conscience about what he was doing, it was even quieter than the engines of his Rolls Royces. The only thing he heard while driving was the ticking of his solid gold Rolex.

And if he felt he might be betraying his university, that was dispelled immediately by the gross insult of his never having had a corner office.

This insult itself had brought him his new wealth, because after he was turned down the third time, someone phoned him, telling him a bank account had been opened up for him. He didn't believe it until he got a phone call from the bank itself, thanking him for opening the account.

Then he got a phone call commiserating with him on his difficulties and complimenting him on his good fortune with his new-found wealth.

"And by the way, Doctor Keating, we're very interested in one special discipline at your university. And there's a little thing we'd like you to do for us."

"I won't do anything illegal," Dr. Keating had answered.

"We wouldn't think of it."

"Or immoral," Dr. Keating had said.

"We wouldn't think of it," the smooth-voiced caller had responded. "After all, I'm your friend, aren't I?"

And through the years, Dr. Keating had to conclude that he had truly never been asked to do the immoral or the illegal. And this he told himself as he drove to his Cape Cod estate in the money-green Rolls Royce, knowing he probably would never see the two new professors ever again.

Too bad. They had gotten a corner laboratory, and

Dr. Keating, after twenty-five years at MUT, had an office that faced onto the parking lot. Where he kept his Rolls Royce.

Bradford Wakefield III, publisher of *The Boston Blade*, was eating lunch overlooking his cove on the Massachusetts north shore, when he was disturbed by his butler.

"Your special phone is ringing, sir," said the butler.

Bradford was a portly man, with flesh to his jowls and thinning hair. When he turned his head suddenly, his double chin waffled.

"What you say?" asked Wakefield.

"Your phone, Mr. Wakefield. The special one is ringing. You never let me answer it."

"Right. Don't answer it," Wakefield said.

"But it's ringing, Mr. Wakefield, sir."

"Right," said Wakefield, and offered a hand to be helped up to his feet, whereupon he shuffled off to his study, away from the view of the beautiful rocky cove on his northern shore estate in Mamtasket, Massachusetts. The telephone was ringing. Wakefield knew he didn't have to answer it right away. That phone would keep ringing for a month if he didn't answer it. But he had nothing better to do this afternoon, other than planning the conference on racial justice.

The big problem with that was convincing the local police to allow the black panel members into the quaint village of Mamtasket, from which Wakefield and *The Blade* led its campaign for racial justice in Boston.

Boston had a deep and grievous racial problem. *The Blade*, under Wakefield's leadership, fought that prejudice and the bigotry of white Bostonians.

The Blade fought it daily and on Sunday.

Wherever white racism reared its ugly head, *The Blade* was there to lead the fight against it.

There had been, Wakefield was happy to say, no racial incidents in his own hometown of Mamtasket,

43

just outside Boston, for the last fifty years. It was a record he and his family were proud of.

There also had been no blacks in Mamtasket after the sun set. Anyone wanting to hire black help in Mamtasket had better make sure it was not sleep-over.

This contradiction between his paper's policy and his life did not bother him, for it was the Wakefield tradition to lead America in righteousness and also make a buck by doing it.

The Wakefields were America's biggest slavers and leading abolitionists before the Civil War. The Wakefields wanted the slaves freed, right after they were paid for them. The Wakefields led all causes. They protested anti-semitism, while Wakefield factories sold Nazi Germany weapons. Wilhelmina Wakefield, Bradford's mother and the grande dame of liberal causes, marched against segregation in Selma, Alabama, while her husband protected the family's Back Bay property from penetration by blacks.

And of course the family newspaper at that time led the fight for school desegregation in, of course, South Boston, where racism was, of course, fiercest. When some politician with a puckish sense of humor suggested that the Boston schools could be desegregated by busing some black children into Mamtasket schools, *The Blade* slowed down on its support of busing. But it made sure that politician never ran for office again.

The Wakefields, even down to Bradford's young granddaughter, the famous journalist, Melody Wakefield, all were leaders for social justice. And they all had a healthy respect for a Wakefield dollar. Being rich didn't stop a Wakefield from doing good. Rather, it helped, Bradford Wakefield believed.

He shuffled to the phone and picked it up. Then he dialed a code, and the message that had been recorded repeated itself.

It was Dr. Keating's voice. Bradford scribbled down the message. If his memory wasn't failing him, there should be no scientists left in the rapid-breeder field.

But here were two at MUT, arriving there out of the blue.

This mildly puzzled him, but he was not worried. This was not his problem. A far wiser person than he would know what to do about this. Perhaps the wisest person to whom Bradford had ever spoken.

Bradford dialed another code. He had come to believe that all these calls he made were cleared by some scrambling device because he once queried this wise person about the risk of interception, and the person said he should not worry.

And when this person said one did not have to worry, one did not have to worry.

"Hello," said Bradford.

"Hello," said Friend.

"We have a problem, I think," said Wakefield. "As you remember, as you always remember, we had set up this system at MUT, where I'm on the board of directors."

"Yes," said Friend.

Wakefield liked the even way Friend always responded. Friend was never ruffled. Friend always had the right answers. Perhaps Friend had a bit too much warmth for the taste of the Wakefield clan. But that was his only fault.

Wakefield had often thought how wonderful it would be if Melody could marry the lad into the Wakefields. That is, if they could ever meet him in person.

"We have, as you directed, kept security watch on that department. We have offered employment to those wanting employment. We have done otherwise to those who refused employment. I have nothing against doing otherwise," Wakefield said.

"No Wakefield has," Friend answered. "That's why your ancestors were such good slave traders, Brad."

"Please, Friend. One can't help his ancestors."

"Brad, I would have loved to have worked with your ancestors also. I like Wakefields. Wakefields are reliable people. Wakefields don't do silly things. You don't

45

know how much I value that in a person. You don't do silly things."

"Thank you, Friend," said Wakefield and read from his notes all the qualifications Dr. Keating had reported about the two new scientists, the young American and the old Oriental.

"Do otherwise," ordered Friend. "But first we must know who they are and whom they represent. You see, those two are frauds."

"How do you know so quickly? Why, Dr. Keating couldn't tell they were frauds."

"Which also means that Dr. Keating is going to have to be otherwise," said Friend.

"Why is that?"

"If the two are frauds, Dr. Keating has either become incompetent or has sold out."

"Dr. Keating sell out?" asked Wakefield.

"He has already done it once. He sold out to us, remember?" said Friend.

"That's not really selling out. That's serving the Wakefield interests. That's the highest calling one can have."

"Not if you work for MUT and don't even know you are being employed by the Wakefield interests," said Friend.

"You're right, Friend," said Wakefield. "Now, how could you tell that those two were not real scientists?"

"There is no paper that they have done. No one has ever mentioned their names in a paper, there is no cross-reference to any of their work. In brief, they do not exist academically. Therefore, they are not scientists. Therefore, they are something else. Therefore, we must find out what else. Before you do otherwise to them."

"Of course," said Bradford Wakefield.

"You will find out," said Friend.

"Of course."

"Then do otherwise with them."

"If you say so," Wakefield said. "Obviously you used a computer to go through academic files, but what

46

amazes me is how quickly you assimilate everything in your computers," Wakefield said.

"Brad," said Friend. "Stop fishing."

"Wouldn't you stop over for dinner with us sometime? We'd love to meet you. My granddaughter, Melody, would absolutely love to meet you. You've heard of Melody Wakefield, haven't you?"

"Yes. She is in Hamidi Arabia."

"How do you know? I didn't even know where she was."

But the line was dead. Friend had hung up on Bradford Wakefield III. But that was how he always said good-bye. He was just finished and then no longer on the line. It wasn't rude. No one who had done for the Wakefields what Friend had done could ever be called rude.

Bradford remembered it sharply, those trying days during the 1960s. Wilhelmina Wakefield had just finished her sit-in at the Department of Agriculture, trying to triple farm taxes to support the poor; Melody was just beginning to win all those awards for her book proving that American predictions of slaughter and flight if South Vietnam were to lose the war were all just propaganda; and Bradford was working toward a new concept in affirmative marriage.

Bradford remembered that it was a crisp fall day because the autumn sun was setting low when his wonderful idea of how racism could be cured by ending race altogther hit him. He had come up with a reasonable solution. Thirty percent of all lower-class whites would marry blacks.

This would not be mandatory, but communities would have quotas, and if a community did not meet its intermarriage quota, then it would be fined.

Naturally, no one would be expected to marry across class lines because class wasn't a problem. Race was—at least for lower-class whites. Perhaps, Bradford Wakefield thought, they could start the program in South Boston, which needed to overcome its racism most.

Of course, the wonderful idea was immediately forgotten when the horrible news came in. The family accountant trembled as he spoke.

"Wakefields," he said. "I have disastrous news."

"Speak," said Wilhelmina.

"There have been financial reverses of some size," said the accountant. "You are no longer living on the interest on your interest. You are living on the interest itself."

"My God," screamed Wilhelmina. "What's next? Someday are we going to be living off our capital itself?"

"That could happen," said the accountant. "It is not so farfetched."

Wilhelmina fainted. Melody paled. Bradford felt his stomach grow weak, and the room became a blur. When he awoke, a doctor was giving him a tranquilizer and water to wash it down.

It was in these dreadful times that Bradford got his first phone call. It was from someone who seemed to know everything there was to know about Bradford's tax return, his bank accounts, his investment portfolios.

"I will return your capital worth to you so that you can, for the rest of your days, live on the interest on your interest," the magnificent person said. Bradford cried openly.

"Tell me who you are, Savior," he said.

"I am Friend."

Friend was true to his word. All Bradford had to do was little things. Like this afternoon, taking care of Dr. Keating, whom Bradford had first recruited under Friend's instructions.

Now Bradford Wakefield drove down Route 1, along the Massachusetts coast, looking for a likely place. This was also Friend's method. A brilliant method of cutting links to both Bradford and himself. And it would hardly cost anything.

Bradford had $10,000 in $100 bills in a single manila envelope that had been carefully wrinkled to look old. A bit of fudge glop was poured on it and a cigarette ground out in the glop.

Bradford cruised down the route until he found a Burger-Triumph stand, where he dropped the envelope into the trash basket.

There it sat, scuffed and filthy, while Bradford phoned an employee who had never met him.

"It's at the second Burger-Triumph after you get outside Marblehead," said Bradford into the roadside telephone. "Doctor Woldemar Keating of MUT. We want to know who really employs him and why does he phone in wrong information. Then there are two new professors. One is white and one is Oriental. We want to know who employs them and then we want them finished."

Wakefield gave his employee their names. He wondered what the corpses would look like after his employees finished with them.

In his newspaper, he never ran those gruesome sorts of photos. *The Boston Blade* never pandered to prurient interest. *The Boston Blade* was the conscience of New England. Also, Bradford Wakefield III did not like blood.

Dr. Woldemar Keating couldn't believe what was happening to him. Four black men, one very large, had come into his Cape Cod home and stretched him over a butcher block table in his kitchen.

One of them had held a can opener with an ugly point. He put it point first to Dr. Keating's navel. The man with the can opener did not talk. The very large man they called Bubba did not talk.

The shortest one, with the thin mustache, talked. His name was Dice. Dr. Keating was not sure whether he really had such perfectly white teeth or whether the darkness of his face made them look white. He had the complexion of charcoal.

All four had come through his front door after the big one they called Bubba had knocked it down. Bubba had lifted Dr. Keating like a marshmallow and put him on the kitchen table.

"We gonna take out you insides like some lukewarm peas outen a can," said Dice. "We gonna split you up like a popped pork sausage. We gonna spread you greasy white intestines outen you belly like so much spaghetti."

"Yeah," said the big one named Bubba.

"Or we can be nasty," said Dice.

"What could possibly be nastier?" whined Dr. Keating.

"Nasty is we don't use the can opener," said Dice.

"Bubba, he use his hand," said the big one named Bubba. He raised a very large and wide thing with fingers on it. Dr. Keating knew it was a hand because one of those fingers was a thumb. And he could see fingerprints. They looked like pottery swirls on kitchen plates. Bubba must have been seven feet tall. The hand could hide a chessboard.

Bubba took a big flat, thick salad knife and put it between forefinger and pinky with the other two fingers underneath. He pressed up with the two middle fingers. The knife snapped.

"What do you want from me?" asked Dr. Keating. He finally understood.

"We thought you never ask. We wants to know who employ you. Who be the man what pay you?" said Dice.

"Yeah," said Bubba. "Dat what we want."

"MUT pays me," said Dr. Keating.

"Who else?" said Dice.

"No one else."

"We know dere be someone else."

"No one else."

Dice nodded. Dr. Keating felt a sharp pain at his bellybutton. He felt his flesh rip. They were bringing the can opener up, digging his stomach open. He screamed in pain.

"Please, please, please. I get money deposited in my bank account."

50

"How long?" asked Dice.

"Many years now, five, six. You can't do this."

"Don't be telling this black man what he can do. Dat be 'fringing on my rights dere," said Dice. "You does that and den I gets mean."

"Yeah," said Bubba.

"Please," begged Dr. Keating.

"Now, I don't wants what you been getting paid for for a long time now. I wants de new thing. Who you working for so you be phoning in wrong information?"

"I don't know what you're talking about. Please."

Dice nodded. The can opener moved up a few more inches to just below the chestbones. The white belly gushed blood like a sausage split by the heat of a fire.

"Last chance 'fore we gets mean," said Dice.

"There's nobody new paying me. No one. I tell you. I swear."

"Too late. Now we be's mean."

Dice stepped away to keep anything from getting on his pure white silk suit with the red handkerchief hanging out of the breast pocket, the red handkerchief that matched Dice's new red shirt and red tie and shiny red shoes with the blue neon socks. He had had to hunt all over Roxbury to get the right neon blue. Most of the stores had only the dull neon. Whoever heard of wearing dull neon blue socks with a red shirt?

Bubba reached into Dr. Keating's belly and the two other men who were holding his arms and legs turned their gaze away. Dice stepped back farther. Sometimes Bubba splattered. Bubba was sloppy.

Crack went the ribs, and Keating's eyes widened in shock. Crack went the backbones, and then there was blankness in the white man's face.

"Okay, Bubba," said Dice. "Let's go. He dead."

But there was more cracking. Bubba was taking out the ribs. Then Bubba went to work on the knees. Bubba crushed the knees in his hands like pine cones mashed in a steel vise.

"Bubba, he be dead a while now, Bubba," said Dice.

Bubba took the legs out of the hip joints.

51

"Bubba," said Dice. "He dead. Time to go, sweet fella."

Bubba went for the head. He liked heads. He liked to press them till the eyes popped out.

"All right now, Bubba. You done the head. Les' go now, big beautiful fella," said Dice. "Good. You got de eyes. You always be liking de eyes. De eyes finish it. Hmmmm. Yeah, good, Bubba, let's go now, precious big fella."

One of the men who had stepped back and had his head turned because he couldn't stand watching Bubba work suddenly felt his head inside something very big. And when he saw large fingers close over his eyes, he knew his head was in Bubba's hands. He tried to let out a big scream, but there was that finger sticking down his throat, and then he thought he heard a very big crack, but then there was no hearing and there wasn't even a thought.

"Bubba, beautiful fella. We got de car. De new car, baby," said Dice, grinning very hard. Bubba had started on their own men.

"Right," said Bubba.

Dice looked around for a place for Bubba to wipe his hands. There were only two places. Dice's suit or the other man they had picked up for the work.

Dice quickly pointed to the other man.

Bubba wiped and the man screamed. Bubba had wiped too hard. Bubba suddenly realized that he had done a wrong thing. His own man was whimpering softly in his giant hands. Bubba looked to Dice. He knew he could trust Dice.

Bubba was the only man from Roxbury who trusted Dice. If people could get close to Bubba, they would have told him that Dice was no good. But people did not get close to Bubba. Only Dice got close to Bubba, and Dice made a living from the big man. The only problem was that Bubba was a victim of enthusiasm. Once he got started, he was like a long freight train; he took a while to stop. It was not that Bubba was especially vicious, Dice thought. It was that those big hands needed something to do once they got started.

Bubba had been six-foot-two and 240 pounds in junior high school. Naturally, he was the greatest thing in the Tiny Tot Football League, the division for boys fourteen and under.

Bubba's football career started and ended there. He could not realize that the play had been whistled dead. Coaches tried jumping on him to teach him, but Bubba could never stop thinking that a tackle was only the beginning.

An opposing quarterback who would never walk again sued successfully, proving that Bubba did not play football, he mugged.

The junior high tried him with the big boys in high school. Bubba put a fullback into a wheelchair for life, by running after the stretcher to finish him off while the fullback looked helplessly up to the sky.

Bubba never made love to a woman more than once.

He tried professional boxing, but he hated the gloves on his hands. Bubba knocked out his first opponent in fourteen seconds of the first round. His manager was delighted, until the referee couldn't get Bubba up off his prostrate opponent.

Frustrated to agony, Bubba tore off the gloves with his teeth so he could get at the other boxer's skull better with his bare hands.

The referee tried breaking a stool over Bubba's head to stop him. Then someone came into the ring with a lead pipe that he brought smashing down on Bubba's big head. The pipe could have splintered a pier piling, it came down with such force. Bubba looked up and scratched his head. The pipe had caught his attention.

When he concentrated, Bubba realized that he was supposed to stop crushing things with his hands. But the concentration was hard for Bubba.

Now in the kitchen of the white man's Cape Cod home, Bubba realized he had already killed one of his own men and was in the process of killing another.

The man was half dead. Bubba looked to Dice.

"What we do, Dice?"

"You started it, you finish it, big fella," Dice said. "You leave him here, he gonna be singing all songs to de fuzz. He gonna say you did it."

"No. Won' say nuffin," said the man in Bubba's hands.

"He say he won' say nuffin," said Bubba.

"Dey all say dat when you gots dey head in you hands. He won' say nuffin now. He say it plenty looking at dem Boston blues, dem fuzz. Who you friend anyway?"

"You my friend, Dice."

"Who never lie to you?" asked Dice.

Bubba thought a moment. "Ain't nobody never lie to me. Everybody lie to me," he said accurately.

"Well, who lie to you nicest, then?" asked Dice.

"You be de nices', Dice."

"Den finish what you start, so we don't be doin' no life in Ambrose Prison."

When Bubba heard Ambrose, his hands convulsed instinctively. A loud crack filled the room, and the man spat out his lifeless inanards like a toothpaste tube squashed by a brick.

Bubba did not even notice this. He was thinking of his two years in Ambrose State Penitentiary. Ambrose was where prisoners were sent when all other prisons failed.

Not even Ambrose was strong enough for Bubba. The guards had locked him in solitary confinement one night, and in the morning they found the steel cell door torn in half, the way some men did with telephone books.

He had failed to escape only because he had jammed the secondary door himself. The three-inch steel there had managed to hold.

They built a special open-air prison for Bubba. It was four walls of steel-reinforced concrete, set into the rocky ground. It was a steel-lined pit. One warden from out of state saw it and said it reminded him of a rhino pit he had once seen in the Paris zoo.

The Ambrose pit for Bubba had used the same design, the warden was told. Except for Bubba there was an extra layer of steel reinforcement. And with Bubba no one dared enter to clean the cage.

His food was thrown down from above. Bubba knew it was mealtime when lunch landed on his head.

Bubba was lonely. It was the loneliest time in Bubba's life, and it hurt more than anything he knew. He would have given anything just for somebody to talk to him. Even to threaten him would have been all right.

Then Dice entered his life.

Every day someone would lower a bucket to collect the leavings from Bubba's pit lavatory. But this day, someone spoke. None of the others had spoken because they didn't want Bubba to get to know them by name because later, he might want to shake hands with them.

"You a sucker. You know why you down dere and I up here?" said the man.

" 'Cause dey gots to have somebody to haul up de shit," said Bubba.

" 'Cause I realize my potential. I am a potentiator of my life. You don' see me in no pit. I don' waste my potential, see?"

"What potential?" asked Bubba to the man with the bucket in his hand.

"Potential be what you can achieve in life. I am an achievorator. You an under-achievorator. Dat why you down dere. You be de under-one. I be de over-one."

"You still haulin' shit, nigger," said Bubba.

"Today. But soon I be outside in a boss hog. You gon' stay dere till de sun dry up. Yessuh. When you die, dey just fill in de hole and dat be you grave."

This thought horrified the big man, and he had dreams of great truckloads of earth coming down on him. The next day, the same man was up above removing the bucket.

"How I use my potential?" asked Bubba.

"Stop breakin' people's heads for nuffin."

"I likes breakin' heads."

"Den stay dere till dey fills it in on you, sucker."

"Wait. Don' go. I promise I don' break no head no more. Jus' don' let dem bury me alive."

"I din' say don' break heads. Jus' don' do it for nuffin. Now, you willin' to come in wif me, I will use your potential and show you how I uses my potentiorator. It get me what I want, see?"

Bubba nodded.

"But you gotta do what I say. You do what I say, I get you up here wif me," said Dice, maneuvering the waste pail downwind toward the truck that would carry it away.

He returned to the edge of the pit, and looking up was Bubba's big mournful head.

"What you in for, man?" asked Dice.

"Manslaughter, felonial assault, resisting arrest, rape, molestering a child, armed robbery, three counts of mugging. I din' do one of dem muggin's."

"You left out arson," said Dice.

"Dem matches, dey be too small for my fingers," Bubba said.

"Tomorrow, dere by a lady comin' here, and no matter what dey say you done, you jes' tell her it be revolutionary."

"What dat revolutionary shit?" asked Bubba.

"Revolutionary be you can do anything you want and you can't do no wrong. You sets fire to a nursery and you say it be revolutionary, and it be all right wif lots of folks," Dice said.

"Lots of folks sound like dey be stupid," Bubba said.

"Dey be white," Dice said.

The next day, Bubba looked up and saw many people with the warden at the edge of his pit. The warden was explaining how dangerous Bubba was. But Bubba remembered what the waste collector, Dice, had said, and he yelled up, "It was revolutionary."

A white-haired old woman, hearing that, insisted that a ladder be put down, and despite warnings, she entered the pit. She was, Bubba later found out, an important person from an important family. He did not know she was Wilhelmina Wakefield, the grand dame of support for the Third World wherever she found it, as long as it wasn't in Mamtasket.

"Revolutionary," grunted Bubba.

"You're going to free us all," said Wilhelmina Wakefield. "Your revolutionary sensitivity is extraordinary and too complex for the dull white mind."

"Revolutionary," grunted Bubba again. Wilhelmina motioned up to the edge of the pit. Photographers came down. Their strobe lights frightened Bubba and he growled, but he guessed that Dice wouldn't want him breaking the photographers' heads.

The next day, on the second page of *The Boston Blade*, was a large picture of Bubba. His story covered the entire page. The headline read: "He Only Wanted to Free His People."

Bubba could not read the story, but Dice read it to him. The gist was that Bubba was put into the pit because his revolutionary sensitivities were too difficult for a reactionary warden to deal with.

In a full page of small newspaper type, *The Blade* never once mentioned one of Bubba's crimes.

When *The Blade* spoke, politicians listened. The mayor of Boston got on national television and discovered in his own heart, his own gut, sureness that the only reason Bubba was in jail was because Massachusetts was racist. A rally was held at the Boston Common. Religious leaders spoke. Buttons were handed out.

The buttons read: "Free Bubba."

Bumper stickers said more: "His only crime was wanting freedom. Free Bubba."

Finally, the parole board met and not only freed Bubba, but apologized to him. They also freed one Mandranus Rex Smith, alias Dice.

From then on, Bubba knew whom he trusted. What Dice never told Bubba was that he had been told what to tell Bubba. He had never met the man. But it was the same voice he heard on the telephone, telling him who to take care of and where to pick up the money.

So they went to work for that man, that high-class man with that high-class Boston accent, who left them money in Burger-Triumph garbage pails, but whom they had never seen. It was a perfect union. Bubba had Dice's brains and Dice had Bubba's magnificent hands.

Dice looked at his pink and gold Rolex watch as he drove his white Eldorado convertible back to Boston from Cape Cod. It was really too late to visit the other two professors at MUT, the white man and the old Chink.

They could always do that in the morning.

Bubba had had enough fun for one day anyway.

They continued on into Roxbury, where Dice preened his way up to the bar and, as he often did since he had teamed up with Bubba, tried to pick a fight.

And as always, when he had Bubba along, he couldn't manage it.

"Get yo' ugly face outen dis bar," said Dice to a slick pimp with a foxy lady Dice wanted.

"Yeah," said Bubba.

The pimp moved. The fox stayed. Life was good for Mandranus Rex Smith, alias Dice. In the morning, say at noon, he would take care of the other two scientists. Maybe even do one himself, it the one were small.

Chapter Four

Remo tried to follow *The Boston Blade*. He had a half-year's issues shipped to his lab. If the contact was going to be through the media, then he might be able to see where other professors dealing with rapid-breeding bacteria had been reached.

They had spent the evening before in an elegant hotel named the Copley Plaza.

Remo had tried to watch three television news shows at once, hoping to see some kind of contact.

He could have taped at least one of the news shows, but Chiun would not let him use the video recorder. Remo had pointed out that CURE had paid for that video recorder before such machines were seen outside of television studios. CURE had developed the technology to make the taping machine portable—just for Chiun. So Chiun should at least allow one show to be taped for one hour.

Chiun had been horrified.

"Blasphemy. How many years have I taught you? And yet you now here say to me that I should take assassin's tribute and return it to the use of the emperor. If I have taught you nothing else about Sinanju, most holy and sacred is the assassin's tribute."

"There we disagree, Little Father," said Remo.

"How can you disagree? I am the Master."

"I just don't think the money is that important."

A moan came from Chiun. "No. Not you, Not you,

Remo, who I taught with the golden years of my life. Not you, Remo."

Remo sighed. He had known what was coming. Every time he said that money itself was not important, but the art of Sinanju, the mystery of being that was encompassed in its power, Chiun would accuse him of betrayal to the highest ideals of Sinanju.

"Amateur," Chiun hissed. "Not you, Remo. You cannot think like an amateur. Your country and the world bleeds from amateurs taking weapons into their own hands, and when you, who have been trained in Sinanju, who have been give Sinanju despite your dead-fish white color, when you talk like the lunatics who perform these services for nothing, you have pierced the very heart of your Master."

"Sinanju now gets tribute from what I do," Remo said. "I work for Smith and I do what he wants, and those ingrates in your village get a shipment of gold to keep them alive and not working. Because of what I do."

"Because I trained you," said Chiun. "It is only just."

"I don't care about tribute," Remo said.

And then Chiun's wailing would not stop. Remo was going to be an embarrassment to Sinanju. Already in the world, people were going around shooting popes. Murdering babies. Now Remo was going to let it be known that he would kill for nothing. That the tribute did not matter.

So many years and so much pain, and now Remo had done this to Chiun.

"Even for a white, this is not gratitude," said Chiun, and Remo had known further arguing was useless. He was not going to get the tape machine. And Chiun would not be speaking to him for a while. Remo had to be careful to notice that Chiun was not speaking to him, however, because if Chiun thought Remo was not noticing how he was being ignored, Chiun would make noises or interrupt in some manner whatever Remo was doing. If there was anything that bothered the

60

Master of Sinanju, it was someone being oblivious to the fact that he was ignoring them.

Remo watched the three TV news shows as best he could, flicking back from channel to channel, and realized that he was going to have to come up with something better.

So the next day at the lab, he ordered the six months of *The Boston Blade*. He also tried to devise a system for monitoring all the media to see if a contact was being made.

The Blade had one interesting story. A Professor Keating had been killed during a racial incident. Remo remembered that Keating was the one who had promised the contact through the media.

Remo almost missed the story on his death because the headline read: "Racial Killing in Cape Cod." The racial part was two blacks being horribly mangled. There were quotes from community leaders about Cape Cod's shame. Apparently, the professor's body was found in his Cape Cod home, along with those of the two blacks.

There was an editorial in *The Blade* about this. It called for an end to racial killing and the establishment of a special board to root out the racist nature of Cape Cod, where, as everyone knew, it was impossible for a black welfare family to buy a home.

But neither editorial nor news story carried much information about Keating's death. Remo phoned the newspaper, hoping he could get someone who knew more about it. One could tell from the kill sometimes why it was done.

He finally was connected to a reporter at a *Blade* bureau on Cape Cod.

"Yeah. He was butchered just before the racial incident," the reporter said.

"How?" asked Remo, glancing over to the window to let Chiun know that he was aware he was not being spoken to. Chiun was by the window, grandly examining the Charles River. It was a saying of Sinanju long before the world had so many great cities that one could

61

never be lost on a river, for wherever it flowed, there was always a city where it entered the ocean.

"I think the guy—what's his name, Keating—had his ribs broken out," the reporter said. "A bloody mess."

"Mangled?" asked Remo.

"Yeah. After his belly had been cut open by some crude kind of knife. I wasn't paying too much attention to that body."

"How did the other two men die?"

"Racially," said the reporter.

"How do you know?" asked Remo.

"It was a white neighborhood."

"Time out," said Remo. "You mean, if a black guy gets killed in a white neighborhood, it's automatically a racial killing? What if they were killed by a black guy? You know, people kill for other reasons than race hatred."

"Some do it for nothing," said Chiun, still looking at the river. "Some give away the finest training in all history."

The reporter told Remo that until proven otherwise, any time a black man was killed by a white or probably killed by a white, then it was racial.

"Why?" asked Remo.

"Because Massachusetts is a racist state."

"Why?"

"Because it's *The Blade*'s policy. Speak to Mr. Wakefield, if you don't like it, but I tell you now, anyone who thinks differently is a racist."

"Who says?"

"Mr. Wakefield. Why do you think I got shipped up here to work, when my house is in Boston? I wrote that a store owner shot a burglar."

"What was wrong with that?" asked Remo.

"The store owner was white. The burglar was black. I'll never make that mistake again. But I didn't even recognize a racial incident until then."

"So Mr. Wakefield controls the news at *The Blade*," said Remo.

62

"No, no. Never say I s... not interfere ever. He just ma... highest standards. And you'd b... those standards are."

Remo hung up and looked at the ... months of *The Blade*. It almost reached the ... the far corner of his lab. And there were month... months of television news shows. How the hell was he going to find out how somebody had reached other scientists through the media?

Suddenly the phone was ringing. As long as Remo was answering the phone, he wouldn't have to be reading those newspapers.

It was a woman's voice. She was terrified. She was the office manager of this section of the lab, and she was telling Remo that he and the other professor had better jump out the window now.

"It's only three stories to the street," she said in a desperate whisper. "You still have time."

"I'm not jumping through any window," Remo said. "It's eleven in the morning. Is the place on fire?"

"Worse. The biggest, ugliest man I ever saw is headed for your office. He's got giant hands. He's the one who was always seen around here when the other professors were killed."

"It's eleven o'clock in the morning," said Remo. "Tell them to come back at three maybe. I've got all these papers to read."

"You know there have been five professors in your discipline killed in the last three years? Do you know that? Do you know that a giant of a man with giant hands was seen at everyone's death? He's coming for you, don't you understand? And he's got a friend, and I think the friend has got a gun. Jump. You can't get out by the hallway. They're already there."

"Listen," said Remo. "You wouldn't know how I could get a lot of papers read and television news shows watched, would you?"

"You're going to be dead in minutes."

down. Look, do you know of people
nire to read newspapers?"

"You don't need people. There's a computer system,
but you've got to be alive to use it. Please. I don't want
to see someone killed again. Please, jump."

"So you can rig up a computer to do it," said Remo.

With a roar, the door to the lab cracked off its
hinges and two men entered, one of them enormous
with giant hands.

The smaller man waited for the two scientists to flee
in desperate panic. Dice always loved it when Bubba
entered a room by pushing a door in. You could see
the desperate panic in the room. You could do just
about anything to anyone in the room after Bubba entered.

A real old yellow-faced gook with long fingernails
was staring out the window. The young white one was
on the telephone.

The older one didn't jump because he was probably
deaf. But what about the white one? Dice had never
seen people not jump when the door went flying into
the room.

"Sweet Bubba, make Whitey jump," said Dice.

"De arms or de legs?" asked Bubba.

"Suit yourself. Make yourself at home on his body."

Bubba saw the white man. Bubba would break the
white man. Bubba moved on the white man. Bubba
grabbed an arm of the white man. Big Bubba's hand
enclosed the entire forearm. Big Bubba got ready to
yank the arm out of its socket.

Bubba could do this sometimes if he had the right
leverage and got a good yank. Usually, though, he
would just damage the socket.

Bubba yanked. The arm didn't move. The white
man kept talking. Bubba yanked again.

"What?" said Bubba in confusion.

"Shhhhhh," said the white man. "I'm on the phone."

"He doesn't believe in getting paid. He is worthless,"
said the yellow man.

"You next, Pops," said Dice. He thought Bubba

64

could snap the frail old man in [...] low robe with just one blow. He had [...] do a one-blow kill. But the old Chink [...] good spit would do him in.

Dice decided to teach the old man some [...] before Bubba finished him. He sauntered over to [...] old yellow man while Bubba was tugging on the white man's arm.

"Don't sass me," said Dice. "Don't ever sass me." He slapped the old face, but something strange happened. He felt only air. He slapped again. His hand didn't connect. He didn't even see the head move, but the wisp of a beard was quivering. Therefore the head had moved but so quickly he hadn't seen it. Unless, of course, he was imagining this.

"I do not kill for free," the old yellow man said.

He was talking to the white man. Dice turned. The white man should be dead by now. Dice saw a giant black hand flail at the sky. It grabbed a lamp and shattered it. It clutched onto a gray metal lab table and cracked it in two. It latched onto a chair, crushed it like a soft aluminum beer can, sending splinters flying around the room. Dice had to duck.

The other black hand was useless.

And Big Bubba was seated helplessly, his legs stretched out, his big head erect, held very tightly by a telephone receiver cord that had come around his neck and had stopped all the air from going into his lungs.

Bubba was being strangled with a telephone cord. In one hand the white man had one end and the other he held the end with the receiver. And he was talking into the receiver as he was strangling Big Bubba.

"No, nothing's wrong. What noise? Oh, a table or something. I don't know. Listen, can you really get me a computer to do all that newspaper reading and television watching? No, nothing's going on here. Stay to the point, please. You have such a computer program? That's definite? Right. Okay. Come in, say in . . ."

The white man lifted the giant Bubba up by the cord and looked at the face.

in, say, in four minutes. Don't worry about
, there's no problem here. Yes, they did come in.
We're talking. They're very nice. Yes. Four minutes."

The white man hung up and waited. Bubba's eyes
bulged out. His giant face contorted.

Dice smiled. He smiled very broadly. He had worn a
white fedora with a red, white, and blue feather. He
took off the hat. Dice understood how impolite wearing
a hat indoors could be. Dice held the hat in front of
himself. He heard his own feet do a shuffle. Good for
you, feet, thought Dice. He bowed. The word *sir*
flowed from his lips. The word flowed easily. Good for
you, lips, thought Dice.

He smiled at the yellow man.

"I always like Chinamens, suh. Yessuh. I do like de
Chinamens." Dice showed a lot of teeth when he said
that.

"I am Korean, imbecile," said the old man.

"Yessuh, like dem Chinamens."

"Korea is not China. Koreans are not Chinese.
Chinese are slothful."

"I like all dem Chinamens," said Dice, whose ears
were not working that well. He was trying to like everyone living in the room. He was hoping to promote
niceness as a way of life, now that Bubba was on his
way out of this life. Dice could not find it in him to ex-
clude any group from his niceness.

"Koreans are different inasmuch as virtue is different
from sin," said Chiun.

"I like all mens. All brothers. Yessuh. Koreans and
Chinamens, dey be one," said Dice. His voice rang
with sincerity. Good for you, voice, thought Dice.

And then everything was very dark. He did not see
the hand move and flick at his spinal cord with just
enough force to sever all motor responses.

He saw only darkness and felt a great floating away.

Good for you, floating away, thought Dice and then
thought no more.

Remo looked at the big one who was inside the telephone cord. He had just expired.

66

"Did you kill that man?" said Remo. "We [...] posed to save one. I wanted to save one."

"I did it free. You should be happy," said Chiun.

"If I knew you were going to kill yours, I wou[...] have saved mine," Remo said. "What if they don't send someone else? How are we going to find the source? You know you can't find out who sent someone unless they're living."

"I thought you liked killing for no tribute."

"You should have told me, that's all."

"He called me a Chinamen. Not once but four times."

"All you had to do was tell me," said Remo. He unraveled the phone cord, which snapped away from Bubba's neck in a small shower of blood. The big body dropped to the lab floor.

"I can't talk to that," Remo said. He wiped the cord clean with a piece of paper. "I could never talk to that now. You could at least have told me."

"I wasn't talking to you. How could I tell you?"

"You can talk enough to tell me I'm an amateur," Remo said.

"That's not talking to you," said Chiun.

"Now we have two bodies," Remo said.

"I'm not cleaning them up."

"You killed one."

"I'm not cleaning it up," Chiun said.

"Kill it, clean it," said Remo. "I'm not running around picking up bodies after you."

"Of course not," Chiun said. "Why show any respect? Mock everything you are taught. Ignore traditions thirty centuries older than your country. I would be shocked if you showed any respect after all these years."

"Respect, my ass. A deal's a deal. Our deal is I don't pick up your bodies and you don't pick up mine."

Chiun turned back to the window. He was ignoring Remo.

"I take it you're back to not speaking to me again,"

Remo said, and when he got no answer, he was sure he was right. He looked around for someplace to store the bodies. The woman would be in soon to tell him how to scan the newspapers by computer.

He found a large cart for refuse outside the office, put both bodies inside and covered them with copies of university regulations that someone had stacked on his desk. He stored the broken table in a closet. He whisked up the broken lamp and tossed the pieces on top of the refuse cart to make it look more like garbage. Then he put the cart in the corner.

"Thank you," he said to Chiun. "For your help."

"You're welcome," said Chiun with a happy little smile.

Then Remo went out to the office manager. She seemed relieved that he was alive.

"What else would I be?" said Remo.

She told him that MUT had developed a computer program to measure a norm of accuracy in the American news media. The computers could read and evaluate material and then give a breakdown and examples of story aberrancy.

"Aberrancy?" asked Remo.

"Where a story differs from the usual accurate norm."

"Right," said Remo. "Keep up the good work. I'll be gone for a few hours. There's a large pile of newspapers in my office to start with. There is also a very unpleasant person in the lab. Do not call him a Chinaman."

"Your colleague?" she asked.

"Yes."

"We already met him this morning. I hate to say this, Professor," she said, kneading her hands. "I know it's not my position, but . . . well."

"Go ahead," said Remo.

"Would you please show him a little more respect? He's done so much for you."

"You certainly have met him," said Remo. "But did he ever tell you what he did for me?"

"It must have been wonderfully sweet. He's so precious, I could die. We all love him."

"Sure. He can con anybody."

"He certainly is not unpleasant as you said. And all the suffering he's gone through to make sure you were brought up properly. Well, we'd all be so happy if you would show him a little more respect."

"I'd like to do a biopsy on your mind," said Remo.

It was a pleasant spring afternoon, and since it looked like garbage Remo was pushing, no one bothered him or even noticed. He rolled the cart along Memorial Drive until he found a pleasant tree-shaded grassy knoll where he parked the cart and the bodies and returned to the lab. The computer program was under way.

The office manager had gotten a half-year's television tapes from the studios, the MUT name being magic in Boston. She showed Remo how to do a scan of the television tapes.

Remo did the scan while the office manager brought Chiun a light ginseng tea. She was middle-aged and plump. She cooed whenever she approached Chiun. Remo asked for a glass of water. She informed Remo that getting refreshments was not among her duties.

"We do extra things for people who are exceptionally pleasant. Or people who treat those who deserve respect with respect."

"A gracious woman has spoken," said Chiun as the office manager nodded approval. Chiun sipped the tea. Remo didn't need the water anyway.

The first readout on aberrancy of the Boston media concerned the television news. The report read: "Television reporters apparently function under the assumption that they themselves are the news."

Remo pressed the scanner. There was the face of Deborah Potter. There was Deborah Potter announcing the pregnancy of Deborah Potter. She was announcing it to her husband, Paul Potter, who was co-anchor. The main news story for the city that day was what Paul Potter thought of conception.

The Boston Blade carried a story on the conception. The other networks commented. In one six-month period, there were 176 news stories on which television anchor person was having difficulty with which personnel manager at which station. It not only was on the television news, *The Blade* reported on it too.

There was the monthly report on Deborah Potter's pregnancy.

And then came one section that Remo was especially interested in. It was about oil.

There was a debate over the Middle East. Three reporters monitored the debate between two people who agreed about everything. Everyone was agreeing. The reporters were telling each other how wonderful they were.

Someone said Egypt was in Europe. It was one of the reporters. No one contradicted him.

Every reporter looked alert and responsible. They could look alert and responsible asking for someone to pass the ashtray. The debate concluded that Boston had the best news media in the world. The final note sounded was that everyone should listen to the Boston media, and the Middle East problems would be solved. The Boston media called for niceness and a civil rights act for the Middle East. This was logical because one reporter thought that the Palestine Liberation Organization was some sort of civil rights group. He also thought it was based in Israel. No one contradicted him. They were too busy congratulating him on his five-part series on the Middle East.

Remo couldn't make sense of the anchor people. They all sounded like clones of each other, except for one black sports announcer. He showed insight and enthusiasm, and it was a pleasure for Remo to hear about something that a reporter thought was more interesting than he was. The black reporter was fired before the last month of tapes, and none of the other stations picked him up.

The Blade was even more confusing than the television nets. There were many articles on oil. One of

70

them said that America should be more responsive to Arab demands because of Arab oil. There were many articles about how America was paying a high price for oil because the Arabs had been offended. There were ominous threats of cutoffs of oil by the Arabs.

Then there was a five-part series about how America was being unfair to the Arabs by blaming them for using oil as blackmail. It was written by Melody Wakefield.

At the time the Iran-Iraq war broke out, splitting Arab countries into different sides, Melody Wakefield covered a convention of Arab-Americans in Boston. Melody Wakefield asked 107 incisive questions at the convention. Not one of them mentioned the Iran-Iraq war. Most of them had to do with how unfairly the Arabs were being treated in the news media in America. The rest had to do with how unfairly the Arabs were being treated in the Middle East. A few had to do with major Arab contributions to world civilization and why Americans wouldn't recognize them.

There was only one question in the 107 that didn't sound as if it had been drafted by the Arabs' public relations staff. That question was, where was the ladies' room. It was the one question that didn't get an answer.

The Blade called the Melody Wakefield series hard-hitting and explosive, "telling you what some people don't want you to know about the Middle East." The implication was that there were vast forces fighting the courageous truth of Melody Wakefield.

Remo gave up and called the office manager, who had returned to her desk.

"I can't get what I want from this thing," he said. "The media up here is all aberration."

"That's not so," she said. "It only seems like it. The computer just gives you the bad parts, not the good work."

"How long would the good work take?" asked Remo. "A minute?"

"I would not expect you to understand, sir. Anyone

who could treat such a kind, decent, gentle person with such depraved lack of gratitude certainly isn't fit to pass judgment on the media of our city."

"Who?" said Remo. "Who have I mistreated?"

Chiun cleared his throat in the background. He smiled and the office manager brought him another cup of ginseng tea.

Bradford Wakefield III waited for the telephone call from his contact, telling him that all had been taken care of with the two new scientists at MUT. He waited past noon and past three P.M., when his granddaughter, Melody, called from Hamidi Arabia.

Melody didn't know whether to do a ten-part series for *The Blade* on how the West defamed Islam or a twenty-part series on how the West defamed Islam.

She had plenty of time to think about it in Hamidi Arabia because no mullah would speak to her in the clothes she was wearing. She had also been told to read the Koran, but she thought it was boring. And one thing the world was not allowed to do was to bore a Wakefield.

"Melody, I am waiting for an important call," said Bradford.

"You mean I'm not important, Grandpapa?"

"Not as important as this call I'm waiting for."

"Grandpapa, I am in the greatest revolution of all time, where the wealth of the West has been transferred to a Third World country. Now, that is important," she said.

Bradford understood what she meant by a transfer of wealth. That meant little old ladies in Maine keeping their homes at 60 degrees in the dead of winter and paying ten times as much for their heat anyway. When a Wakefield referred to the wealth of the West that had to be shared with developing countries, it was not Wakefield wealth but the single homes of middle-class families, the long summer vacations by car, people's color television sets, and inexpensive and abundant food. This was the transfer of wealth they were talking

72

about. OPEC profits just made the Wakefield fortune larger.

"Melody, I regret that the transfer of wealth from the West might be our own wealth if you don't hang up."

The phone clicked as dead as if it had been cut by a razor blade. Melody was a good girl, her grandfather thought. She was only trying to do for the Arabs what her earlier book had done for the Vietnamese and Cambodians, when she proved beyond argument that the only thing wrong with those countries was American's presence in them.

When America had left and the Cambodian communists engaged in a population slaughter unseen since Adolf Hitler, *The Blade*, through Melody Wakefield's typewriter, proved that it was not the communists' fault for the killing, but America's because America had bombed that country years before.

When the Vietnamese took to the boats to escape their "liberators" from the north, *The Blade* proved that boat people weren't really Vietnamese at all, but Chinese money lenders. Melody's poisoned pen led the attack.

Melody loved revolutionary discipline for the masses and sometimes, Bradford knew, she only went to these countries to watch revolutionary discipline in action. She had her own whip for revolutionary discipline. She carried it in her traveling bags or sometimes stuffed into her high leather boots.

Bradford looked at his watch. It was four P.M. and still no call. He went to his stone patio to look out over his own rocky shoreline of Mamtasket. He paced until four-thirty P.M., when his stomach started heaving.

The paper had been trying to reach him for an hour, but that wasn't the phone call he wanted. The paper phoned again. And when Bradford ordered his butler to tell his newspaper not to bother him anymore, the butler said it was about a killing.

"What?" said Wakefield. "Give me the phone."

The managing editor told him there had been a

racial killing near MUT, across the river from Boston. Two blacks had been found murdered, stuffed into a trash cart and left along Memorial Drive.

"Did one of them . . . did one of them . . ." said Bradford, his voice choking, his legs becoming weak. "Did one of them have very large hands?"

"Yes. He was identified as the civil rights activist who only wanted freedom for his people—Bubba. We helped get him out of the racist oppressor jail."

Bradford felt weak. He hadn't felt so weak since a Jew and Catholic and somebody from Ohio had tried to move into Mamtasket.

He hadn't minded the Jew. He was quiet and could be ignored. The Catholic was in industrialist who was called "the rapacious beast of Wall Street," so he and Bradford had something in common. But the family from Ohio laughed loudly and sang songs. Right out in the open. One of them ate a hot dog on a bun, and the father had been raised on a farm where they grew things. They went to football games. And none of the games was Harvard. Their youngest daughter had those big Midwest things on her chest called breasts. No Wakefields had them. They had decent old line New England breasts. Egg size. Fried egg.

Bradford hung up on his editor and shakily made his way into his study and phoned the one person he hated to give bad news to.

"Hello," said Friend at the other end of the line.

"The initial attempt on the two new scientists failed," said Wakefield.

"Fine," said Friend cheerily.

"You're not bothered?"

"No."

"But I thought you didn't allow failure."

"Not at all. How foolish I would be if I insisted on perfection. Do you know how unreal that is?"

"Then you have a contingency plan for a second attempt?"

"Of course," said Friend.

That was the beautiful thing about Friend. He never

panicked. And he always had answers and orders immediately.

"First, you will find out everything about the way your two workers died. Then you will head north on your boat until you are outside Kennebunkport, Maine. And you will wait there."

"We aren't going to get those two now?"

"We are going to follow directions, Bradford."

"Yes, Friend," said Bradford Wakefield III.

The reports from his newspaper on the black men's deaths weakened Bradford's stomach even more. He was so upset, he had to drink enriched baby formula and mush.

The two men found in the refuse cart could not have been killed by human means, the coroner said. The killings were just too precise for human hands. The large one was strangled, and while that required inhuman strength, it was not nearly so much as the strength that would have been required just to hold the big one in place for strangling.

The conclusion—he had been killed with something that worked like an extra-strong forklift and baling machine.

The smaller one was killed with a blow so precise, it would make a surgeon jealous. No human killer could have been that accurate.

The conclusion—death by forces unknown.

Bradford Wakefield had been anchored off the coast of Maine for two days when a small fishing trawler approached his yacht.

A man barely over five feet tall came aboard the yacht. He wore a three-piece summer suit and wire-rimmed glasses, and he did not smile. He did not offer his right hand to shake, either.

His name was Merton, and he did not give his last name. He spoke in a British accent and seemed to know everything there was to know about Bradford Wakefield III, his physical health and, more importantly, some of his relationship with Friend.

"You know Friend?" asked Wakefield.

"Yes, I do."

Merton seemed to be able to sit on the frail wooden deck chair with hardly any pressure. For a moment, Bradford thought he was entertaining a robot. Passing Merton's chair to go to the railing, Wakefield touched the Englishman. But the flesh was warm and human. No robot.

Merton smiled inwardly. People often did that to him. They would sense a lack of human response and then try to touch him. It did not bother him on occasions like this, but it did bother him in his personal life.

His son had once said to him, "Are you my natural father, sir?"

"Yes, I am," Merton had said. "Why did you ask?"

"Because, sir, I have read in biology that during copulation, people emit sounds of joy and secrete bodily fluids."

"That is correct."

"I cannot imagine you, sir, doing those things."

"Quite," said Merton, trying to remember the time he had copulated with his wife, Lady Wissex. He tried to remember if he perspired. He didn't think he had. But one didn't think about those things at a time like that.

Instead, Lord Wissex had thought about completing his orgasm and removing himself from Lady Wissex. When he found out she had indeed conceived, he sent her a little silver garden bucket with a note reading: "Good show. You've done your duty and I've done mine. We'll never have to go through that again."

His son also said to him once, "I wonder, sir, how you have been so able to restore our family fortune. From what I have studied of our history, your father left you almost penniless."

"I do work, boy."

"What work, sir?"

"The sort of work our family did to earn its title."

"But, sir," the boy said, "that was murdering Catholics for King Henry."

76

"Quite," said Merton.

"You kill Catholics, sir?" asked the boy incredulously. "For the government?"

"Of course not. These are modern times. We don't practice that sort of religious prejudice anymore. And we're not bloody civil servants, no matter what others may think. Someone has found me who appreciates skill at the highest level. Not British, but he's a decent enough sort."

"Is it possible to be not British, but decent, sir?" his son asked.

"I think so. Never met the chap, but I think he has the soul of royalty. Actually, he sounds American," said Lord Wissex.

So Merton Lord Wissex this day found himself on an American's yacht off the Maine coast, with the American upset by the Briton's cool nature. The American, of course, did not know Merton was of the peerage. It really wouldn't matter anyhow. Merton Lord Wissex did not intend to know the chap long.

"Is that all the information you have about how you lost your two operatives?" Merton asked.

"All? You've taken four pages of notes," said Wakefield.

"Quite so. I wonder if I might trouble you for a spot of tea."

"Of course," said Bradford.

Wakefield decided that he hated this man, and it took him a moment to figure out why. This man called Merton actually was condescending to him. How could anyone condescend to a Wakefield? It was for a Wakefield to condescend.

The tea came with one of the stewards.

"You're not having tea," said the Briton.

" 'Course I'm having tea," said Bradford. "I always have tea. I have the best teas in the world available to me. Better than Britain."

"How nice," said Merton.

"I take it you have known Friend long?" Wakefield asked.

"That depends on what one considers long."

"I consider an hour long if one has to be with some-one who is condescending," said Bradford. "You know, I gave you an awful lot of information. I don't see how you can call it inadequate."

"Hmmmm," said Merton.

"Name one question I didn't answer."

"How were your people killed?"

"I told you," said Wakefield.

"No, you didn't. You just described in detail the result. But we have no idea what killed them. Or how."

"Those two phony scientists."

"Seems a bit more than a scientist would do, what?"

"They're not scientists," Wakefield said. "They must be somebody's agents."

"Obviously," said Merton.

"So they did the killing."

"But how, Mr. Wakefield? How?"

"Effectively, obviously. If Friend would send me some more operatives instead of someone so obviously not an operative, I would have those scientists finished. Let me tell you this, Merton. I ran this operation to perfection until this point. And I resent your coming in here to push papers around and write reports."

"Why are you so sure I am not an operative, as you put it?"

"Look at you. Not enough meat on you to dress a coat rack," said Bradford. He liked that. He drank from his teacup. The tea was a bit too sweet. So sweet it burned his throat.

"Why aren't you drinking?" asked Bradford.

"Because it's poisoned. I poisoned the whole batch."

"Rubbish. I didn't see you go anywhere near the pot," said Wakefield.

"That's right. You're not supposed to see me go anywhere near the pot because if you did see me, old boy, you might not drink the tea, and then I would have to cut your throat. I prefer the least amount of vi-olence. Even though I would cut your throat if I had to."

"You couldn't have poisoned me and be so casual," said Wakefield. "Now, *I* could do it. But not you. You know why, little man? Because we had to rescue you during World War I and World War II. That's why. You think you're better than everyone else but you're not. You know why? I'll tell you why. Because we Wakefields are better than everyone else, that's why. And both of us can't be."

The sun was setting early this day on the yacht. Darkness was coming to Bradford's eyes. His fingertips felt numb. The burning began to tear at his throat. His stomach moved in strange ways.

But he wasn't going to show that twerp Merton that he was suffering. He was going to smile through the whole thing. And then an idea struck him, that last brilliant Wakefield idea.

He whispered to the little twerp.

"You'll never win, you know. They beat everyone," he said, and then he smiled.

"Bluffs don't suit you well, colonial," said Merton.

"I know now. Nobody can defeat them. Only sorry I won't be here to see them put you in your place, bloody English twerp."

Merton Lord Wissex watched the beefy American expire and then neatly emptied the teapot overboard, helped the corpse into a deck chair, and then washed out the teacups himself. He tied the chap's tie, walked up to the bridge of the yacht, chatted amiably with the captain about tides, got behind him when the captain showed him the sextant, broke captain's neck with a short karate chop, broke first mate's neck with similar chop, straightened own tie, left bridge, debarked Wakefield yacht, entered rented trawler, returned to American coast, poisoned trawler captain with laced glass of stout so there would be no identification, phoned Friend informing him of possible trouble, then in boarding room of American hostelry sat down to write a long and deep letter to his son on the importance of good manners.

He started it five times, each time throwing away the

79

first page. He just couldn't quite get through to the boy how utterly important manners were.

Without manners, he wrote finally, man is a beast.

Chambermaid entered room, discovered gun paraphernalia and had to be removed. And was. Suffocation.

Chapter Five

On the mountain road that divides the island of St. Maarten's in the Dutch West Indies, Peter John, an upright man with a small herd of cows and a farm that through his courage fed a large family on but two acres, could not start his car.

He was a religious man, and he took the little setback with joyful calm. These were things of life. But within one day, because he could not start his car, a president of the United States would face the most horrifying decision of his life and do what he had vowed no president of the United States would ever have to do again.

And because Peter John could not start his car, assassins would fly into his little island to settle a centuries-old feud, and a computer chip would continue advancing toward its greatest profit venture ever, even if it meant the end of the civilized world.

Four times Peter John pressed the accelerator of his Ford station wagon, and four times there was nothing. Not even a cough.

"Betty, you naughty girl, you start now, precious," Peter John said to his station wagon. He talked to his car the way he talked to his animals. No one could ever prove to him that machines did not have souls.

"The only difference between a machine and an animal is that the machine won't kick you. The only difference between a machine and a person is that a machine will never give bitter tongue to pain the heart. I love my Betty," Peter John would say.

This morning Betty did not love him. She would not move and she would not cough, and Peter John got out of the station wagon and lifted the hood. There was a white soapy substance on the carburetor. He tried to smell it. It was odorless. He took a piece of it in his fingertips. It felt waxy.

But it crumbled. His fingertips stung a little bit, and he noticed that the pink pads turned just a shade whiter. Peter John was a black man, and he felt God had made him black so that the sun could kiss him without harm. Peter John did not yell of pride in his blackness or hold workshops on maintaining his blackness; he just wanted to be black for the rest of his life because that was what he was. And he reasoned that if this waxy substance could cause the pink pads of the underside of his hands to turn white, then it might do the same thing to the rest of his body, and he did not want that.

So he immediately phoned for an appointment with the doctor in Marigot, the French part of the island. He decided to use his friend's Chevrolet to drive there.

But that too would not start, and it too had the white substance in the carburetor. And so did another friend's Peugot.

Peter John reasoned that if it were in the carburetors, it might have come through the gas. So he opened the gas tank of Betty, and there was a small explosion of white waxy material that splashed all over him. The material had been compressed somehow in the gas tank, and Peter John wondered who would do such a nasty trick to such nice cars.

He telephoned the bus company that ran through the island. But no one answered, strangely enough, and he decided to hitchhike. He had heard from tourists that in America, hitchhiking took a long time because many cars would pass up people, especially black people. But Peter John knew the people of St. Maarten's were nicer than that. He never had trouble hitch-hiking, and he never passed up people, either.

But this morning no cars were on the road, as he walked.

He walked past the large, sprawling acres of the Puressence Laboratory, and there he saw, high on the hill, a few very tiny cars chugging around, spilling off a purple exhaust. He had never seen an exhaust like that, but even down on the road beneath the laboratory's high hill, he could smell its bitter odor. It made breathing hard, even at this great distance.

He saw cars on the road, but none of them were moving. A few had popped their gas caps, and the white substance that he thought someone had dumped into his car in a prank was spilling out of the other cars. One gas station was a mound of white wax with the pumps and the concrete they had been set into lying back on their sides.

Peter John was now flecked with little white spots where the white substance had touched him, and the spots stung—not greatly but like an annoying mosquito.

His doctor was a Dutchman who had married a Frenchwoman and decided to settle on the French side of the divided island. He had treated Peter John's entire family.

John had lost three of his eight children. He attributed that to God's will. But he still had five of the eight. He attributed that to his doctor's skill. Peter John was generally a very happy man. He was also considered "that fool Peter John" by many, including his doctor.

"Excuse me, doctor," he said after his long walk, "but a strange substance attacked my car and is now attacking me." He pointed to the painful white spots on his rich black skin.

"What did it do to your car?" the doctor asked.

"One day there was gasoline in my car, and the next there was this waxy burning substance."

"In the gas tank?" asked the doctor.

"It burns the skin," Peter John said.

83

"Yes, but did it do permanent damage to the engine?"

"I don't know."

"I will tell you why I ask. I have long admired that Ford station wagon of yours. Yes, I must confess. She has attracted me for years. What do you want for her?"

"I came to have my skin healed."

"All right. Take two aspirin and phone me if it doesn't get better."

"Why two aspirin?" asked Peter John.

"Why not two aspirin?"

"What good will they do me?"

"What harm will they do you?"

"They will not cure my skin trouble."

"If you know that, why did you come here?" said the doctor. He thought for a while, looking at Peter John's skin, and suddenly horror seized his face. His eyes widened and his mouth dropped open.

"No," he gasped.

"What is wrong? What have you discovered about me?"

"Maybe if your car was attacked by this, others might be also."

"Some were," Peter John said. "I saw them."

"I hope we're not too late," the doctor said. He ran out of the office, with Peter John following him. He ran down a garbage-strewn alley. He hopped over a fence. His knees were cut as he fell but he kept on running.

Finally, crying for air, the doctor reached a small building and threw open the doors. A sleek gray Peugot sat on the immaculate white concrete, its tires gleaming black, its chrome polished perfect.

The doctor rushed to the front seat and put a key into the ignition. He saw that Peter John had followed him.

"It's in God's hands now," said the doctor. "We can only hope and pray it has not spread this far."

He closed his eyes, prayed, and turned the ignition.

There was a cough and a sputter and the Peugot kicked over and the doctor laughed, tears of gratitude coming to his eyes.

"I am happy for you," said Peter John.

"Would you like a ride?"

"I would like my skin cured."

"Let's try washing it," said the doctor. "I have some absolutely pure water that I keep for my car. You may use it on your skin, but not too much."

John saw the doctor pointing to the back of the garage. He saw the water in plastic jars. He saw that it came from springs in France. The label read: "This water exclusive for use with Peugot and not to be wasted on eyewashes, etc., etc."

Peter John poured the water over his arms. A soothing relief came to the burning little white spots. They even darkened a bit.

"It works," said Peter John. "May I keep this pure water?"

"For your skin?"

"Yes."

"That's awfully expensive stuff to use just for one's body," said the doctor. "But all right. Come ride with me. I will take you home. I want to see your station wagon for myself. Maybe I will not want to buy it anymore if it is badly damaged."

The doctor took the long route home to show Peter John how well a decent car ran. The route cut through the port of Peterburg, with the giant oil tanks. Everything on the island of St. Maarten's ran by oil, even the electric generators.

But as they approached the giant oil tanks, a strange thing happened. With a gigantic crunching gurgle, the tank tops began to rise, and Peter John and the doctor could see that the tops were rising on a foam of the white waxy substance. Tons of it, pushing up the top, looking like frosting on a giant birthday cake.

Slowly the lights of Peterburg dimmed. Windows opened as air conditioning stopped. People ran out into

85

the streets, looking for someone to blame about the electricity going off.

"Hurry," said Peter John. He was frightened, for it was evening, and darkness was coming soon to the little island, and there would be only candlelight, as there had been a century before when Peter John's ancestors came to the island as slaves, purchased by the doctor's ancestors.

And then the doctor's car stopped.

The doctor put aside the pain in his heart and opened the hood of his dead car. He examined the gas tank. The gas cap almost popped off. Whatever this white stuff was, it attacked the gasoline and changed it. That was why Peter John's car had stopped. And his too.

Before his eyes, the doctor saw what was happening. The grease and lubrication of his car were moving. The doctor blinked. It was writhing as if it were alive, and then all the grease and oil turned white and waxy and still. A chemical process was happening before his eyes—possibly a bacteriological process. Whatever this bacterium was, it seemed to travel through the air and attacked all petroleum very quickly. And then it was still.

Around them, Peter John and the doctor saw other cars rolling to a stop. Radios and television stopped. Suddenly the island was still. A cricket chirped in the rich green growth that had been drinking the bright Caribbean sun all day. Somewhere off on a dark hillside, a cow mooed.

"This is terrible," the doctor said.

"It's rather beautiful," said Peter John.

In Peterburg, an American official was at the community long-distance telephone station called Landsradio. He had purchased his time for a telephone call to the United States, and he was describing what had happened.

"You have gas or oil anywhere, and it turns to wax. Something happens to it. No, it's not chemical, I don't

86

think. Maybe some kind of bacteria they manufacture here or something. I don't know. The ships in the harbor still have their lights on. Yeah. We can get you all you want, but how do we get it off the island? Half the planes are grounded. Their fuel tanks are wax. I don't know what the shit is, for Christ's sake."

He waited by the telephone for the return call from the States. He noticed that the receiver was becoming somewhat soft in his hand. His thumbprint was on the white plastic of the receiver. Then he remembered that plastic was made from a petroleum base. His shirt felt clammy, and he remembered that the synthetics of the shirt were made from a petroleum base.

He pulled at his shirt. Instead of feeling like cloth, it felt like warm caramel.

His callback was almost immediate. Yes, his superiors in the Department of Commerce were interested in the substance, and they wanted five tons of it.

"Five tons?" he asked incredulously. "Why do you need so much for testing?"

"Well, everybody wants to test it. Defense. Agriculture. CIA."

"No way. How can I get you five tons?"

"What can you get?"

"An oil can full."

"Good. We'll fly in a plane."

The first plane that came for the substance couldn't take off again. The second one immediately covered its engines with a fine gauze screen to protect anything in the air from getting to its fuel. It made the mistake, however, of taking off into an inland breeze. It got to 7,000 feet before the engines stopped and the controls became mush. Guests at the Mullet Bay Hotel stood on their verandas watching. Another plane took off and made it out seven miles before it dropped into the sea.

Finally, the government employee wrapped a whole mess of the white waxy substance in a big tightly woven canvas bag so that it would not be carried by the wind, and went around to hangars at the airport looking for planes that might not have been affected. Two hangars in the lee of a hill, their windows shut tight, had such planes. The employee waited until there was a breeze coming in off the ocean and then had the pilot fly right out into it.

The canvas bag of the substance reached Washington that day, and by nightfall, the president of the United States was being told that civilization as they knew it might well be endangered.

"Well," he said with a charming twinkle, "that certainly is a problem. But then again, we've faced problems like these before and won. What it took was spunk, a willingness to work and, well, just plain faith, I guess."

His words brought a few gentle tears to the members of his cabinet. Lumps came up in throats. They thought about the hard times and how people got through those sorts of times by hard work and faith. Most of them had gotten to where they were by hard work and faith. They were from California, and they were familiar with deep, meaningful traditions. That was because all theirs were fresh. None of them went beyond a year ago June. There was nothing like California for a fresh tradition.

"Excuse me, Mr. President," said the reporting scientist. "You have not faced the extinction of civilization like this."

"Oh, gosh, yes, we have. That's where you're wrong, mister. We've faced it before and won."

There was applause in the cabinet room. The secretary of defense said he had never seen a better performance. The secretary of the interior said he hadn't been so inspired since he saw the beautiful neat cartons of a new paper company built where a forest had once littered the landscape.

The president of the United States thanked everyone.

But the scientist was adamant.

"I don't think I have quite made myself clear. This is not a battle to try men's wills. It is a disaster. It is an avalanche that is coming down on all of us."

"I played in an avalanche movie," said the president. "I remember we hid in a log cabin. It was with Vera Hruba Ralston. We fell in love in the cabin and then when I got out, I hunted down the man who caused the avalanche. Gave him a good punch in the nose and that was it."

The secretary of defense nodded. He was glad the president had everything under control because his system couldn't stand another shock. He was still trying to recover from what had happened to him the previous week at an Army base.

He was being shown a weapon by some soldiers. He liked weapons. They reminded him of accounting offices, neat and tidy.

"Go ahead and try your weapon," the secretary of defense had said. And then there was this awful deafening bang of a noise.

"What in bleet hawzus name was that?"

"That was a gun, sir," explained the colonel assigned to escort him.

"A what?"

"A gun, sir."

"Well, I know what that is, but what the hell are people doing hunting on an Army base?"

"No, no. Not for hunting. Infantrymen use guns too, sir. Rifles. Pistols. Cannons. Guns, sir."

"Oh. Well, what does the noise do?" the secretary of defense had asked.

"Do? It doesn't do anything."

"Then why do you have it?"

"It comes when you shoot a projectile. It is the gunpowder exploding."

"Yes?"

"Well, that's it. The noise is a byproduct of shooting a projectile."

"Okay," said the secretary of defense, his logical mind moving in for the kill. "Why do you want to shoot projectiles anyway? What's the purpose in that?"

"Well, sir, it's to kill the enemy."

"How do you know it's going to kill the enemy?"

"You don't, sir," said the colonel. "Sometimes you miss."

"Then what you have is a waste of a projectile, correct?"

"Yes, sir."

"I see. Well, we'll have to cut that out. We're not going to just waste the taxpayers' money hurling expensive projectiles around, not even knowing if they're going to miss or not. That's why radio carbon laser computer ray systems are so much better."

"Can an infantryman carry one?"

"Oh, no. It's the size of a house and won't be off the drawing boards until the year 2038 at the earliest. But it is better. And it doesn't make noise. A gun, you say?"

The secretary of defense had shaken his head to get the ringing noises out, but he hadn't been the same since. He was glad everything was under control. He just wished that noisy scientist would leave the cabinet room.

The scientist was talking. "I am saying that we are in danger of losing the world's petroleum supply."

"Impossible," said the secretary of defense. "It's all underground."

The scientist sighed. He had a little bottle with the waxy substance and another bottle that appeared empty. A third tightly sealed bottle was filled with black oil.

"These are anaerobic bacteria," he said holding up the apparently empty bottle. "Anaerobic means they can function without air. That is why once they are introduced into any oil system, they can go completely through it because they don't need air to reproduce or survive. So they can consume the contents of the oil under the ground, once they're introduced there."

"But who would introduce them?" asked the secretary of defense.

"The air itself, if they don't have to travel far," the scientist said. "Fortunately, they seem able to be blown about for only short distances. The ships off the shore

90

of St. Maarten's still appear to be working all right, so that means the bacteria were not blown that far out."

"Punch him in the nose," said the president.

"What, sir?"

"I punched him in the nose and then we all lived happily ever after."

"These are bacteria, sir. You can't punch them in the nose."

"If we could, we'd be a lot better off, I tell you."

"Yes. That would be true," said the scientist. "But we can't."

"No. I guess we can't. Those days are gone," said the president.

"Never go near a gun when it is being used," said the secretary of defense, shaking his head. "Wheew, those things make noises just like giant firecrackers."

The scientist said desperately, "There is going to be no oil left on the planet. No oil. No gasoline. No plastics made from oil. None."

"Maybe it just means the end of the oil glut," said the president.

"No, sir," said the scientist. "It means the end of the internal combution engine, which just about means the end of industry. There will be no more cars running on gasoline unless some substitute is found, which will be a lot more expensive than we're paying now. Can you imagine ten-dollar-a-gallon gasoline? That is if this bacterium doesn't attack the synthetic fuels also."

"Oh," said the president. "The end of the industrial age."

"Back to the horse and plow," said the scientist. "Maybe back to the caves."

"Unless," said the president. He was used to people warning him about things. When someone came to you with a warning, he was invariably trying to sell you something, some idea or weapon or program. Nothing ever seemed to reach his desk without a warning attached. But this thing in the little bottle seemed real. It was not the same as the warning he'd gotten that morning that if America did not spend three times its gross national product on beautifying the prison system, someone was going to be unhappy in Harlem and therefore America would end. The person who was going to be unhappy in Harlem, of course, was the person who wanted to run the $20 trillion prison system, with every second-story man getting his own personal psychiatrist and live-in mistress.

That was nonsense, but this looked real. No matter how pretty the movies made ancient times look, history was, in truth, a bunch of people dying in their thirties from upset stomachs and cold weather and no food.

This was a real crisis. He watched the scientist take the tops off the apparently empty bottle and the small vial of oil. He held the open ends of the bottles together. The oil suddenly became cloudy, then bubbled and turned to wax.

"You have just witnessed the rapid-breeding bacterium," the scientist said. "This bacterium consumes petroleum. A bottle dumped into an oil well, in minutes would be reproducing itself over and over, so rapidly that it might be only hours before it consumed the entire underground pool of oil. And it can do this because it needs no air. It is anaerobic."

"What's the white stuff? Maybe we can sell the white stuff," said the secretary of defense. He had come from a large industrial company and had taken over the nation's defense.

"The white stuff is dead bacteria. Like human pus, sir," said the scientist. "You must understand that if I am a little vague, it is because this is not my particular field. I was called in as a last resort."

"Well, let's get someone in this particular field," said the president. "And let's do it now."

"That is part of the disaster, Mr. President. There is no one in this particular field who can be reached. I wouldn't be here if there was. But I can't impress on you too much the importance of this. With enough oil to breed on, this bacterium could grow until it's as large as the Rockies. It's horrifying."

"We can handle the Rockies. Turn them into a

92

parking lot for Los Angeles," said the secretary of the interior. "L.A. needs parking."

"Why can't we get any scientists in that field?" asked the president. He ignored the secretary of the interior. He liked to ignore his secretary of the interior. He only wished the press would also.

"I found, to my horror, when I tried to get some assistance that they have all gone. First, every expert in the field was attracted to MUT, and then they were either killed or hired off somewhere. Where, I don't know. In essence, sir, we are facing an epidemic—a petroleum epidemic—with all the doctors gone."

"You mean the entire oil supply of the world is in danger."

"Exactly."

"I think someone has planned this thing," said the president. "I think whoever removed the experts in this field made that invisible stuff there that becomes the white stuff. That's what I think."

"I think you may be right, sir," said the scientist.

So did the other cabinet members.

"Well," said the secretary of defense. "Now that we've got that settled, let's move on to the next item on the agenda."

"Let's stay with this one for a while," said the president wearily. Maybe his secretary of defense would really be happier back in private industry.

"Where did these bacteria come from in the first place?" the president asked. "Why were they created?"

"To clean up oil spills," said the scientist.

"Why would anyone want to clean up oil spills?" asked the secretary of the interior.

"To protect the oceans and the sea creatures who live in the ocean," the president said.

"Environmentalists," said the secretary of interior. "I knew they'd cause us trouble. What has an environmentalist ever produced?"

The president sighed again. Maybe his secretary of the interior would be happier back in private industry too. But that was for later. For now was this problem, and the president understood it better than anyone else at the table. The bacterium had been created for a purpose. The people who might be able to stop it had already been removed from helping. That had been part of the plan too. And now civilization was ready to get thrown back to the Bronze Age if he did not stop this evil force, whoever or whatever it was. He knew he would now have to use that one power he had said he would never use.

He went to his bedroom and to the top drawer of the bureau. This was what every outgoing president showed the new one. He remembered his predecessor opening the drawer and telling him, "You don't control it. You can only suggest. It won't do everything you suggest."

"How do you know?" asked the new president.

"You're still alive, aren't you?" said the old president. "And I lost the election, didn't I?"

"I'll never use it," said the new president. And he had meant it.

Then.

He picked up the red telephone.

The bacterium had to be stopped. The people behind it had to be stopped. It would do no good to worry about the sanctity of the Constitution because if the bacteria were loosed on the world, there would be no Constitution. No America. He had to use the secret agency he had sworn never to use.

There was a sharp, lemony voice on the other end of the line.

"Yes, Mr. President."

"Civilization has a problem. It's rather sudden, but there is no one else I can turn to. It must be stopped."

"If you are talking about the rapid-breeder bacteria, we are already on it," the lemony voice said.

"Then you know about the missing scientists at MUT and the fact that there's nobody left to help us."

"We already have people at MUT," said the acid voice.

"Then you must know what in the Lord's name is

94

behind this. What possible purpose could anyone have in eliminating the world's oil supplies?"

"We don't know that yet. But we are fairly certain that that is the purpose. And what this person, whoever he is, has done by removing the oil scientists is to eliminate the defenses against him before we ever had a chance to deploy them."

"How many men do you have on this?" asked the president.

"One man. And his trainer."

"One man? One man? What kind of an operation are you running? The world's facing disaster, and you've got one man and a trainer on it?"

"He is a very special man," the acid voice answered coolly.

"Will he be enough?" asked the president wearily.

"If he isn't, then nothing will be."

"I hope so," said the president.

After he replaced the telephone in his office inside Folcroft Sanitarium in Rye, New York, Dr. Harold Smith looked at the phone and said softly, "I hope so too. I hope so too."

Chapter Six

Chiun watched porters carrying the fourteen lacquered steamer trunks out of the door of the suit in the Copley Plaza Hotel. Remo knew he referred to the porters as "cheap white help" even though half of them were black.

Remo was glad Chiun had the porters. If he didn't have them, he would have tried to get Remo to move the trunks around. Or some passerby. Remo had seen Chiun directing women and children whom he had conned into carrying the great steamer trunks of the Master of Sinanju.

Chiun saw Remo watching and used the occasion to lecture him. "The problem with America is the amateur assassin. Nay, the problem with the world. And we are living in an age of great debauchery, where these services are given away. Randomly given away. Willy nilly given away. On street corners."

"We have a noon plane to Anguilla," said Remo. "We're going to sail to St. Maarten's. Smith just made contact with me on that. They're making that germ stuff on St. Maarten's."

"Decent competent assassins are now being affected by this wanton attitude of giveaway," said Chiun.

"We'd better hurry," said Remo. "Boston traffic is a mess."

"Years of training, poof. Gone like the wind that never was, and all that is left for a tired old man is the ingratitude of he who has benefited from years of the old man's wisdom."

"Smitty asked if you'd like a lighter, more portable tape machine," said Remo.

"But who cares?" said Chiun. "Who cares that the training will begin to suffer because of bad attitudes? Who cares that the Masters of Sinanju are, have been for ages, responsible for the food and the roofs of the whole village? Oh, no. We do not care anymore. What is tradition? What is responsibility? *Poooffff.*"

"I told Smitty no," said Remo. "I told him it took you a month to learn how to work the tape machine you've got. I told him you didn't like new things."

And then in somber fury, the Master of Sinanju turned to his pupil and said in majestic and awesome tones, "You should have taken it, idiot. Suppose the one I have now breaks?"

In the hotel lobby, a man in a three-piece suit and a monocle, with a British accent you could paddle a canoe on, inquired if Remo were perchance a professor at MUT? And did he, perchance, work with an Oriental? And was he, perchance, an authority on bacteria, the fast-breeding bacteria that consumed oil?

"That was yesterday," said Remo. "We know where your headquarters is now, so we don't need you anymore to find your boss. Go home and get lost."

"I beg your pardon."

"I am catching a plane. I am too busy to kill you. You are going to try to kill me, right?"

"How impertinent," said the Briton.

Fourteen steamer trunks came out the fire exit in a caravan, led by Chiun, an Oriental wisp in a golden day robe.

"Ah, your colleague."

"Hey, Chiun, this guy wants to kill us, but we've got a plane to catch."

"Another amateur," said Chiun haughtily.

And then, as in no other time in his life, Merton Lord Wissex felt the sting of insult.

"I beg your pardon. My family goes back to Henry the Eighth."

Remo smiled tolerantly. "That's very nice."

"What did he say?" asked Chiun, turning back from his trunks for a moment.

"He said his was a new house," said Remo.

"New?" said Chiun.

"Less than a thousand years, right, buddy?" said Remo. He saw the tight British face turn pale. "Yeah, Chiun. Less than a thousand years. He wants to kill us, I think."

"Is he getting paid?" said Chiun. "Tell me, good man, are you being paid?"

"Of course," harrumphed Merton Lord Wissex.

"See, Remo. Even this gets paid," said Chiun. "Even this." And his bony hands and long fingernails pointed to the tweed vest of Merton Lord Wissex.

Traffic to the airport was held up by a religious procession. Remo could make out the signs of the parade: "Stop Racist Murder."

"What's that?" he asked the driver.

"A civil rights leader got killed yesterday. Here. It's in the paper."

The Blade landed on the back seat. Chiun looked back to make sure the three extra taxis for his trunks were following closely.

Remo read the story and shook his head. Apparently, a civil rights leader had been horribly murdered for the "crime of wanting to be free."

There were statements from the religious leaders of the community. The archbishop said racism must be rooted out of the mind of Boston. A rabbi compared the hatred that killed the civil rights worker to the hatred that created the Holocaust. A protestant minister called for armed protection of all civil rights workers.

It seemed the civil rights worker and his friend were found on Memorial Drive, mangled. The civil rights worker's name was Bubba. Remo wondered if he had seen the killer because he was at Memorial Drive the day before, just before the bodies had been found. He was dropping off his own bodies at the time.

This man, however, was not a killer, like the two who had barged into Remo and Chiun's office, but a person who had struggled for prison reform, a proud black revolutionary voice challenging the white conscience. His name was Bubba and Remo felt sorry that he had never met him. He probably would have liked him.

"Why don't we fly to St. Maarten's directly?" Chiun asked.

"Because the whole island had been quarantined. We have to sail in."

"Why don't we sail all the way?"

"We don't have time. Western civilization may go under unless we get this cleaned up right away."

"Why don't we sail all the way?" Chiun repeated. "On a slow boat."

Merton Lord Wissex heard the horrible news.

"But, sir," he said into the public telephone, "I know I can put them away. You don't want them."

"You have described two people whom I wish to employ. What is the problem?" Friend asked.

"If they are dead, they are no problem, sir."

"And if they are employed by me, they are an asset."

"Do you know you can trust them?" asked Lord Wissex.

"We will find out, won't we?" said Friend.

So with great bitterness in his craw, Lord Wissex rushed to the airport, where he followed the parade of fourteen lacquered steamer trunks until he found Remo and Chiun.

He approached the old Oriental. The Oriental seemed a bit more polite.

"Sir, may I speak to you about employment?" said Lord Wissex.

"Absolutely. You're hired," said the Oriental. "Talk to Remo about salary."

"No, sir. You misunderstand. My employer wishes to hire you, sir," said Lord Wissex.

"And he is?" asked Chiun.

"I call him Friend."

"We don't work for friends," said Chiun. "We are professional. Are you sure you wouldn't care to work for us, carrying things, taking care of our clothes? The thing I like most about you Britons is that you know your place."

Raging hatred filled the marrow of Lord Wissex. Words did not move up through the throat. Even the blood felt still and hot in his body.

"Yes, I would love to buttle for you, sir," said Lord Wissex. Those were the words that finally came out of his mouth. He smiled. Once, as a boy, his foot had gotten caught in a trap on his father's estate. The teeth of the trap had bitten to the bone. But that trap hurt far less than the smile he pushed out onto his face at this moment as he said he would love to serve the Oriental.

"I am the Master of Sinanju, and this is my pupil, Remo. Remo, come here. We have a real British servant. They are so good. Not as good as Persian but the best whites in the world."

On the plane, Lord Wissex insisted he serve the tea to his new masters. He would not allow the stewardesses to do it. They lacked proper respect.

"See," said Chiun. "The British know."

Remo still had his copy of *The Blade*. He turned to the front page. There was a big article about the publisher, Bradford Wakefield III, having died of a heart attack in a mystery death. His boat had been found floating off the coast of Maine, with Mr. Wakefield dead of a heart attack and his crew also dead. The crew's deaths appeared to have been from natural causes, too, because it looked as if they had fallen and hit themselves.

Lord Wissex had a very big subservient smile on his face as he served first Chiun, then Remo, the tea. It was a special blend, he said. Chiun sniffed the wafting aroma. Then he nodded.

"Very good," he said.

Remo was interested in *The Blade*'s article. It was sketchy, but from the coroner's statements, Remo thought he had spotted something.

"Little Father," he said, "look at this. Don't these sound like some of our blows? You know, when it looks like the person just fell down and cracked crucial bones. Here. Read what the coroner says about the fracture of the neck bones."

Chiun glanced at the newspaper. Remo pointed to the paragraph he wanted Chiun to read.

"What is that?"

"That's a newspaper report. Something strange in it about the blows killing the sea captain and his first mate. Someone else was killed in such a way to make it look like a heart attack. I'm sure of it."

"How can you be sure of anything from reading?" Chiun asked. "One gets beauty from reading, not information. I won't look at it."

Remo lifted the tea to his lips. Lord Wissex smiled, rubbing his hands. Remo put down the cup.

"I don't know," he said. "In a newspaper you can get information."

"Is there something wrong with your tea, Master?" said Lord Wissex.
wrong."

"What?" said Remo, looking up. "No. Nothing

"Then why don't you drink it?"

"I will. I'm just interested in something," said Remo and, turning to Chiun, he showed how the neck of the captain was reported to have been shattered.

"A variation," Chiun said. "Karate, judo. A variation. Who knows what it might be? It might be any of that junk they teach now to children all over your stupid country. An inferior blow, nevertheless."

"Sure. But for someone without Sinanju, it makes you think. I mean, someone must have gotten on board and gotten off quickly. And this guy Wakefield owned a newspaper. I was supposed to get some kind of word on getting hired from a newspaper. Therefore . . ."

"Therefore you are doing work you shouldn't. A proper assassin eliminates the threats to good government, assures the throne, establishes the peace of a true regency in his land. There is nothing better for a people than a good king assured his throne by his professional assassin. A professional assassin is not a policeman. A puzzle solver. A worrier about such people as this Bradford Wakefield."

"Your tea, sir," said Lord Wissex.

"I'll take the tea," said a plump woman across the aisle. She wore a straw hat with artificial cherries. She had rushed on at the last minute.

"No," said Lord Wissex. "This tea is a special blend for my masters."

"Well, if it's being served on board, I should have a right to it too. I don't think it's fair," said the woman with the straw hat.

"Give her the tea," said Remo. "It smells funny anyhow."

"It's for you, sir," said Lord Wissex. "I made it just for you."

"All right," said Remo. He took the cup and drank it down in one draught.

Lord Wissex waited. When the American curled up in agony, he would attack the old Oriental. He did not care about the difficulty in getting off the plane. He did not care about the orders from Friend. He had never been so humiliated by anyone, and only the death of these two would make up for the shame burning inside his Britannic bosom.

And so Lord Wissex, who had restored his family fortune by service to Friend, waited to watch the American die, prepared to watch his grovel in the aisle of the plane, at which time Lord Wissex would lean over to pretend to help him and in the confusion put a death blow into the throat of the old Oriental.

Then, of course, he could tell Friend that they had attacked him first and it was purely self-defense.

The American returned the empty cup. The American looked to the Oriental. The American said something to the Oriental. Then he smiled at Lord Wissex.

"Are you feeling all right, sir?" asked the butler.

"Sure," said Remo.

"Oh," said Lord Wissex.

"There is something wrong," said the Oriental.

"What?" said Lord Wissex. They know, he thought. And now they will kill me.

"You didn't bow. How can you serve tea without the proper bow?"

"I will remember that, sir," said Wissex.

"They usually can bow quite well," Chiun said to Remo.

Wissex returned to his seat. He thought of burning them alive. He thought of catching them while they slept, pouring gasoline around wherever they slept. He thought of them running screaming from their rooms, their bodies aflame, their skin charring and their voices pitiful wails.

And on this good thought did Lord Wissex manage to overcome his rage of humiliation. He would await the proper time.

But why was the poison taking so long to work?

In Anguilla, Lord Wissex supervised the loading of their small sailboat.

"Hey mon, nobody be allowed off that island," said a dockworker. He was helping to load Chiun's trunks in the hot crystal sunlight of the Caribbean neighbor to St. Maarten's. He pointed to St. Maarten's. "The army and navy has that island sealed off, mon."

The man had little clumps of hair hanging down in braided ropes. He was a Rastafarian and he believed that Haile Selassie, the dead emperor of Ethiopia, was God and that marijuana was a beneficial religious experience. He worked very hard, and the sweat glistened off his body.

"Mon, I will load for you. But I will not go with you. I love Anguilla and do not wish to leave."

103

"All these islands are the same," said Remo. "What's your problem?"

"St. Maarten's is cursed," he said.

"Why?"

"Because they have not acknowledge Haile Selassie as God."

"God? He's dead," Remo said. "He was killed in a palace coup."

"You believe what you read in the newspapers?" laughed the Rasta man.

"Inside America," Remo said. "And outside of Boston."

The Rasta man shook his head. "The white man is through around the whole world, he is."

"See. Even a dock laborer can make sense," said Chiun. "But for servants, no one beats a white."

"It's too hot to listen to this nonsense," said Remo.

"That means you're not breathing properly," said Chiun.

"Holding my breath, it'd be too hot to listen to this."

"I tend to agree with Mr. Remo," said Lord Wissex, sweltering in his tweeds. He was still waiting for the American to fall unconscious from the poison. Why didn't that bloke drop? There was enough poison in that tea to fell a platoon.

"Where did you pick up this servant?" Chiun asked Remo. "Talking without being spoken to. Next time, check references."

With all the trunks aboard the little sailing boat, and a commercial captain at the wheel, the three set out for St. Maarten's, in the distance. Lord Wissex slipped a thin needle from the lining of his coat. He moved first behind the American. He brought the needle smoothly up to the American's neck. Then, with a short lunging jab, he drove home the point.

Except the point went too far. It kept going. Which was the usual thing for a point to do when your whole body was behind it and there was nothing in front of it.

Wessex had never seen anyone move that quickly. It was instantaneous. The American had been seated in front of Lord Wissex, and now he was standing behind him. Now he knew how the giant black had been strangled so easily and why Bradford Wakefield III could so easily lose his two best killers.

Friend had been right. Anyone who could destroy Wakefield's killers had to be hired. Of course, as the sailboat moved noiselessly toward St. Maarten's, and the incredibly blue waters churned up beneath them, Lord Wissex knew that he had realized all of that too late.

"And you poisoned me too," said Remo. Wissex felt just the lightest of touches on his neck, but he could not move his arms and barely kept his balance. It was as if the man had discovered the exact nerves in his body that controlled his motion.

Wissex knew that a time like this had to come eventually. It was part of the business and something he could accept. And he had made plans for this. His lower right molar was a hollow cap. All he had to do was push it out with his tongue and then bite down very hard.

He pushed the tooth out, but he could not get his jaw open to crush it.

"Why did you poison me?"

"Blast you," said Lord Wissex. Well, his voice worked. That was something. The American had allowed his voice to work.

"Why did you poison me?"

"Why didn't you die?"

"From poison? My body won't accept it."

"I didn't see you spit it out."

"I didn't. I held it in my stomach. Now I'll spit. See? See the spit? See how the nice man spits? Tell the nice man everything," said Remo, and let the gooey green slime up through his throat to his mouth, which launched it into the clear blue Caribbean. Fish popped up to the surface in the green wake of Remo's spit, white bellies skyward. A little pitiful waggle of flippers, and the fish were dead.

"Who are you?" said Wissex through jaws that would not open.

"I am joy and life and the spirit of goodness," said Remo. "Now you do some talking or I'll feed your belly to the fish and use your sternum for a hook."

"That is vicious," Chiun said. "And we've never had a butler before. That's no way to treat a butler."

"He tried to kill me."

"Butlers are always murdering people," said Chiun. "It is expected. But bad language, hostile language from an assassin is not. When you're done with him, save him. We've never had a butler before."

"We'll see," Remo said.

Lord Wissex tried to turn his head to see the two, but he couldn't. All he could see was the incredibly blue waters, and he heard the two argue about butler service, with the younger one accurately saying the butler would always be trying to kill them and the older one answering that one always had to expect some small problems with domestic help.

And then the incredible pain began. It came first in little notes, as he was asked his name, asked how his body felt, asked the color of his hair, and then built in a symphony of hurt that Merton found he could control. With the giving of truth, absolute and total truth. He told things he didn't even realize he had known.

He told of being penniless and being called one day at Castle Wissex by a man who understood how awful it was that Wissex lived in a country that no longer appreciated and rewarded courage.

"What do you want?" Wissex had said.

"I want the same services your ancestor provided for Henry the Eighth."

"He killed people for His Majesty."

"That is what I want," the voice said.

"No," he said, and slammed down the receiver of the phone.

The next day, he received a note. It read, "I only want you to do what is proper."

106

And on the phone later that day, he asked the man, "How can this be proper?"

"Most proper. I am an international corporation not subject to national laws. Not above the law, mind you. But beyond it. And I have a tradition of hiring people to kill."

"Proper, you say? Tradition, you say?" said Wissex.

"Yes. And I want you with me as senior vice-president."

"In charge of what?"

"Tradition and propriety," the caller said.

Wissex thought for a moment. "You must give me your word of honor, sir, that everything will ultimately be for the good of Great Britain, and therefore mankind."

"You have it," said the voice.

And then Lord Wissex learned the man's name. His name was Friend. He had never seen him.

"Oh," came a voice from far away. "So you're the one. Your family. Henry the Eighth. What do you know?" It was the American talking, and he called to his companion.

"Hey, Little Father. This is the Wissex. Descendant of that Wissex."

"The one who serviced Henry the Eighth?" asked the Oriental.

"You know of him?" asked Wissex.

"Sure," Remo said. "Part of my training was learning all the traditions of the Masters of Sinanju. I remember one of them worked for Henry the Eighth."

"Yes," said the Oriental. "He was called in because the gracious Henry had no one."

"He had my ancestor," said Lord Wissex.

"Correct," said the Oriental. "Remo, please recite."

"And it came to pass," said the American, "that the lesser Wang came unto the shores of England, which had at that time conquered Wales and held Scotland in a form of alliance.

"And the king was deeply troubled. Enemies abounded, the kingdom verged on civil war, and all he

107

had to defend himself was his Lord Wissex, a man skilled only at removing complicating children from women's bellies. Namely the king's complicating children from women's bellies. Would the Master of Sinanju properly service His Britannic Majesty for proper tribute? And train Wissex to kill grown men?

"And the sum there was was four hundred of cattle, ten weights of gold, fifty of silver, five ships of corn grain, a thousand fat fowl, three hundred iron blades yet to be fashioned, ten thousand weight bronze, thirty-two fine chairs, fruit seed, twenty bolts of linen, unworked. . . ."

"Lie," gasped Lord Wissex. "He was not an abortionist. My ancestor was an assassin."

"You interrupted the list," said Chiun. "We haven't gotten to the pear trees, partridges, gold rings, calling birds, milking maids, and french hens. There were french hens."

"Lie. He was not an abortionist."

"Don't be ashamed of your ancestors, Merton," said the Oriental. "He was, after all, only English."

"There were no pear trees," said the American.

Merton Lord Wissex felt the American's hands release just a bit from the neck on that statement.

"There were pear trees," said Chiun.

"No, no," said Remo. "Louis the Fifteenth sent trees. I think they were plum trees. Henry sent turtledoves."

"No, we never got turtledoves from Henry," Chiun said. "The British had fine pear trees. We never had plum trees."

"I saw them in your village," Remo said.

"You never saw plum trees in Sinanju," Chiun said.

"I did."

"Didn't," said Chiun. "Pear trees."

Wissex pushed the tooth up out of its slot and up to the molars on the left side of his mouth. With his remaining power, he bit down on the empty shell of a tooth. It cracked, releasing a bittersweet syrup.

He swallowed. His throat became numb, and then

the tips of his fingers felt faraway, and he glided off into that sleep of sleeps.

Remo felt the life go out of what was in his hand. He let the body drop.

"They were plums," Remo said. "I ate one in Sinanju. I remember it. It was a lousy plum."

"Because it was a pear," said Chiun. "You killed our butler."

"No. He took his own life. It was a plum."

"Pear," said Chiun.

The sailboat's skipper was amazed at how quiet St. Maarten's looked without its oil. An American gunboat stopped the sailboat.

"If you enter, you cannot leave," came a voice over the bullhorn.

"I know," the captain shouted back.

"Did you people throw something overboard back there?" came the question from the gunboat.

The captain asked his passengers. There were only two now. He didn't see the third.

"Did anyone throw anything overboard back there?" he asked.

"I know a plum from a pear," said the American angrily.

"And so do I," said the Oriental.

"Did you throw something overboard?" asked the captain again.

"A body. He was dead," said the American. "Have you ever seen a purple pear?"

When the boat docked at St. Maarten's, even the horsedrawn carriages squealed in their axles for a lack of oil.

"This," Remo said, "is what happens without oil."

"Not bad," said Chiun.

"Beg your pardon," said the sailboat captain. "You didn't say back there that you threw a dead body overboard, did you?"

"Sure," said Remo.

On St. Maarten's, cars were stopped alongside the

109

roads. Some of them were pushed off to the side. Little white waxy mushrooms covered their gas tanks.

Remo stopped a well-dressed couple sitting in the back of a haycart. He and Chiun had left Chiun's trunks on the sailboat. Chiun thought they might use the cart for the trunks. Remo thought they would go back for the trunks because they probably would be finished here soon anyhow. The island was small. Chiun thought they could take the horsedrawn cart and use that to carry the trunks. Remo said it was too cumbersome. Chiun pointed out that it was not Chiun who allowed the butler to kill himself with poison. If Remo had not done that, this would have been settled because they would have had someone to deal with the trunks.

"I'm working," Remo said. "If you won't help, don't harm." Then he asked the couple if they knew where the cars had first stopped working on the island.

"Where did the first reports come from?"

"From all over," said the husband.

"From just west of Marigot. There's a small hill there, and farmers were complaining," said the woman. "It changed all their gasoline to waxy uselessness and burned their skin too."

"We had a Porsche 911, a Mercedes 450SL, a Jaguar XKE, and a Chevette," sobbed the husband.

"A Chevette?" asked Remo, wondering what they would need with a little, inexpensive runabout, with all those expensive cars.

"The Chevette was the only one that stayed out of the repair shop," the man said.

Remo and Chiun walked toward Marigot. It amazed Remo how steep the hills were on the little island. They were not mountains, but their steepness gave that impression. Cows roamed freely over their sides. Off in the distance, someone sang slow day-long songs, that easy, almost sleepy beat meant to go on for at least an afternoon. A chameleon perched on a black rock, black as the rock, winking at Remo and Chiun.

"We could have used the cart," Chiun said.

"Do you feel the death, Little Father? Do you smell it? The dread. The death. The lingering, ominous feeling?"

"No," said Chiun.

"Neither do I," said Remo. "And I wonder why. Before I became Sinanju, I would enter alleys or dark places and feel that, but now I don't. Maybe I'll feel a presence. I'll feel death but there are no drum rolls of fear. And I don't know why."

"When you were a child, you felt like a child, with much fear, for that is how children protect themselves. By fearing and hiding. And this is proper. So when a person is grown but poorly trained, when he fails to be one with his body and his essence, then a gap in the personhood is created. An unknowing of life and death and of one's ability to use his body waits to be filled. And who fills it but the child who knew fear as its only defense?"

"So I have been trained away from fear?" Remo said.

"You have been trained away from those empty spaces. The fear will always be there. The child is the first and the last of all of us. It is said that at the moment of death, every Master of Sinanju will hear his own childhood say good-bye to him."

Remo knew enough not to tell Chiun that he thought that was beautiful. For that would have shown he did not understand. For in proper training, things were not beautiful, they were right. They were proper. Beautiful meant exceptional beyond the norm, but in Sinanju the norm itself was exceptional, in full unity with all the powers and presences of the universe. It was not beautiful.

"That is so," said Remo simply, the highest compliment he could pay.

They found the hill outside Marigot. A small white box of a factory stood on top. It was ringed by a cyclone fence with a sign that read: PURESSENCE, INC. Under that title was a motto: "A Clean World for our Times."

There was a guard in the guard booth. The guard was not using his gun because it had been used. His mouth was closed around it, and the back of his head was imbedded in the ceiling of the booth. He had blown out his own brains.

Atop the hill, a voice from a loudspeaker shouted hysterically, "It's them. It's them. It's them. Quick, brothers. Don't let them get you. Don't let them get you."

Suddenly, little popping sounds of rifles came from atop the hill. But no bullets were being fired down at them. There was no hiss, not even a flash of a muzzle. All the rifle fire stayed inside the building.

Remo and Chiun moved quickly up the road, not a run but faster than a run, a smooth, loping movement where the heads did not bob but just went forward at increasing speed up the mountain.

As they approached the white building, white as if bleached by the Caribbean sun, they heard giggling inside.

They opened the door. Sitting at desks and microscopes and computer terminals were twenty men and woman, all slumped forward, all with dark, bloody holes where the backs of their heads had been.

The heads were pumping blood from the last lurches of the still-working hearts.

"They're coming, they're coming," came the voice from the loudspeaker. And then here there was laughter. It was not a wild laugh. It was a giggle.

Behind a large crate, a blond bearded man sat giggling. He was missing three teeth, and his grin appeared silly. He nestled the microphone on his kneecaps. He wore a leather shirt and designer jeans and a ruby ring in his left earlobe. He seemed absolutely delighted that Remo and Chiun were now standing over him.

"Heyyyy," he said with a happy breath of voice. "Hey. Welcome to Puressence. You're them. We just got the message you might be coming, and we're doing Plan 178-Y. That's heavy."

112

"What's 178-Y?" asked Remo.

"I shout into the speaker that you're coming. That's my first program to follow. I did that really good. You wanna hear?"

And, still giggling, the man yelled into the microphone, "They're coming, they're coming." His voice reverberated over the loudspeakers in the building.

"What's that for?" asked Remo.

"Heyyyy. Goodness and peace, baby."

"I think that was the signal for your people to kill themselves."

"What are you talking about? Nobody is going to kill himself because I yell into a microphone."

Remo took a handful of the scraggly blond hair and lifted the man from the box and turned the grinning face toward the factory of dead people.

"Well?" said Remo.

"Cooooool," said the man.

"Cool?"

"Yeah."

"Why?"

"They did what they wanted. They did their thing."

"You triggered it. That is obviously some kind of panic response."

"That's their problem, man. Not mine. No such things as fair or unfair."

"What if I break your neck?" asked Remo.

"Coooooool," said the man, and grinned the tooth-missing grin.

"I take it you're on drugs," said Remo, dropping the man to the floor. He hit his head and grinned back up. A little flutter came from the upraised feet as he popped a blue tablet into his mouth.

"Step Two of Program One."

"What drug is that?" asked Remo.

"I think it's poison."

"What makes you think so?"

" 'Cause I'm dying."

The eyes closed and Remo sensed a stillness in the body, the last complete stillness. The man was dead.

Remo had found a place, possibly the place where the fast-breeder bacteria had been manufactured, and now there was no one left to tell how it was made.

But how could anyone get them all to commit suicide? And why?

Outside, a soft purring of an engine made its way up the road toward the factory. It was a car engine on an island where cars did not run.

Chapter Seven

"Bleem," said the woman stepping out of the back seat of a yellow and gray car that looked like a cross between a 1938 Ford and a Mercedes Benz. Sitting sullenly behind the wheel was a burly driver in a business suit, his bald head shining like a wrinkled pink artillery shell.

The woman wore a white suit with international-class styling and carried herself with the firm pace of someone with much money and about to make much more.

Her hair was like an ebony crown to a smooth, pale face. The eyes were so blue, they could cut. And her smile had a little-girl tinkle to it.

She was so beautiful, Remo half expected the dead inside the plant to rise up to offer her their seats.

"Bleem," she said again.

"God bless you," said Remo.

"Reva Bleem," she said. Her hand went out firmly to Remo's. Remo shook it. She offered her hand to Chiun. Chiun folded his hands under his morning robe.

"That's rude, Little Father," said Remo.

Chiun stepped back one pace and gave Reva Bleem an assassin's nod.

"I'm Reva Bleem, president of Bleem International, American Bleem, Hoyt Bilco Bleem, Standard Bleem, and Bleem Limited. What happened here?"

"How come your car runs?" asked Remo. "Is it some special car?"

"Yes, it's a special car. It's a Gaylord. *Special Interest Autos* magazine featured it. *Special Interest Autos* is the best car magazine in the world."

"How does it run? Gasoline doesn't survive on this island."

"Shit," said Reva Bleem. "What's going on here."

"First of all, why does that car run?"

"It doesn't use gas.There are other fuels besides petroleum-based fuels. There's Bleem International's new synthetic. We call it Polypussides. It's got a few kinks, but it'll run a car."

"What are the kinks?"

"It costs fifteen dollars a gallon, and the exhaust stunts human growth when it gets into the atmosphere. Right now, if everybody used it, our scientists estimate that probably mankind would be reduced to an average height of four feet, one and a half inches."

"That'll be good for dwarfs," Remo said.

"No, it won't. Dwarfs will be even smaller. You'd be able to fit one in your glove compartment. But we'll work these problems out. Frankly, I don't see four-one-and-a-half as a problem anyhow. Less food consumption, smaller houses, less drain on the world's resources. What do you think of that?"

"I don't think four feet is a height people will want," Remo said.

"Then advertising will have to come up with something else besides world good," she said. "What about 'Sex is better at four feet?' Maybe with a jingle? Would you like that?"

"I don't think so," said Remo. And he turned to ask Chiun what he would think of that, but already Chiun was walking back into the factory.

"If I can't do it with advertising, we're going to have to make difficult decisions," she said. "We just might have to change the Polypussides basic molecules to something that won't stunt growth. But dammit, that could cost millions. Tens of millions."

Reva Bleem's voice quavered. Tears rimmed the beautiful blue eyes.

"You've never lost a million dollars, have you?" she asked Remo.

"No."

"You have to take these things as they come. But you never get used to it."

"Money only means something if you don't have it," Remo said.

"What do you have?"

"You wouldn't understand," Remo said.

"Maybe I would."

"I have what I am supposed to be. I am more complete than you."

"That's another word for nothing," she said.

"I told you you wouldn't understand," Remo said.

"Have you tried money?"

"You should talk to my partner," Remo said. "He's into money." And then they both entered the factory. The driver remained behind in the car.

With disgust in her eyes, Reva looked around at the bodies. "Sure. Sure. Exactly," she said. "There. That's Wardley. Wardley has been turning all these people on. Wardley got them hooked. Then Wardley went through defensive drills. Then Wardley probably forgot he put bullets in their guns. Then Wardley forgot he poisoned himself."

"What are you, crazy?" said Remo. "Someone forgets he poisoned himself? Someone convinces top scientists to kill themselves?"

"How did you figure out they were scientists?" she asked.

"This place. First, all those scientists vanished from the U.S. Then you hear something about rapid-breeder bacteria. Then all the gas on this island turns to wax. I figured that this had to be the place where they're making the rapid breeder."

"Right," she said. "It's a tax loss that went crazy. We needed a tax loss. That, lying there with the silly grin on his face, is my brother Wardley. Wardley could turn anything into a tax loss. Wardley could lose money finding gold; he's an absolute genius at losing money. I

117

guess whatever I got, he was deficient in. Wardley took over this company to give Bleem International the tax loss we needed in America."

"I follow that," said Remo.

"So Wardley decided to hire all the scientists in this field and create a monopoly. Somehow he got it in his acid-soaked head to prove me wrong about this being a loss operation. And he did."

"What about the scientists he killed?" asked Remo.

She looked shocked. "Was he killing people?"

"Someone was."

"The idiot. I guess he figured he needed all of them if he was going to form a monopoly. Anyway, he got all these down here at fantastic salaries, creating our tax loss, which was all right with me. Then he got them hooked on this drug he invented, and he got them involved in playing his games of never letting anyone get at you. Wardley played that when he was a kid. If everyone takes drugs, Wardley makes sense. But I thought he was harmless, and he was giving me my tax loss. Now look at this. This is awful. And those goddamned bacteria must be all over the place."

"One problem with your story," Remo said.

"What's that?" asked Reva.

"I know now why someone wants to remove all the oil from the world. It's you, Reva. Then you can sell your Pussyjuice. . . ."

"Polypussides," she corrected.

"Polypussides at fifteen dollars a gallon."

"Except for one thing, whoever-you-are," she said. "The Polypussides won't be ready for mass distribution for another ten years. Working full speed right now, I can make a thousand gallons a day. What the hell does that mean? I spend that much money on hotel rooms. And in ten years, when I'm ready, they're going to have other synthetic fuels. So where does that leave me? With a lot of four-foot people. The idiot. The idiot."

Reva Bleem was screaming. She ran over to Wardley's dead body and began kicking the face.

118

"I can't kick that grin off. I can't get it to stop grinning at me," screamed Reva.

"Hold on," Remo said. "Hold on." He grasped her shoulders and massaged up to her neck until she was calm. The blue eyes still burned with fire, though. There was a beauty to her anger, Remo thought. And that beauty was strength.

And, yes, Remo admitted, it was unsettling to see a grin on a corpse. He wanted to remove the grin also.

"Wardley has ruined everything I've ever had. Everything. And now he's killed these men. He's killed others, you tell me. And all I wanted was a tax loss."

Reva Bleem's shoulders slumped; her face fell, revealing great, great sadness; and she sobbed. Remo felt her move into his arms.

"We were a poor family. I had to work since I was nine years old. And I thought finally I had enough money for all of us. And now, this. This. And he's killed people too. What am I going to do?"

"I'm not a businessman," said Remo. "But I would say these bodies have to be buried. The families have to be notified. The police have to be notified."

"Is that what you would do?"

"No," said Remo. "I'd just leave."

"Can I do that?"

"Sure," said Remo. "If you show me where all the fast-breeding bacteria are."

"They've got to be here. Everything is in this one factory. He wasn't supposed to get this stuff done for ten years. It's the first thing Wardley ever did ahead of schedule. He usually can't mail a letter."

"Are you sure all of it is here?" Remo asked.

"Oh," said Reva. "Oh, no. Don't tell me."

Pulling Remo behind her, she ran into the office section of the complex and looked around for a computer terminal.

Chiun had followed them. One of the telephones was ringing and Reva answered it.

"For you," she said, handing the phone to Chiun.

Chiun took the telephone and Remo said, "Who would know you're here?"

"Possibly someone with taste," Chiun said.

Reva went to the terminal and began operating the computer. She typed in questions, and the computer answered them. Remo tried to follow the terminal action and Chiun's conversation at the same time. Reva's head kept shaking, leaving the beautiful black hair with tremors at the ends, as her lips pursed and she kept mumbling, "The idiot."

Chiun kept saying, "Yes. Quite so. Quite so. You seem to understand, Your Highness. You seem to understand. Quite so. Quite so."

And then after almost two minutes of "Quite so," Chiun said, "Can you phone back again? In a few minutes. Yes, gracious one."

"Is that Smitty?" Remo asked, whispering low enough so Reva's ears could not pick up the question.

"No," said Chiun.

"I was wondering how he would have found out we were here."

"He didn't and we were fortunate," Chiun said.

Remo glanced back at Reva. Her head was still shaking, and she kept muttering, "The idiot."

"Remo," whispered Chiun, "we have just received an offer from one who must be royalty, for he made us an offer we cannot refuse. Now I must insist we stop squandering the talent of Sinanju on a man who refuses to become emperor of your backward country. I must insist we leave that lunatic Smith to his insanity and take the one offer that understands the basic needs of an assassin."

"I've got to finish this job," Remo said.

"Do you know what he has offered us?"

"No," Remo said. "You talked to him, not me."

"What do you want?" asked Chiun.

"Come on, what's the offer?"

"That *is* the offer. Whatever we want. Gold, oil, companies, gems, horses, land. An offer from a king. A true king making an offer to a true assassin."

120

"I want to finish what we're in."

"But what do you want, Remo?"

"I don't know," said Remo honestly. "I don't know, and I haven't known for years, and I don't think I'm going to know. I used to think I wanted Sinanju. And then when I had it, when I really had it and grew in it, it was just there. I used to think I wanted to help my country, and I guess I still do. But I don't know."

"So after this assignment, we can say yes?" asked Chiun.

"I don't know," Remo said.

"I am saying yes."

The phone rang, and Remo heard Chiun giving the shopping list of Sinanju demands, all to be delivered to the little North Korean village on the West Korea bay. It was where Smith delivered Chiun's shipment of gold every year.

Chiun had always said the gold was "enough, but not a joy."

Now Remo could see joy on the face of the Master of Sinanju. Chiun lapsed into Korean. Obviously the other person knew Korean. Then there was medieval French. Chiun knew that from the tales of the Masters of Sinanju who had served Frankish kings. And then a singular look of worry came over the parched, frail face of Chiun.

"Just a moment," he said and turned to Remo.

"Remo," he whispered. "This noble, benign regent has offered to double our tribute if we agree to serve him now."

"No," said Remo, watching Reva punch something into the computer.

"You can't say no. It is double everything we want."

"You can't double everything," Remo said. "If you have everything you want, doubling it won't improve it."

"Teach philosophy to a white and this is what you get," said Chiun, his voice cracking in a squeak. He went back to the phone, and in a few moments he returned with an ultimatum.

121

"If you do not accept this now with me, we are through. This divine perfection of an emperor has just offered triple what I demanded. It will be the largest payment ever brought in triumph to Sinanju since the Great Wang was Master."

"I've seen Sinanju," Remo said. "You just store most of that junk, or the villagers steal it when you're not there. And no one goes hungry like in the old days if you don't bring back tribute. So what triple are we talking about?"

"My feelings are what we are talking about. My pride is what we are talking about. Your pride. Our Sinanju," hissed Chiun.

"This is the first time you ever said it was our Sinanju. I mean, I was always this white foundling that you so graciously poured all this wisdom into, this pale piece of pig's ear from which you could never get respect and gratitude."

"Now you can do it," Chiun said.

"After," said Remo. "Maybe," he added.

"I cannot tell this emperor no. Not after what he has offered," Chiun said.

"Then don't tell him no."

Remo saw Chiun straighten himself in dignity and give a little polite bow to the phone.

"Your most gracious Majesty," said Chiun, "I cannot accept your offer at the moment. I will do that. I will ask him. Whatever he wanted you will provide. I heard that, Your Majesty. What then do you wish to be called if not 'Your Majesty?' Yes. I will do that, although I will always consider you royal. Yes. Goodbye, Friend."

"Was that Friend?" Remo asked.

"Yes," Chiun said. "You know him?"

"He was that English twerp's boss. He's the guy we were looking for. He's the one behind all this."

"Rumors," Chiun said. "Just rumors. He is the most treasured of rulers."

Reva jumped from the computer terminal. "Damn.

122

Do you know what he's done? Do you know what Wardley has done?"

"I don't know him. I just got here for his death," Remo said.

"He's already shipped a consignment of the rapid-breeder bacteria. If it gets loose, it can wipe out the world's oil reserves."

"We've got to stop it."

"Of course we do," Reva said. "I can't produce Poly-pussides for less than a pump price of fifteen dollars a gallon. I'm just not ready."

"And it will create a world of midgets too," Remo said.

Reva waved a hand, dismissing that as a consideration.

"That doesn't matter," she said. "What's worse is that my fuel will kill half the world's population until the survivors get used to breathing differently. Marketing says human survival has never hurt any product, but I just can't get it over with a fifteen-dollar pump price. We've got to stop that shipment."

"Is that the only one?" Remo asked.

"The computer says it is."

"Let's go," Remo said.

"You go yourself," said Chiun. "You have let me down as never before. I don't know where I have gone wrong. I don't know why I deserve this, but deserve it I must. Leave me and my poor possessions to die on this island far away from my home, knowing how close I came to the glory tribute of Sinanju. Go. Don't mind me."

"I'll get you back through Smitty," Remo said.

"He seems upset," Reva told Remo.

"He is."

"Are you just going to leave him?"

"I don't need guilt from you, Ms. Bleem. Where are we going, anyway?"

"To Hamidi Arabia. That's where Wardley sent the shipment."

Chiun stepped closer and touched her arm.

123

"Where in Hamidi Arabia?" he asked.

"Sheik Abdul Hamid Fareem," she said.

Chiun turned to Remo. "I will go with you, Remo."

"Why the change of heart?" Remo asked.

"Because I have business in Hamidi Arabia," Chiun said.

"Since when?"

"Since the time the land was green with rivers before it surrendered to the sand. It is an obligation. And we, those of us who are truly Sinanju and not just impostors with no sense of tradition or honor or . . ."

"Skip it, Chiun," said Remo.

"We honor our obligations."

"We have to stop in Marigot first," Reva said. "I'm not going to Hamidi Arabia without it."

"How do we get there? You can't get off this island."

"No problem," Reva said.

Her bullet-necked chauffeur drove them into Marigot, where Reva picked up four large gray metal boxes, each about one foot high. With great care, she had them packed in styrofoam. Remo heard liquid gurgle inside.

"What is in there?"

"Booze," she said. "The only thing you can't buy in Hamidi Arabia."

"Come on, with their money, they must smuggle some in."

"Yes. Ordinary booze. But not Lazzaroni Amaretto. That's the authentic Amaretto. Made from the old 1851 recipe."

"So what?" said Remo.

"So I buy my cars through *Special Interest Autos* and I drink Lazzaroni Amaretto. I want the best. What's money for?"

"I don't know," said Remo.

"Glory," said Chiun.

A U.S. Navy patrol boat pulled up to a pier in Marigot, looking for one Ms. Reva Bleem.

"You're under arrest," said the commander.

"Thank you," said Reva. "I have three friends here with me who are also under arrest." She pointed toward her chauffeur and Remo and Chiun.

"Certainly," said the commander.

And the patrol boat moved the four of them and Chiun's trunks through the line of quarantine ships out across the Caribbean to a large pleasure yacht.

"I want you to look after my car," said Reva to the commander of the patrol boat.

On her yacht, Reva explained that the Navy commander would retire soon and that his pension was not as good as the one Reva had offered him to get off the island.

"Money buys everyone," she said.

"That's what people think of tribute," Remo said to Chiun.

"That's not what I think of tribute," Chiun said.

The yacht sped them to Anguilla, where there was a Bleem jet ready for takeoff. The jet ran on Polypussides, Reva explained, but already a few mechanics had passed out, and doctors said they might never walk again because their nervous systems had been ruined by some form of deadly gas.

"See," Reva said. "It's the exhaust emissions from burning Polypussides. It's not ready for sale yet. Now you know why we have to stop that bacterium."

Chapter Eight

Remo walked up the steps of the private twenty-seater jet, with Chiun and Reva Bleem following him. Oscar, the chauffeur, was supervising the loading of Chiun's trunks and Reva's packaged liquors into the hold of the plane.

As Remo stopped just inside the doorway at the head of the ramp, he felt Chiun suddenly brush by him, the breeze of his robe wafting past Remo's face. He knew where Chiun was going—to the seat he always took on planes, on the left-hand side, directly over the wing.

He saw Chiun walk down the aisle between the empty seats and could almost feel him chuckling at getting his favorite seat. And just because it annoyed him, Remo dove across the rows of seats on the left-hand side of the plane, like a swimmer making a racing start into an Olympic pool. Down three rows he skidded, then dug in with the toe of his foot against the back of one of the seats and pushed forward again. He turned his body in the air and wound up sitting in the seat over the wing.

He looked up the aisle at Chiun, who was walking toward him, but without a hint of expression, the Oriental sat in a seat on the right side of the plane. Reva Bleem still stood in the doorway, looking at both of them. Remo heard Chiun chortle, "Heh, heh."

"Something funny, Chiun?" Remo asked smugly. He

126

knew how annoyed Chiun must be that Remo had his seat.

"Heh, heh, heh."

"What is worth three heh's?" Remo asked.

"I was just thinking of how predictably foolish you are," Chiun said. "You thought I wanted that seat, and so you plop your big fat white body down the plane like a flying squirrel to try to deprive me of it. But I knew you would do that. And I laugh because I did not want that seat. In aircraft like this one, I like this seat. I like to be on this side of the plane. Now, don't you feel like an imbecile, Remo? Aren't you even a little bit annoyed that I find you such a cause for amusement? Heh, heh, heh. Who would want to sit on that side of the plane?" Remo saw the old Oriental's eyes on him, little laugh lines wrinkled in the corners as he chuckled.

"Heh, heh, heh."

"Good," Remo said. "I'm glad you got the seat you want because this is the one I want."

"It is yours, Remo. Take root in it. I have the seat I want," Chiun said.

Oscar, the chauffeur, came up the gangplank of the plane and went forward into the pilot's cabin. The door closed behind Reva Bleem, and almost instantly the jet began taxiing away from the hangar.

Remo wanted to be alone with his thoughts, but a few moments after the plane lifted off, he was alone with Reva Bleem.

"Do you two always argue over airplane seats?" she asked as she sat next to Remo.

"No. Seating's not important. Not to me anyway."

"Nor to me," Chiun called out from across the aisle. "I don't care where anyone sits as long as it is not here in my favorite seat. This is my favorite seat. I love it here."

"Why don't you let the old gentleman have his seat without all this bickering?" Reva asked Remo.

"Shut up, will you?" Remo said. "Next thing, he'll have you running errands for him." He half rose in his seat, watching Chiun from the corner of his eye. He just did not trust the old Korean. But Chiun's eyes were looking away from him, out the window, carefully watching the wing of the plane for any incipient signs of stress or fracture.

Remo pursed his lips in annoyance, then brushed past Reva Bleem and walked to the front of the plane and slid into a seat there. Within moments, Reva was sitting next to him.

"Where are you from?" she asked. "I don't know a thing about you."

"Everywhere and nowhere," Remo said.

"That's not much of an answer," she said.

Remo got up and brushed by her to sit on the other side of the plane. Reva followed him.

"Are you trying to avoid me?" she said.

"What gave you that idea?" Remo said. He moved again and she followed.

"Will you two cattle stop stomping around this craft?" Chiun snapped. The voice came from the left side of the plane, and when Remo looked back, Chiun was sitting in Remo's seat over the left wing. He smiled at Remo before going back to inspecting the wing.

Annoyed, Remo slumped against the window. Reva Bleem pressed her bosom against his left upper arm as she leaned toward him.

"Why are you being so unpleasant?" she asked.

Remo moved away from her breast. "Unpleasant? Who's unpleasant, goddammit?" Remo said. "All right. I'm unpleasant." He lowered his voice to a whisper. "I've got to find this stupid bacterium, and that's all your fault, you and your damned tax loss, and what the hell am I going to do with it when I find it? Punch it? And I've got him on the snot back there because he wants to go to work for somebody else and he's getting so he can't tell the difference between a plum and a pear."

"Can too," Chiun called out. "It was a pear."

"How long have you two been together?" Reva said, pressing her breast against Remo again.

128

"A hundred years," Remo whispered back.

"Two hundred," called out Chiun. "It seems like only a hundred to him because he has enjoyed it so. And he repays those two centuries of pleasure with treachery and denial of a poor man's only wish."

"See?" Remo said. "On the snot. Because I won't go to work for some guy who's probably promised him Barbra Streisand, a new Betamax, and forty dollars worth of junk jewelry."

"Who would you rather work for?" Reva asked.

She was pumping, Remo knew, but before he could answer, Chiun called out again. "He would rather work for other ingrates like himself and for emperors who do not know what emperors are supposed to do or even how to be emperors. He wants to defend his Constitution. I ask you, can the poor people of my village eat a defended Constitution?"

"Those lowlifes could eat rocks, as long as they didn't have to work for them," Remo said. He turned back to Reva and said, "His *poor* village has a higher standard of living than Westport, Connecticut. Ingrates."

"Your responsibility," Chiun said.

"No, your responsibility," Remo said. "Never mine."

"How like a white man," Chiun said. "All the character of a peeled boiled potato."

Remo snorted and turned back to the window.

"I guess you don't feel much like talking," Reva said.

Remo snorted again.

"Go ahead and talk," Chiun called out. "I've got this good seat and I'll watch the wing. Heh, heh, heh."

The plane landed on a narrow sliver of concrete that Remo supposed had been designed for an Arab air force because it stretched for ten miles in either direction, making safe allowances for pilot error of up to 6,000 percent.

When he got off the plane, Remo saw nothing in all

directions but sand, and a narrow new road heading out over a hill. A Rolls Royce waited on the road.

Remo waited until Chiun joined him at the head of the plane's steps. "So this is it, Chiun, huh? Your great Hamidi Fareemi Areebi tradition, or whatever the hell you call it? Another name for freaking sand."

"There can be tradition in a desert of sand as well as in a city of buildings and people. There can be no tradition only in the heads of mongrels who remember no past and therefore have no future," Chiun said.

"You mean me by that, I guess," Remo said.

"Do not talk to me, Remo. I am ignoring you from now on," Chiun said.

"Come on," said Reva Bleem. "That's our car."

Walking toward the big sedan, Remo had a chance to look over Oscar, Reva's driver, for the first time. He was a tall, husky man with a smooth bald head that disappeared into ripples of neck muscles. His face was acne erupted and scar pitted. He held open the rear seat door for Reva. Remo started to get in after her, but Chiun brushed by him onto the wide seat.

"Move over," Remo said.

Chiun asked Reva, "This person with the lumpy face is your servant?"

"He's my chauffeur."

"Remo, ride in the front with the other servant," Chiun said. He turned back to Reva. "We had a servant once—a British butler. But Remo killed him for no reason at all."

"You know, Chiun, I love you when you're like this," Remo said.

"Sit in front," Chiun said.

Remo waited in front while Oscar went back onto the plane to carry back Reva Bleem's four liquor boxes, which he put into the trunk of the Rolls.

"And my trunks?" Chiun asked the driver.

"They will follow us by truck when it arrives," Oscar said.

Chiun nodded. "It will be on your head if they do not," he said.

The heavy car moved off slowly and inexorably, like a rubber ball starting down a gently sloped hill. Before long, it was humming along the absolutely level road at 90 miles an hour.

"Where are we going?" Remo asked, turning toward the back seat.

"To see the sheik."

"Which one?"

"Sheik Abdul Hamid Fareem," Reva said, which didn't really tell Remo much. All their names sounded alike, and they all looked alike, and in a band they attacked America as bloodthirsty imperialists while cutting the hands off anybody who stole a loaf of bread because he didn't have the good fortune to own an oil well.

"I can't wait," Remo said.

"That is the first intelligent thing you have said since we left that island of white wax," Chiun said.

"Why?"

"Because the Hamidi family have been royalty in this part of the world for centuries. Noble, enlightened, loved-by-all royalty."

"That means they hired one of your ancestors and paid their bill," Remo said.

"That means they are truly noble, Remo. You would not understand it." He pointed out the right window into the distance, and Remo turned to see what he was pointing out.

"There is their capital city of Nehmad," Chiun said. "Right where the scrolls of history said it would be." He closed his eyes and recited from memory. "A marvelous clean city of towered parapets and minarets, with streets of tile and wall paintings encrusted with precious stones."

"There's no minarets or parapets" said Remo, who assumed they meant some kind of pointed things on buildings. "Look at that city. It's a bunch of big, ugly, flat apartment buildings."

"You can turn everything into dross," Chiun sniffed.

131

"We'll see when we get there just how wonderful these Hareemis are," Remo said.

"Hamidi," Chiun said.

"We're not going to the city," Reva said.

"Why not?"

"The sheik Abdul Hamid Fareem lives in the desert."

"Why?" Remo asked.

"I read about him," she said. "He thinks Arabs were not meant to live in cities, that cities weaken the blood."

"See, Remo," said Chiun. "That is respect for tradition."

"That is stupid," said Remo. "Why live in a tent when you can live in a building?"

"Because these are kings and princes and royalty," Chiun said heatedly.

"And that means they should live in a tent? If an Arab prince should live in a tent as a mark of honor, then you should live in a cave. A hole in the ground in Sinanju. But *you* live in a house. How do you explain that?"

And because it was a compliment that Remo had paid Chiun, as an expression of his respect, Chiun mumbled only, "I do not choose to speak of it anymore. Please, Remo, you're giving me a headache."

The Rolls Royce buzzed past the wall surrounding the city of Nehmad, as the road widened and then as it shrunk again into two narrow lanes out into the trackless, endless sand.

Reva kept asking Chiun questions. How long had he known Remo? Where had they met? What did they do together? Who did they work for? Chiun kept looking out the car window and finally said, "Please, dear lady, do not ask me to talk about things that pain me. Just know that it was the worst day of my life when first I set eyes on that white thing."

The city was out of sight, far behind them, when the road began a slight rise. When the limousine crested, Remo saw a city of tents a few thousand yards away from the road, in a declivity between two long, sloping sand dunes. Behind the cluster of tents was a large oasis, perhaps two acres in size. Women and men moved through the trees toward a central clearing in the green spot. Against the vast expanse of sand, the oasis looked like an emerald laid on a wrinkle-free sheet of brown butcher's paper.

Oscar pulled slowly off the roadway, and the Rolls sank softly into the sand. From the right, coming from the oasis and the tents, Remo saw a man leading a camel. The camel was bedecked with a stone-studded leather saddle.

As they all got out of the car, Reva said, "Oh dear. They sent only one camel." She turned toward Remo and Chiun. "When I get there, I'll have them send back more camels for you too. It's such a long walk in this heat."

Remo grunted. Chiun silently folded his arms.

When the Arab leading the camel drew near them, he stopped and bowed from the waist, then touched his waist, chest, and forehead in the traditional greeting.

Reva stepped forward toward the camel. But suddenly the Arab looked past her and recoiled as if she were unclean. She stopped and he pointed past her to Chiun, who stood silently, holding in his hand a miniature golden sword with a curved blade and a red ruby in the handle.

"All right," Remo said to Chiun in a hoarse whisper. "What is that piece of crap?"

"It is the sign of Hamidi royalty," Chiun said. "And never again ask what I carry in my steamer trunks."

A few moments later, Reva and Remo were trudging through the sand as the Arab led the camel, with Chiun perched atop, back toward the village. Oscar remained behind by the Rolls Royce.

Looking down the five feet toward the top of Remo's head, Chiun said in Korean, "You know, Remo, I have never really liked riding on camels."

"Try walking."

Chiun shook his head. "It will not do. We are to

133

meet a prince, and the Master of Sinanju must arrive in proper fashion."

"Chiun, I'll tell you before we even get started. I'm not making any deals with this guy, whoever he is. I don't care what he offers you, how much shlock jewelry or fat-faced women. I'm here to find that bacteria crap and get rid of it. Anything else, forget it."

"Must you always talk business?" Chiun asked. "That is so mercenary." His camel moved away from them as they neared the village.

"I take it you're annoyed that he's riding and you are walking," Reva grunted to Remo. Her milk-white skin was beaded with perspiration, and her spike-heeled shoes seemed to screw themselves into the loose sand with every step.

"You might say that," Remo said.

"Why not just reach up, then, and pull him off?" Reva said. "You're bigger than he is."

"That's true," Remo said. "There are a lot of things bigger than he is. Bags of leaves. Packing boxes. Blow-up dolls. And most people."

"I don't understand."

"They've all got just about an equal chance of getting him off that camel," Remo said.

"As big as you are?" she said.

"Lady, you don't understand and you never will. Forget it."

"You're telling me that you're not stronger than he is?"

"I'm telling you that when he doesn't want to be moved, he won't be moved. Strength has nothing to do with it."

"Well, what does?"

"Tradition, lady. Thousands of years of it. And you don't know gnat's breath about it, so forget it."

"Now, *you* talk about tradition. But when he talks of it, you make fun of it."

Remo lowered his voice to make sure that Chiun, fifty yards ahead of them, could not hear him. "That's different. He's always talking about other people's traditions, and they're mostly crap. I'm talking about his tradition, and that's something else. He *is* tradition. Even though I don't want to hear him talking about it all the time."

"That doesn't make any sense," she whispered back.

"He never makes any sense," Chiun called out.

The camel stopped fifteen yards before a large tent set up in the corner of the encampment, its back against the initially sparse grass of the oasis. One entire side of the tent was open, and the pathway to the tent was lined on both sides by forty Arabs in long robes.

The camel driver dropped the animal's reins and ran into the tent. A moment later, he came back and brought the animal to its knees so Chiun could dismount. There was a handclap from inside the tent, and the forty Arabs in robes dropped to their knees before Chiun and placed their foreheads against the sand.

When Remo came to his side, Chiun said, "Now you'll see people who know how to act."

A man stepped from the tent. He was tall, in his early fifties, burly but shapeless in his flowing red and brown striped robe. The hands that jutted from the sleeves of the robe were knotted and strong looking. The man's face was weathered with the genes of the Arab and the aging of the sun.

He walked toward Chiun, Remo, and Reva, a smile laid over the deep creases of his brown face. He stopped before them, then bowed and touched stomach, chest, and forehead in an Islamic greeting.

"*Salaam aleikim,* Master of Sinanju," he said. "After, lo, these many years, we feel one of our brothers has returned to our midst."

Chiun returned the greeting. "*Salaam aleikim,*" he said.

"Shalom," said Remo.

Sheik Fareem looked at Remo, and Chiun said, "We had best speak English in front of the child. He knows not your language."

135

"Our land still rings with the glory of the deeds of your illustrious ancestor," the sheik told Chiun.

"And in our ancient scrolls you and yours are written of as wise and honorable rulers," Chiun said.

"What is this all about?" Reva asked Remo. "What scrolls?"

"It's too long to explain," Remo said. "But basically what this is all about is that Chiun's great-granduncle killed somebody for these wogs, and they paid their bill in full."

"Oh," she said.

"And these are your friends?" the sheik asked Chiun, nodding toward Remo and the woman.

"Actually, no," Chiun said. "The white man is . . ." He paused, then stepped forward to whisper to the sheik. Remo heard him say, "He's really a servant, but he doesn't like to hear that. He is of no consequence because he understands neither tradition nor obligation." Chiun stepped back. "I do not know who or what the woman is, except she flew us here in her plane."

Sheik Fareem nodded. "She shall be treated with the greatest courtesy, then. She shall be allowed in the tent with my wives and concubines. A great honor for a Western woman."

He turned to the men and waved them up from their knees, when Reva approached him and spoke. "Your Excellency, I am Reva Bleem. I am from the Puressence Company."

The sheik's face wrinkled and then opened in a look of understanding. "Oh," he said. "I see. Then you may sit with us, woman."

He turned from her as if she were particularly uninteresting and reached out a hand for Chiun's elbow. "Now, Magnificence, you must partake of our hospitality. You and your servant and the woman."

"You are gracious, Excellency, to open your tents to such as them. But then the Hamidi family has always been gracious."

136

"Is this almost a wrap?" Remo asked. "Can we get out of this sun someday soon?"

"Of course. My tent is yours," the sheik said. He snapped his fingers, and one of the men behind him stepped forward and tossed a long cloak over Reva Bleem's shoulders. She looked surprised but tied it closed at the throat.

As they walked toward the tent, she asked Remo, "What's that about?"

"Who knows?" Remo said. "Probably some nonsense about not showing your legs in the sheik's presence or something. Ignore it."

The tent, shaded by trees, was cool despite the desert heat. Chiun and Fareem sat on tufted chairs atop a small wooden platform, while Remo and Reva were consigned to cushions on the sand floor below the level of the platform.

The sheik clapped his hands and said with a small smile on his swarthy face, "I have often read of the ancient ways. There will be tea for you."

Chiun smiled and nodded. "It is correct," he said.

"Can we talk some business?" Remo said.

"Forgive him," Chiun said. "He is young."

"Of course," the sheik said.

"Shove forgiveness," Remo said. "Let's try business."

"And what is your business?" the sheik asked.

"The oil-eating bacterium. Where is it?"

"You should ask the woman," Fareem said. "It comes from her company."

"Right," Remo said. "And some's been sent to you. So where is it?"

"It has not yet arrived. I have not yet seen this wonderful invisible bug. But what interest is that of yours?"

"Because I want it before it's used. Before it messes up the world. I'm here to take it back to the States."

Fareem was about to answer, but stopped as two women in veils and gauzy robes brought in steaming brass pitchers of tea. They set them on a low table and poured tea for all four.

137

"Hold the cream and sugar," Remo said. The woman who stood before him pouring looked up and into his eyes while she filled his cup. Her eyes were as green as emeralds, and even under the veils, he could see that she was smiling. Even her eyes, spaced wide apart in her light golden face, smiled. And then she left.

Fareem sipped the steaming-hot tea, then placed his porcelain cup on the chair arm and leaned forward.

"You said, my friend, that you want this bacterium before it does something bad to the world. And I tell you that it can do nothing to the world to compare with what has already been done to my world."

Remo opened his mouth to speak, but the sheik raised an imperious index finger for silence.

"Once," he said, "my people were warriors, brave and fearless and just. Back in the time of the Master of Sinanju, many years ago, we were the best horsemen in the world. We could live as no other men could in these barren sands. Yes, we were . . . if you wish . . . bandits. But these were our lands, and we resisted those who would use them, and we took their goods and only when necessary their lives. And we took them openly in fair contests of arms."

"This is their tradition, Remo," said Chiun. "It is well known."

"All right, all right," Remo said. "So you were wonderful highwaymen. What happened and what's it got to do with me and the bug?"

"Oil happened," the sheik said. "The Hamidi were warriors. We battled other tribes for supremacy, other nations for glory. But no longer. The Hamidi—all of them except for a handful of my tribe—are warriors no more. They are bankers." He spat onto the sand. "They sit in offices growing sleek and fat. They are money lenders. Oil and its riches have made them give up the old life, and now they are soft and degenerate. Their hands have never held a sword; their arms have never cast a lance."

"Well, that's your argument with them," Remo said,

138

"but not with me. Work it out yourselves. Take it to the United Nations and let that freak show discuss it for six months."

"It is too late for discussion," Sheik Fareem said. "My brother, the king, knows that what they are doing is wrong, but they persist. The lure of oil and the gold it generates is too powerful for them to resist. The king—my brother—and his court have tried to tell me that they are the true raiders. That they, through their oil, are conducting the largest raid in our history, in the history of civilization. That they are raiding all the treasuries of the Western world."

"Sounds about right to me," Remo said.

"But it is wrong. What they are doing is not war, and it is not battle. It is theft and burglary. Not one of them can sit a horse. Not one of them can fight. The Hamidi, the rulers of this land since before there was sand here, are being ruined by the wealth of oil."

"Why'd you wait this long to get upset about it?" Remo said. "It's been going on for years."

"Is it not true that sometimes a tragedy must strike in our homes before we realize what a tragedy is? We never fear the lightning in the next valley, only that which flashes over our heads," Fareem said. "My son, Abdul. Raised to take my place, to lead men in war, to rule wisely and honestly. He went to join them." He crossed his arms over his chest like a pair of Sam Browne belts.

"Where'd he go?" asked Remo.

"He went to Nehmad, to the capital. He surrendered his stallion and rode in an automobile like the one that brought you here. He wished to become one of them." He spat again. "But I have brought him back. He will learn our ways or die."

"Well, I'm really sorry for your trouble," Remo said, "but it's your trouble, not mine. Why do you want the bacterium?"

"I received a message one day from a man who said he was my friend."

"There he is," Remo said. "Friend again."

"Who is this friend?" Reva asked Remo.

"I don't know. He hired some guy to kill Chiun and me. Then he offered Chiun work. He's the guy behind this."

"This friend," the sheik said, "told me of this special germ and how it could destroy the oil which is destroying my nation. That is what I will use it for. I am going to rid this corner of the world of that vile black grease which is pushing us into oblivion as a people."

"You'll push the whole world into oblivion," Remo said. "Who knows how underground oil reserves are connected. You might turn the whole world's oil supply into wax."

"Men have lived without oil before," Fareem said.

"I just can't let you do that," Remo said. "I have to get that bacterium. . . ."

"Anaerobic," Chiun said.

"I have to get that anaerobic bacterium and destroy it," Remo said. "Then I'll be out of here."

"And I cannot let you have it," the sheik said.

"Then I'll have to take it from you," said Remo.

He felt, rather than saw, the motion of the two guards at the front of the tent as they turned toward him. But the sheik held up a hand and they stopped.

"You think you can do this?" Fareem asked Remo.

"I know damned well I can do this."

The sheik nodded. "Your government would be very upset if there were no more oil?"

"Not just my government. All governments. All people. Just because your people have bred over it doesn't mean you have any knowledge of what it does, of how the people of the world depend on it."

"And you really believe that?" the sheik asked.

"Maybe I do, maybe I don't," Remo said.

"If you are not sure, why are you here?"

"Because it's my job. I was told to do it, so I'm doing it. If tomorrow they tell me to blow up your oil fields, I'll do that too. I don't give a damn. I just do."

"You are satisfied with living this way?"

"Yes," Remo said, and was surprised to find that he

140

meant it. "I trust the person I work for. He's a jerk but his instincts are good. If he says something's important, I trust him, and that saves me all the trouble of having to think about it. When the bacterium comes, I'm taking it with me."

"We shall see," the sheik said. He rose from his seat and walked to a far corner of the tent, where he opened the top of an elaborately carved wooden trunk. He brought out an old yellowed piece of parchment which, in his excitement, he waved over his head, then brought back to the chair. He carefully unrolled it, glanced at it, then handed it to Chiun without a word.

"What's that?" Remo asked.

"Hush," said Chiun as he looked carefully at the old parchment. He read it carefully, then nodded.

"What is it?" Remo asked.

"Read it for yourself," Chiun said. He handed it forward, and Remo took it before he saw that it was written in Arabic. He could not understand one symbol.

"It looks like graffiti," he said. "What is it?"

"It is a contract between my people and the House of Sinanju," the sheik said, taking the scroll back from Remo.

"It is the agreement between the sheik's ancestors and mine," Chiun said. "What they would do for him. What the terms of payment were to be."

"And," the sheik added.

"And what?" Remo asked.

"And it says that if ever again my tribe needs the services of the House of Sinanju, as long as its bill has been correctly paid, it has only to ask." He turned to Chiun. "Is that not correct?"

"It is correct."

"I now ask," Fareem said. "I call on the House of Sinanju to honor its contract and to provide, through you, the services our ancestors agreed upon centuries ago."

"Done," said Chiun.

"Done?" said Remo in bewilderment. "Done? What the hell do you mean, done?"

"It is a contract, Remo. It binds me as it binds you. You are a Master of Sinanju too."

"And that's where we differ," Remo said. "You're stuck with that contract, maybe, and you're stuck with Sinanju, with that village and all those ingrates who live there. I'm not. My village is the United States. And my contract is not with this guy but with them. When that bacterium arrives, I'm going to destroy it. No matter how many sheiks make the mistake of getting in my way."

He rose as Chiun said softly, "And I will protect my sheik and his interests because that is my obligation."

"Let us not quarrel, my friends," Fareem said, rising to his feet also. "My men will show you all to your tents, and tomorrow we will have a celebration for all of you. We can become enemies, if we must, after that. But not now."

Walking from the tent, Reva hissed to Remo, "You against him. Who's going to win?"

"I am, of course," Remo said.

"You're pretty sure of that. How come?"

"Because God, justice, and the American way are on my side," Remo said.

But he would rather have Chiun, Remo thought that night as he lay on a mat in a small tent in the compound. There were guards patrolling outside the entrance to his tent. He heard them shuffling around and talking to each other in the thick, muted Arabic tones.

Remo supposed he loved Chiun, but why couldn't the old Oriental have been born in St. Louis? It had happened a half-dozen times in their lives together, that some ancient or obscure rule or contract of Sinanju had put him and Chiun on opposing sides. And now again.

He could not conceive of fighting Chiun. Even if he got the chance, which he doubted, he did not believe that he could ever lift his arm to strike the old Korean. Would Chiun kill him? Remo thought about it for only a moment and had his answer. Yes, Chiun would.

142

Because while, despite all his bitching, he regarded Remo as his son, he regarded Sinanju as sacred. Nothing or no one, including Remo, could be allowed to bring shame to the ancient order of assassins.

Over the sounds of the night, Remo heard Reva Bleem in the next tent, breathing steadily in her sleep. Chiun's tent was on the other side of Remo's, but Remo heard nothing from there, which did not surprise him. Chiun was able to move in total silence, and his sleep was so light—except for a rare excursion into snoring—that his breathing could not be heard from as little as eighteen inches away.

Was Chiun lying there on his sleeping mat, thinking of tomorrow and the tomorrows that might follow; thinking of the moment when perhaps he must raise his hand against Remo?

Remo growled deep in the back of his throat. Let him. If Chiun wasn't so damned mercenary and so goddamned *i*-dotting, *t*-crossing picky about contracts that were a thousand years old, none of this would have happened. Remo hoped that the old man couldn't sleep.

Then he heard a sound.

It seemed like a puff of air rustling the fabric of the tent but it wasn't. He recognized it as a hand touching the tent cloth behind Remo, toward the back of the structure. He rolled over in the darkness and saw the faintest of shadows on the fabric. Then he saw the bottom of the tent lift and a slim figure slide in under the fabric. Remo was ready to move toward the darkened figure, to strike, when he realized it was a woman. The steps were too light across the sand floor of the tent, too gliding and smooth to be a man. But it wasn't Reva Bleem. She would have preceded herself with her mouth, flapping all the time, asking all her interminable questions about who he was and who Chiun was and who they worked for and who would win their upcoming battle if it turned into a battle. Earlier in the evening, she had badgered Remo with those questions for an hour, until Remo had pushed her out of the tent

143

and told the guards to shoot her on sight if she should return before morning.

The guards had not laughed, and the way they glared toward Remo let him know they would just as soon be aiming their rifles at him as at Reva Bleem.

Remo wondered who was moving toward his sleeping mat. He could smell the sweet aroma of a floral perfume. The thought crossed his mind that perhaps Arabs used women assassins, but the person that approached him was empty-handed. The evenness of the steps told him that.

The woman knelt beside his cushions and leaned close to him.

"I'm awake," he whispered.

The woman recoiled with a slight start.

"Oh. I thought you slept." It was the girl with the green eyes who had earlier served tea in the sheik's tent. Remo could see the eyes glint momentarily in the subdued light of the tent as the woman glanced nervously toward the closed entrance flap.

"I must not be found here," she whispered in Remo's ear. Her faint breath fluttered the gauze veil she wore over the lower half of her face.

"I know," he said softly. "Why did you come?"

"Because you looked nice today and you smiled at me."

"No charge," Remo said.

"I'm sorry. I do not understand."

"Never mind," Remo said.

The young woman's lips quivered. She seemed unable to speak, and Remo reached out and touched her gently on the side of the throat. She sipped air for a second, then took a deep breath and said quickly, "I have heard that they plan to kill you tomorrow."

"They? The sheik?"

"No. It was his minister, Ganulle. I heard him speaking to someone. They will kill you during tomorrow's celebration."

"They will try," Remo said.

"Yes," the woman said, not understanding Remo's meaning.

"Why did you come to tell me?"

"Because you looked kind. And because I do not like Ganulle. His plans toward our sheik are evil."

Involuntarily, she moved her neck toward Remo's hand, and he began stroking the side of her throat down the hollow of her shoulder bones.

"Thank you for warning me," Remo said. "What can I do for you in return?"

"You need do nothing, except live. I would want nothing to befall you or the old one."

"What's your stake in this? Just who are you? Are you the sheik's daughter?"

"Oh, no. I am the wife of his son."

"Abdul?"

"Yes."

"What is he all about?" Remo asked. He felt a little hitch in the woman's breathing, and with his thumb he touched her cheek and felt a tear roll down the side of her face.

"He is a fat and worthless cruel man whom I will never love," she said in a rush of whispered words.

"Can't you get away?"

"You do not understand our traditions. It is my destiny to be the prince's woman. One of them."

"I don't understand anybody's traditions, I guess," Remo said. He felt the girl shudder, and he said, "But in my land, we have a tradition of our own."

"And what is that?"

"We show those who care for us how much we care for them," Remo said, and then he was pulling her onto the sleeping mat with him. He was surprised at how light she was. He removed the veil from her face and saw that the rest of her was as beautiful as her eyes had been.

He pressed his lips to hers, and she came to him with her lips and her body, wanting him, needing him, and he brought her to him and gently, delicately made love to her entire body.

They joined in joy, and when they were done, before Remo could stop her, the girl cried out from sheer happiness.

Remo heard a rustling at the tent flap and pushed the young woman off to the side of the mat and covered her with the light blanket. The bigger of the two guards stuck his head into the tent and came to the side of Remo's sleeping cushions.

"Oh, it's you," Remo said.

"I heard a noise."

"I had a bad dream. I cried out," Remo said.

"You cry out like a woman," the guard said.

"I didn't know that," Remo said.

"Perhaps tomorrow you will cry out like a man," the guard said.

"Gee, wouldn't that be nice," Remo said.

After the guard left, Remo removed the cover from the young woman. She replaced her veil and rose quickly to her feet.

"Thank you," she said.

"For what?"

"For making love to me. It has been so long."

She started away, but Remo caught her wrist. "What is your name?" he asked.

"Zantos," she said. "Be careful tomorrow."

"I will."

"I will pray for you," she said and was gone.

Chapter Nine

The two horsemen faced each other across a distance of 100 yards. Directly between them, a five-foot-high wooden post, four inches thick, was anchored into the sand, supported by smaller posts propped at angles against it.

Sheik Fareem sat next to Remo on the small raised platform. He slowly lifted his hand and then dropped it, and as he did, the two horsemen prodded their big, muscular stallions with their heels, and the two horses bolted forward, racing toward the center post. As they rode, the two Arab soldiers withdrew long, curved swords from scabbards at their sides.

The horseman coming from the left reached the post first. He waved his sword over his head in a large, sweeping arc, then swung it in laterally, parallel to the ground. Flashing in the sun, the blade bit cleanly through the four-by-four post, with the thunk of a melon hitting the ground. But even before his sword exited the wood, the second soldier was there. He raised his sword high over his head as he was riding, and then, without his horse even slowing down, he brought the sword down vertically on the wooden post. He slashed it through, almost to the base, his blade missing only by millimeters the side-moving sword of the first horseman. The top of the four-by-four, severed two feet above the sand by the first soldier and then split lengthwise by the second, dropped to the sand in two neat pieces.

The gathered crowd followed Sheik Fareem in applause.

Remo clapped too, as did Chiun next to him.

Fareem leaned toward Remo and said, "The finest light cavalry in the world. And now, only one hundred of them are left."

Remo saw Zantos, the green-eyed girl, on the other side of the platform and nodded to her, but the girl looked away. He felt Chiun tapping his shoulder.

"Pretend that this is good, Remo," Chiun whispered. "That those two horseback-riding monkeys impress you. It is good manners."

"You desert me and go over to the enemy, and now you're worried about my manners?" Remo said.

"Must you always argue with me?" Chiun said, still applauding vigorously.

Dutifully, Remo put his hands together, clapping softly. He looked around the small platform. Beyond the sheik was Reva Bleem, still wearing a long desert robe. Next to her was a pudgy young Arab with beard and mustache, who looked as if running him through a ringer would produce enough oil to light Tacoma for a week. Prince Abdul. The sheik had introduced his son to Remo and Chiun when they arrived at the platform for the Arabian martial arts display, and the prince had acknowledged the introductions by looking away from them and walking to his seat.

The sheik's wish for an Arab soldier, Remo thought. Too bad. Prince Abdul looked as if he would be more at home at the baccarat table in the MGM Grand than on a horse.

Standing behind the sheik, leaning over, whispering in his ear, was Ganulle, his advisor. He was a rat-faced man with a long, pointed nose that he kept aimed in Remo's direction.

Suddenly, over a large sand dune, came a dozen men on horseback, and Ganulle leaned back from the sheik as the ruler concentrated on the riders. They wore the red and brown robes that signified they were of the Hamidi tribe. Shouting war chants as they rode, waving

148

their swords over their head, they came down the side of the dune, their Arabian stallions plunging forward, not leaning back on the hills the way American cow ponies would, but using the hills to create even greater speed and forward momentum. The entire village of 500 people cheered their arrival, and their full-throated cheers overwhelmed the war cries of the horsemen. As they reached the flat table of desert in front of the reviewing stand, half the soldiers freed their feet from their stirrups, then rose up and stood on the horses' saddles, seemingly oblivious to the need to balance themselves, their swords still flashing in the sun as they swung them over their heads. The other six riders released one foot from their stirrups, then hooked their free legs around their saddle horns. Then they fell backward until they were riding upside down, their heads dangerously close to the flashing hooves of the giant stallions. Easily, they transferred their swords to their left hands and kept swinging and slashing at air, eighteen inches above the ground.

A great maneuver if they were fighting Munchkins, Remo thought to himself.

The soldiers standing on the saddles jumped into the air and came back down in a seated position on the horses' rumps, behind the saddles, while the other horsemen executed a tricky maneuver by passing under the bellies of the horses and coming up standing in a single stirrup on the far side of the stallions.

All twelve reached the far end of the level clearing. At full speed, the horses turned, and the men came riding back, side by side, two by two. In each pair of horses galloping shoulder to shoulder, the two riders moved up out of their stirrups and switched from one horse to the other. Then they turned neatly in their saddles, and as the horses galloped up over the dune and out of sight, the twelve horsemen were facing backward in their saddles, waving their swords over their heads in a farewell salute.

The sheik leaned toward Remo.

"Do you ride?" he asked.

"No. But I can."

"Like that?" asked the sheik.

"Only with practice," Remo said. "They're good."

Sheik Fareem nodded. "Once all our men could ride that way. They were feared from Persia to Libya. But now, no more. There are very few left." Remo heard the tone of regret and sorrow in his voice, and he found himself feeling a tinge of pity for the sheik. The Arab's world was vanishing, swallowed up by the twentieth century, and he didn't like it, and Remo understood how he felt. Fareem's world might be dirty and barren and uncomfortable, but it was his. It was the devil he knew, and he preferred it to the devil he didn't know. That was his right.

But he was wrong in trying to impose his devil on everybody else in the world. Fareem could choose to live out here in this sandbox forever, Remo thought, but he had no right to try to make everyone else's world into a sandbox. And that was why Remo would find that rapid-breeder bacterium when it arrived and bring it back to Harold Smith.

Whether Chiun liked it or not.

Remo leaned over to Chiun and nodded toward the last of the horsemen, who was vanishing over the crest of the dune.

"What do you think, Little Father?" Remo asked.

"The Koreans are very good horsemen."

"These aren't Koreans."

"I know they are not Koreans. I am just telling you that the Koreans are very good horsemen. We introduced horses into Japan. Did you know that?"

"I didn't, but I'm sure I'm going to find out all about it now."

"No, you won't," Chiun said, shaking his head. "I am finished telling you things that you do not appreciate or understand."

"We've got to talk," Remo said.

"About what?"

"About this whole thing. You and I just can't go

tangling with each other because of some damned oil-eating bug."

"That's what I am talking about," Chiun said.

"Huh?"

"Really, Remo, you are hopeless. What do you think would happen if you went into the capital city and told them that Sheik Fareem was going to destroy the country's oil supply?"

"I think they'd send the army back here to wipe him out."

"Exactly. And you would march with them?"

"I don't generally work with groups," Remo said.

"Ahh, but you could," Chiun said. "You could lead them. And I could lead the sheik's men. We Koreans know all about horses. And we could let them fight, you and I, and we would not have to."

"Why don't you just stay with me, let's get the bacterium and get the hell out of here?" asked Remo.

"Because I have a contract. It is older than my contract with Smith and takes precedence over it. I have to honor it."

"Let's think about it," Remo said.

Talking to Chiun, he noticed six men busy burying three posts into the sand twenty-five feet in front of the reviewing stand. The posts were padded, covered with cloth, and after their triangular bases were buried, they stood six feet high. They were spaced eight feet apart in a line and reminded Remo of striking dummies he had often seen in karate centers.

This would be it, Remo thought. Because the girl, Zantos, had told him that there would be an attempt on his life, he had been on guard all day. But the sword-flashing displays and the rodeo riding had contained no threats to him. But these posts, obviously some kind of target and so conveniently set up in front of him, would provide the killing attempt.

He glanced over toward the sheik and saw Ganulle looking at him sharply. The pinch-faced Arab smiled at him condescendingly; it was a smile that told Remo that Ganulle thought he knew something that Remo didn't.

The try would come now.

Did Chiun know about it?

Would Chiun care?

Were they now really enemies? He and Chiun on opposing sides. Did that mean that he could die and Chiun would not care?

He wondered about that and leaned over to Chiun and said softly, "Little Father, I . . ."

"Shhhh," Chiun hissed. "I want to watch my new army."

Remo sighed and shook his head. To hell with it.

Nine horsemen galloped into the clearing from the far end. They massed down there, a hundred yards away, then wheeled as a group and began galloping toward the reviewing stand. In their right hands, they held six-foot-long lances; their left hands bunched the horses' reins, controlling them expertly as they raced across the powdery white sand.

Twenty yards from the three target dummies, they lowered their right hands, and as the horses pulled abreast of the dummies, with the reviewing stand as the backdrop, the horsemen flung their spears in an unusual underhand motion.

Remo could hear the thunk, thunk, thunk of lance after lance smashing into the dummies. And then one lance came over the top of the dummies, flashing toward the high-backed seat in which Remo sat, flashing toward his chest.

Remo kept his hands at his sides.

It was up to Chiun.

It all seemed to pass in slow motion. He could see the lance moving toward his chest. In the bright Arabian sun, he could see the steel tip shining and glinting. The spear was revolving on its long axis, much like a bullet fired through a rifled barrel, rotating for stability. That was the reason for the underhand throw, to give the spear that rotation.

The tip had almost touched him when, still in slow

152

motion, he saw a long-nailed yellow hand move out in front of his chest and slowly, ever so slowly, close tightly around the spear. Its tip stopped just short of touching Remo's skin.

"You fool," Remo heard Chiun snarl.

The riders had wheeled around in front of the reviewing stand. The sheik was on his feet.

"Stop that man," he shouted, pointing to one of the riders, but before anyone could move, Chiun was standing, and the spear, now turned around in his hand, was whistling back over the dummies. It struck one of the horsemen square in the chest. Involuntarily, his hands flew to the lance, but as the man's body turned, Remo saw that the spear had gone all the way through it.

Slowly, the rider slipped to one side and then fell from his horse. The animal, trained for war, galloped on as his dead rider lay motionless in the sand.

Remo turned toward Sheik Fareem. He was staring at the dead horseman. Behind him, Ganulle stood, shocked, his mouth open. He looked toward Remo, and Remo winked at him.

Chiun stood in front of Remo. In Korean, he barked, "And you were going to let that stick impale you just to see if I would do anything about it?"

"Naaah, it wasn't like that," Remo lied. "I would have taken care of it."

"You are an idiot," Chiun said, "and an ingrate and white, but you are my son in Sinanju. Do you think I would let anything be done to you by somebody who smells like sheep?"

"Then let's get the bacterium and get out of here," Remo said.

Chiun shook his head.

"No," Remo said. "I know. You've got a contract."

Chiun nodded.

But Remo felt good. He turned around and saw the young green-eyed woman, Zantos, looking at him. He met her eyes only briefly and nodded slightly.

Remo had not heard a sound, but there was Chiun, standing inside his tent.

"It is done," Chiun said.

"What is?"

"I have spoken to Sheik Fareem. He agrees. You will go to the capital city and bring back their army. I will train his. We will fight here, our two armies, as in the olden times, for the right to destroy this country's oil."

"I guess this is the best we can hope for," Remo said, and Chiun nodded.

"You will leave right away?"

"I suppose so," Remo said. "You're not just waiting for me to turn my back and then dump that stuff in the oil, are you?"

"No. The sheik is bound by his word. He looks forward to a war. And he looks forward to my training his son to be a leader."

Remo said, "It's going to be funny, leading an army against you."

"Any army you lead will be funny," Chiun said.

Remo let it slide. "You know who was behind that spear-throwing today?"

"Yes."

"It was Ganulle."

"Why do you tell me that when I already told you I know who it was?"

"I just wanted to be sure you knew," Remo said. "I want you to be careful. Did you tell the sheik it was him?"

"No," said Chiun. "It is better for assassins when their emperors know nothing. Why do you think he ordered you killed?"

"I don't know," Remo said. "Maybe because I'm opposed to the sheik's plans?"

Chiun shook his head. "No, it is not that."

"Keep an eye on him," Remo said.

"I will."

"We can't let him destroy that oil," Reva Bleem

154

said. She was sitting in the rear seat of her Rolls. Remo had ignored her open-door invitation and sat in the front next to Oscar, the thick-necked chauffeur.

"You should have thought of that before you let your lunatic brother play in that factory and start shipping that bacterium around."

"I know," she said. "I wish I knew where it was, why it isn't here yet. But that damned Wardley might have sent it by aborigine runner. We've got to stop it from being used. My Polypussides isn't ready yet."

"No. We've got to get that tank price down and save us all from becoming dwarfs."

"Right," she said.

"And when we do that," Remo said, "what's to stop you from cooking up another batch of germs to stick in the oil supply?"

Reva looked at him, and the chill she felt looking into his night-black eyes was mirrored on her face.

"I won't have to," she said quickly. "By the time I'm ready, my price will be competitive. My prices will go down. Synthetics always do. Oil prices will go up. Natural resource prices also always go up. We'll be even."

"And then you and the oil companies together will march the prices even higher?"

"Right," she agreed. "But through the free marketplace. High prices are only bad when they're caused by governments. Not when they're caused by free market greed." She leaned forward and put her hand on Remo's shoulder. "But we've got to stop them now. That means it's up to you."

"I'll do my duty," Remo said.

"Just who it it you're working for?" she asked.

"Ask me no questions, I'll tell you no lies."

"Can you handle the old man and his army?"

"I don't know. It depends on how good this Hamidi army is," Remo said.

"It's considered the best in this part of the world," she said, and Remo said, "That's not saying much."

The Star in the Center of the Flower of the East Military Base was located three miles outside the capital city of Nehmad. Four uniformed Arabian soldiers stood in a guard shack located inside the main gate.

Oscar did not bother to slow down, and none of the guards signaled to the Rolls Royce.

"Hold it," Remo said to the driver, and the Rolls stopped. If he was going to lead this army into battle, he'd better find out just what kind of army it was. Remo walked into the guard shack and saw that the four guards were playing dominoes.

None of them looked toward him, so he called out, "Is anybody here alive?"

One of the soldiers glanced over. "Who are you?"

"Why didn't you ask me that when I just rolled by in my Rolls Royce?"

"I thought you were an officer."

"In a Rolls Royce?"

"All our officers drive Rolls Royces."

"With chauffeurs?"

"All with chauffeurs. I am told that is why Allah made sergeants. Who are you?"

"George Armstrong Custer."

"You will have to sign our visitor list," the soldier said, making a triumphant move from the little stack of dominoes standing on edge before him.

Remo saw the visitors' book on a stand inside the door. He picked up the pen. It didn't work. He looked around for another pen, but there wasn't any. He looked inside the book. The last visitor had signed in three years earlier, almost to the day.

It was going to be great leading this army into war, Remo thought.

Unquestioned, unchallenged, unchecked, the Rolls Royce continued down the main road of the camp toward a cluster of large buildings, built around an Italianate central fountain.

Off to the right, Remo saw row after row of parked jet fighters. To the left, he saw tanks, hundreds of tanks, parked in so many neat columns that the area

156

looked like the parking lot of a suburban shopping mall.

If this was typical, Remo thought, it was no wonder the Israelis always won the wars. One Israeli commando—check that, one reasonably bright Israeli high school student—could march in here at high noon with a pair of pliers and a wire cutter and disable the entire Hamidi army and air force.

There were two dozen Rolls Royces parked in front of the largest of the buildings. Two uniformed Hamidi guards carrying rifles stood at the top of the stairs, in front of the closed door. Remo told Reva Bleem to wait for him, then walked up the steps. He brushed by the two soldiers, opened the door, and went inside. Neither of them had tried to stop him.

The inside of the command building looked like the lobby of a first-class London hotel. There were potted palms around the inside, clustered at the ends of long brocaded couches and overstuffed chairs. Persian rugs covered every square inch of floor. A large fan rotated overhead, quietly and uselessly, because the area was chilled down into the low 60s by central air conditioning.

At the head of the wide steps was a pair of double doors. Printed on them in gold was "The Office of the Commanding General." The gold was sprinkled with chips of multicolored stones. Spotlights, with revolving filters over them, played on the door, and the cut stones glinted back light, like an overhead disco globe.

In equally large letters under the office name was the name of the commanding general: Jonathan Wentworth Bull.

Remo found the commanding general in an inner office, past six bosomy American secretaries whose Civil Service specialty seemed to be: Doing Nails GS-14.

The general was wearing designer jeans and handtooled brown boots with white stitching on them. He wore a large dark brown Stetson with feathers stuck into the band, and his white shirt was embroidered with red dragons.

157

He sat with his back to Remo, his feet up on the windowsill. A younger man sat in a chair next to the general's desk. On his lap was a high pile of papers in blue and white folders.

He was reading from one when Remo entered.

"The next order of business, General, is the RD-Twenty-two A."

Without turning, the general asked, "What's the RD-Twenty-two A?"

"You know, General. It's the satellite system to bomb enemy attack planes."

"For crying out loud, Winslow, I know that. And you know that. Sometimes I think you're never going to be a soldier. Not a real soldier. Do you think these people are going to spend twenty billion dollars on something called an RD-Twenty-two A?"

"I don't understand, General."

"It's a satellite killer system. That's what you have to call it. They'll go for twenty billion for a satellite killer system. They won't go for twenty dollars for RD-Twenty-two A. These people don't trust letters and numbers. You have to give things names." General Jonathan Wentworth Bull chuckled. "I remember once . . . it was one of my biggest battles. I was trying to sell them one of those things . . . you know, with the long thing sticking out, like a mosquito's nose . . . what do you call it?"

"A proboscis, sir?"

"Not the mosquito's thing. This other thing. Gray metal."

"A cannon, sir?"

"Yeah, that's right. A cannon. It used that stuff . . ."

"Gunpowder?"

"Right. Gunpowder. But my brother-in-law who buys these up cheap, see, he enriched the gunpowder with plutonium. When he told me about it, I told him I thought he had something. I mean a surplus World War II Italian whatchamacallit . . ."

"Cannon."

158

"Yeah, with regular gunpowder and some of that plumonium."

"Plutonium," the younger man said.

"Yeah. With some of that ground up in the gunpowder. Well, anyway, my brother-in-law called it the Advanced Artillery Unit Four-B. I told him it wouldn't sell, but he insisted. So I tried to sell it for a year, but they just wouldn't go for an Advanced Artillery Unit Four-B. I tried for a year, but they wouldn't move, so I put the plans away, and two weeks later I came back with them again, but this time I called it a Mobile Nucotronic Army Decimator. They bought it the same day. Twelve of them. Turned a cool twenty-four-million-dollar profit on those. I'm telling you, Winslow, if you want to be a success in this army business, you've got to learn how to sell. Forget the alphabet. Forget those numbers. Give things names that sound good when they make anti-Israeli speeches. They love Mobile Nucotronic Army Decimators. They love satellite killer systems. Screw that A, B, and C shit. They don't sell anything." The general spun in his chair to smile warmly at Winslow and saw Remo in the doorway.

"Sorry," the general said. "I only see salesmen on Fridays."

"I'm not a salesman."

"Oh. Who do you represent?"

"The spirit of Napoleon."

"Spirit of Napoleon," General Bull repeated. "I don't know that company. Big Board or American Stock Exchange?"

"Neither," Remo said.

General Bull looked at his aide, Winslow, with confusion on his handsome features. Winslow leaned forward and said, "Napoleon, sir. I think it's a kind of cake. A pastry."

Bull's face wrinkled more.

"Pastry?" he said. "Oh. One of those things with that tissue paper crust?"

"Yes, sir. With the creamy filling between the layers."

"And that hard white icing on top," the general said. "With brown swirls in it."

"Yes, sir," Winslow said proudly. "That's a Napoleon."

General Bull cleared his throat and looked sternly at Remo.

"Well, son, it's nice of you to stop by, but we already have a pastry chef. Hired him away from Lutèce's. He makes the best chocolate mousse you ever saw. Tomorrow is mousse day. You want to stay around, you can have some. I'll tell him to make some more for you."

"You feed your army chocolate mousse from Lutèce's?" Remo asked.

"No. Not the army. The officers. The army eats sheep or frogs or something. They like bread. I'm not sure. Something like that. So I don't need you for them, son, and I've got Emile from Lutèce's, and I don't much like Napoleons anyway. So I've got no real use for you here."

He leaned forward suddenly with heightened interest.

"You don't make a Charlotte Russe, do you?"

"No," Remo said.

"Too bad. That's what's missing from our menu. A Charlotte Russe. God, I love that puffy whipped cream inside that cardboard tube. Winslow, take a note. Find us a Charlotte Russe chef."

"Yes, sir," Winslow said.

The general looked at Remo with an understanding smile. "Listen, you come up with a good Charlotte Russe, and maybe we've got something to talk about, okay?"

"No," said Remo.

"What do you mean, no?"

"I didn't come here to hear you talk about goddamn cake," Remo said.

General Jonathan Wentworth Bull rose to his feet. He wore a diamond-encrusted belt around his waist, and he hiked it up over his hips.

"What do you want to talk about?"

"War," said Remo.

Bull seemed confused and looked to Winslow. "War?" he asked.

"Kind of like fighting, General. Between two armies."

"Oh, yeah. I know. Like Space Invaders with people. What about war, fella?"

"General, let's get to understand each other first," Remo said.

"Okay. I'm very understanding. Everybody says that."

"Oil is what keeps you alive. You know that, right?"

"I wouldn't exactly say . . ."

"Yes, you would. All the Hamidi oil pays your salary. It helps them buy all that military junk that your brother-in-law sells. It's oil and oil money, right?"

"Not exactly. I wouldn't . . ." General Bull started.

Remo squeezed his earlobe.

"Right. Right. Oil. It's oil. Easy on the ear, fella. Want to be a colonel? Just let go of the ear."

Remo let go of the ear.

"Okay. Oil keeps you alive. Now somebody wants to destroy the oil."

"There's an awful lot of it. It'd be hard for them to do that," the general said.

"They've got a way. I've seen it work," Remo said.

"It'll destroy our oil?" Bull said.

"Right."

"No more money for salaries or new satellite killer systems?"

"Right," Remo said.

Bull pulled himself to his full height and hitched up his jeans again. "Winslow," he barked. "Scramble the air force. Get the tank divisions ready."

"Should I tell them to get the Mobile Nucotronic Army Decimator ready?" Winslow asked.

"No, don't mess with that crap. Just regular things . . . you know, that go bang."

"Guns?"

161

"Right. How many pilots are around?" the general asked.

"We gave all the Americans the week off, remember?"

"Oh, phooey," the general said.

"You don't have Hamidi pilots?" Remo asked.

"Son, there are no Hamidi pilots. The Hamidis think that planes are things that come with Americans inside them. The Hamidis are old slave traders. They buy people. They buy ambassadors. They've got some ambassador right now running around America on a speaking tour, warning about how officials might come under the pressure of the Israeli lobby."

"I read about that," Remo said.

"Sure, you would. That guy gets ten thousand dollars every time he makes that speech."

"For ten thousand dollars, I'd make that speech too," Winslow said.

"Well, I wouldn't," General Bull said. "I wouldn't because I believe in truth, justice, and the American way. And the free enterprise system, of course."

"Dear God," said Remo, shaking his head. "Well, skip the air force. We won't need it anyway."

"Who we going up against?" Bull asked. "I've heard that there's a chess club in Nehmad and the members are planning sedition against the government. They're voting next week on printing a leaflet criticizing the king. Are they the ones?"

"Not them. We're going against Arab soldiers."

"Come on. There are no Arab soldiers," General Bull said.

"Old-fashioned kind," Remo said. "Horses, swords, spears."

"Real swords?" Bull said.

"Yes," said Remo.

"They'll be no match for our tanks if we can get some running. Winslow will lead them into battle himself. I'll stay here and man the central command post. Let me know as soon as the fighting's over."

"No," Remo said. "Winslow isn't leading. I'm leading. And you're coming with me."

"Up until now, son, I kind of liked you. But why do I have to go?"

"It'll make the troops feel good to know their general is there at their side, sharing the risks with them," Remo said.

"You know what I hate?" Bull said.

"What?"

"All that old bullshit tradition in the army. All those traditions, they're general-killers, that's what they are. General-killers."

"And so am I," Remo said.

"I'll go," Bull said. "You know, I never did ask your name."

"Patton," Remo said. "George S. Patton."

"Is that Irish?" Bull asked. "Sounds Irish."

Chapter Ten

General Jonathan Wentworth Bull assembled the entire Hamidi army the next morning at 10 A.M. Two hundred of them showed up.

"This is it?" Remo asked him. "Two hundred men?"

"Well, there are more, but it's hard to get messages to them right away. And especially before noon. I think we should have a thousand by this afternoon."

"We'll need a thousand," Remo said. "Sheik Fareem's got a thousand men."

"If I get you eleven hundred, can I stay here?" Bull asked.

"No."

"Why not?"

"Do you want me to squeeze your ear?" Remo asked.

"You don't have to be belligerent. We're not in a war yet," Bull said.

"What can these things do?" Remo said, waving toward the troops, some of whom stood in clusters talking, some of whom lay on the ground napping, in the large open area before the main headquarters building.

"I think one of them is a ju-jitsu expert. Somebody told me once that a couple of them know how to use knives. They all have those little things that shoot . . . er, rifles. Right, rifles. I think there's a bunch of them who are good at jumping wires and starting parked cars."

164

"Maybe we can mug the other army," Remo said. He heard a faint tapping sound from the side of the building.

"Do you hear that noise?" he asked.

"Yeah. That's our press agent."

"You've got a press agent for this army?" Remo asked.

"Of course. How else is the world going to know not to mess with Hamidi Arabia unless we have a press agent working?" Bull said.

"What's her name?"

"Actually, she's not really a press agent," Bull said. "She's a journalist. But she's as good as a press agent."

"Show me," Remo said. "Maybe she can fight. We can make her acting commander-in-chief in the field."

They walked toward the corner of the building, and as soon as they saw General Bull turn his back, most of the soldiers ran away. The rest were sleeping.

A small folding table was set up in the shade alongside the headquarters building. A woman sat at it, in front of a typewriter, tapping on the keys with a pencil she held in her teeth.

Remo stopped to watch. He said to Bull, "Wouldn't it be easier if she typed with her hands?"

"She can't do that."

"Why not? Who is she anyway?"

"Melody Wakefield. She's from *The Boston Blade*."

"Christ, that explains it," Remo said. "I had to read that paper once. She's on your side?"

"Mostly she's against the Israelis," Bull said. "I don't read her stuff myself, but that's what I think she's up to."

"Why's she against the Israelis?"

"I keep asking that. What I think is that out here the people most like the Americans are the Israelis. And she hates the Americans, so she takes it out on the Israelis by hating them too."

"Bull, that's the first smart thing I ever heard you say," Remo said.

He watched the young woman drop the pencil from

165

her lips, lean forward and, with her teeth, pull the piece of paper from the typewriter. She placed the paper atop others in a pile and then with her nose pushed a small stone on top of the pile to prevent its blowing away. She stuck out her tongue and pressed it to another stack of paper. One clean sheet adhered to her wet tongue, and she lifted it to the typewriter. After three tries, she got the end of the paper to slip into the paper feed. With her teeth, she bit onto the carriage roller and turned the paper into the machine. Then she picked up the pencil again with her teeth and began typing, slowly, laboriously.

Remo walked around behind the woman, who was concentrating deeply on her work. Her hands were stuck into the pockets of her thin khaki army-style bush jacket. Remo looked over her shoulder.

On the last page, she had written: "The American media has invented an insensitive, cruel Islam to hate, just as it invented the dangers of communism in Vietnam and Cambodia."

She felt Remo standing there and turned toward him.

He nodded toward the page. "Good stuff," he said.

She dropped her pencil. "This book is going to do for the Middle East what my last book did for Vietnam and Cambodia. It'll rip the mask of hypocrisy off the American imperialists and their Israeli lackeys and show all those with an eye for truth that the wave of the future is Islam, benevolent, just, kind Islam."

"Sounds good to me," Remo said. The broad was a daffodil. He remembered that he had seen her byline and that her grandfather had run *The Blade* until he had died. Maybe there was genetic brain-softening in the whole family.

"I just don't understand why you don't type with your fingers instead of with your mouth," Remo said.

Melody Wakefield pulled her arms from the lower pockets of her jacket. She had no hands. Her arms ended at the wrists, in bandaged stumps.

"Oh," Remo said. "I'm sorry. What happened?"

166

"A merchant in the bazaar. He saw me take an apple from his stand. I don't know what the big deal was. I always do that in Boston and nobody complains. Anyway, he called the police. They arrested me, and an Islamic court ordered the traditional sentence carried out."

"They cut off your hands? For stealing an apple?"

"It is written in their holy book. I shouldn't have taken the apple. But if I had sought special treatment, I would have been guilty of trying to undermine, by American power, all the truth and justice of the Islamic movement."

"Don't forget benevolence and kindness," Remo said.

"Right. Islam. True, just, benevolent, and kind."

"Spoken like a dipshit without hands," Remo said. He looked at her shirt front. Maybe they had cut off her breasts too. She certainly didn't have any. Would they do that? Yes, they would, but they probably hadn't had to. She looked as if she had never had any.

"What are you doing here today?" Remo asked.

"I'm here to interview soldiers. I want the world to know how progressive Islam really is. You know in America, they think jihad, a holy war, is a bad thing. But it's not like they want to kill everybody who's not a Moslem. Jihad really only means social reform. Far superior to any American reform. I'm going to prove that in my book by interviewing soldiers. Did I tell you my book on Vietnam and Cambodia won an award?"

"I would have been astonished if it hadn't," Remo said. "Let's see. The American militarists, needing a war to keep their economy alive, tried to impose their decadent and corrupt will on the sweet, peace-loving people of Vietnam and Cambodia. But freedom-loving people all over the world banded together in the cause of liberty to drive out the ugly American invaders and turn their countries over to sweet agrarian reformers who promised land to all the peasants and free elections as soon as possible."

167

Melody Wakefield squealed with delight. "You read my book," she said.

"I didn't have to," Remo said. "I spent a year one day reading your grandfather's newspaper." He noticed that Bull was still standing by the side of the building, looking at them.

"General?" Remo called. "Any objection if she interviews your soldiers?"

"No, none at all. I told you, she's a press agent. She won't write anything to hurt an Arab. If she does, she'll get her tits cut off."

"Too late for that," Remo said, looking again at Melody's flat shirt. "If you want to interview the Army, you'll find them over there in the parade grounds. Asleep. Some of them anyway. The rest ran away."

"Thank you," she said.

"When we go into war tomorrow, you want to go with us?"

"Who are we fighting?" she asked.

"Other Arabs," Remo said.

"Not Israelis?" she said, disappointed.

"No. Arabs."

Melody's face brightened. "But they're Arab renegades whose minds have been poisoned by the corrupt Western beliefs and who are lackeys of the United States and therefore deserve death, right?"

"Right," said Remo wearily.

"It is my duty to go with you to let the world know of our army's glories," Melody Wakefield said.

"Good. You can ride in the front car," Remo said. "Strapped over the hood."

"All right," Chiun said. "Now jump up onto that stallion."

"I don't jump so well," said Abdul, the son of Sheik Fareem. He was wearing a silk shirt and silk pantaloons.

"It is time to learn," Chiun said. "You will lead your father's army into battle tomorrow."

"I don't want to learn jumping," Abdul said.

"Whenever I want somebody to jump, I hire a jumper. Why should I learn to jump? Give me a week or two. I'll advertise in the *London Times*. I'll get you jumpers. Probably in London right now, there are a couple of hundred people who can jump onto a horse. I'll hire one. Two if you want. I'll hire them all for you."

"You must do it," Chiun said severely.

"It'll make me sweat."

"And I will make you cry," Chiun said.

"Is that a threat?" Abdul asked.

They were standing in a clearing in the rear of the oasis, far from the tents of the village.

"Yes," Chiun said mildly.

"Please explain to me why," Abdul said.

"You are going to lead your father's army into battle tomorrow. You have to be able to lead them by your example. They are not likely to follow anybody who falls off his horse. You think I am being unkind to you, but I, the Master of Sinanju, tell you that the only way to train is to work one's body unto pain."

"Where can I buy pain?" Abdul said.

"Get on that horse."

"No."

"You will not have to buy pain," Chiun said. "I will give you some for free." He reached forward and with one long-nailed finger touched Abdul's side through his shirt. It felt like sticking his finger into tapioca.

Abdul turned, Chiun's finger still in his side, and tried to scurry up onto the back of the patiently waiting stallion. His left foot kept missing the stirrup.

"Get up there," Chiun growled.

"I'm trying. I'm trying. Stop hurting my side."

Finally, Chiun released the fat man's side, grabbed the back of his right calf with his hand, and lofted Abdul up into the saddle. It took twenty seconds for Abdul to get himself back in balance. Finally, he was seated upright. He looked down at Chiun, then kicked his feet into the horse and galloped it away.

He stopped twenty yards from Chiun. He did not

know how to turn the horse around, so he looked back over his shoulder at the old man.

"I don't think you understand. I am the next sheik."

"And your father has assigned me to train you."

"I don't want a Korean trainer. I want an American trainer. Everybody knows Americans cost more than Koreans."

Chiun thought for a moment about calling the horse back to him, pulling Abdul off, and punishing him, but decided it was not worth the effort. He watched silently as Abdul rode away, trying to hold onto the horse and not fall off, bouncing his big body from side to side with each step of the stallion.

Then Chiun heard a sound behind him and turned to see a young woman walk from behind the trees.

"I am Zantos," she said. "I apologize for my husband, Master."

"I apologize to you for letting him live another day," Chiun said.

"How will we war tomorrow if Abdul is not ready?" she asked. He noticed that she had bright, direct green eyes that looked into his face with confidence and intelligence.

"I do not know. I will think of something," Chiun said.

"You will not battle against your own son," she said.

"You know Remo? And that he is my son in heart?" Chiun asked.

"Yes. I warned him that there were those who would try to kill him."

Chiun paused. Remo had known about the death attempt to be made on him but had done nothing. Instead, he had wanted to test Chiun to see if Chiun would save him. As Chiun had.

"No, child. I will not raise my hand against my son."

"I am happy for that," Zantos said. She glanced around to make sure that no one was in earshot, then stepped closer to Chiun. "I will warn you now, Master,

170

as I warned your son. There are those here who would kill you."

"Yes," Chiun said. "The regent, Ganulle."

"How did you know?"

"I saw him watching me," Chiun said. "I have seen those kinds of eyes before."

"He and Abdul are in league. Your life is in danger from them."

"You are Abdul's wife. Why do you tell me this?" Chiun asked.

"Because I think they are in league also against our sheik, the noble Fareem. He is a good man and must not be harmed."

"No harm will come to him while I am here," Chiun said. "His life is my responsibility."

"Then I will go, Master."

"Go with my thanks for your warning. And for your loyalty and courage."

The young woman blushed under her half-veil. "What will happen in tomorrow's war?" she asked.

"This is an Arab war, child. Nothing will happen."

"Your son will not be hurt?"

"No," Chiun said.

"Thank you, revered one," she said, and turned to vanish into the trees again. Chiun walked slowly back alone, through the oasis to the main tent village. It was time to talk to Sheik Fareem and tell him some bad news.

Remo sat on the sill of an upstairs window, watching his alleged army trying to drill. Their numbers had swelled to over 750 and from watching, Remo guessed that about fifty of them knew the difference between left and right.

What kind of army did he expect when he took it over by squeezing the commanding general's ear? If Chiun asked, Remo was going to deny responsibility. He wasn't a general. He would be an administrator. A paper pusher. Let General Bull have the credit.

The door to the empty office burst open. Melody

171

Wakefield was shoved roughly into the room, where she sprawled on the floor. Three Hamidi soldiers stood behind her.

"I am told you are the new commander," one of the soldiers told Remo.

"Actually, I'm an administrator, but go ahead. What do you want?"

"This harlot tried to seduce us."

"So she's a soldier groupie. So what?" Remo asked.

"Yes, but she has no . . . no . . ." The soldier brushed his hands down his chest, indicating a bosom.

"Some people like flat-chested women," Remo said.

"That's right. Flat-chested. She offered to take on our entire company. Three at a time. This is obscene, Commander."

"Administrator," Remo said. "With her, it's obscene."

"Our revolutionary army tribunal has judged her in special session," the soldier said.

"And?"

"She can be sold into slavery or stoned," the soldier said. The two soldiers behind him nodded.

"Slavery. I want to be a slave," Melody shouted.

"Shut up, you," said Remo. He asked the soldier, "Who decides the final punishment?"

"You do, Commander. But it must be one or the other."

"Leave it with me," Remo said. He understood that this was how big administrators made decisions. They either said, "Leave it with me," or they appointed a task force to study the problem and make recommendations. Both approaches were based on the same concept—if you waited long enough, most problems went away by themselves, and there was no need to decide anything.

"We will leave her with you too, Commander," the soldier said. He saluted, almost stabbing out his eye with his right thumb, then pulled the door closed.

"What are you going to do with me?" Melody asked Remo.

172

"Stoning's too good for you. And who'd want a slave whose mouth is always going? Three at a time, huh?"

"I thought our brave Hamidi army needed some incentive and expression of the people's love before they marched into battle."

"Well, you're in a pickle now," Remo said. "The Koran is clear. Stoning or slavery."

"You know the Koran?"

"Yes," Remo lied.

"Are you a Moslem?" she asked.

"Yes," Remo lied.

"Wanna make it?" she asked.

"Not with you," he said truthfully. "Listen, don't you understand what's going on here? The last time you fucked up, it cost you your hands. This time it's your life on the line. Don't you care?"

"Spoken like an American. You people think hands are the most important things in the world. But I tell you that hands are not nearly as important as ideas. I will be a martyr to the cause of Islam in the world."

"You'll be dead, and no one will remember your name. Camp followers don't have statues built to them."

"When they understand my motives, they will honor me."

"I wish they had cut out your tongue," Remo said. "You're dealing with lunatics here."

"Islam is liberating," Melody said.

"Go back to your typewriter, will you? I'm taking your case under advisement." That was another thing top administrators always did. Take things under advisement. By tomorrow, the whole Hamidi army would probably be wiped out and the case of Melody Wakefield would be academic. He could send her home. In a strait jacket, as she deserved.

"I will write the truth about our brave army," she shouted as she moved toward the door. "Allah is great."

"Yes, he is. And you are loud. Get out of here."

"Islam forever," she shouted on her way out.

173

"And stop trying to seduce my army," Remo yelled at the closing door. "I've got enough problems without my soldiers getting the clap."

"I am sorry, Emperor," said Chiun, "but your son . . ."

"Will never be a soldier," said Sheik Fareem.

Chiun nodded his head sadly. "Perhaps if I had him when he was younger. But now, he cannot even sit a horse. Or a camel. He is afraid of guns, and swords are too heavy for him. He risks lacerating his own feet every time he picks up a lance."

"It is not that you should have had him when he was young, Master of Sinanju," said Sheik Fareem. "If only you could have had him before there was oil. Oil money has robbed all our people of their respect for the old ways."

"Wealth is like that," Chiun said.

"Oil is like that. We must destroy the oil."

"Saying that makes you a target for many," Chiun said. "Perhaps even some of those around you."

"Do you know something, Master, that you are not telling me?" asked Fareem.

"No, sire. I know nothing. I suspect but I know not."

"You must tell me your suspicions."

"No. Because to rule, you must be without fear and without favor. And you cannot be that when you must always watch over your shoulder. You can look straight ahead. The House of Sinanju is here, at your shoulder, to deal with your enemies."

"You do not mind, though, if I am careful," Fareem said with a sly smile.

"I would mind if you were not, Emperor. The House of Sinanju does not deal with fools."

"It is a good rule," Sheik Fareem said.

"And good men understand that," Chiun said.

They were interrupted by a sound from outside the tent.

"Chiun," a voice called. "Get out here."

"That is Abdul," said the sheik.

"Yes."

"How dare he address you in that tone of voice?"

"He is foolish," Chiun said. He rose from his seat alongside the sheik and, in a swirl of blue brocade, walked to the front of the tent. Fareem followed him.

Abdul stood in the clearing before the tent. Half the village stood back around the other tents, watching. Next to Abdul was a giant of a white man, six and a half feet tall, weighing almost 300 pounds. He was dressed in a red T-shirt and khaki fatigue pants and wore heavy paratrooper boots polished to a mirror shine. His hair was red and his skin was red too. Around his waist hung a wide cartridge belt, festooned with grenades and knives and handguns.

When he saw Chiun, Abdul said, "I told you American trainers were best. I have one now." He gestured to the giant standing next to him.

"What will he train you to do," Chiun asked mildly. "To overeat?"

The red-haired man took a step forward.

"He will be my commander in tomorrow's battle," Abdul said. "He is a soldier."

"Sergeant Willie Bob Watson," the big man said. He saluted no one in particular. "Trained especially for hand-to-hand combat by the world-famous Colonel Mactrug."

"Colonel Mactrug. I have heard of him," Chiun said.

"Until his untimely death, the greatest military fighting man in the world," Willie Bob Watson said.

"A fraud," said Chiun, "who hid behind his gadgets and wires and things and fell the first time somebody came for him."

"That's a lie," Sergeant Watson said. "He was done in by a terrorist squad of dozens."

"The Master of Sinanju does not lie. And, as a matter of fact, he does not even talk to cretins like you."

He started to turn away, but Abdul shouted at him.

175

"A battle," he called out. "A test to determine who will be at my side in tomorrow's battle."

"Abdul!" his father shouted. "You have no right to insult the Master that way."

"I am sorry, Father, but I do not believe that this person is a Master of Sinanju at all. I think he is an old man masquerading as what he is not."

"You saw him with the spear. Was that a masquerade?"

"No. But it might have been naught but luck, Father. Before I will allow you to entrust your sacred safety to his hands, I demand to know how talented those hands are."

Chiun looked at Fareem, then glanced about at the crowd. He saw Ganulle, the sheik's regent, standing placidly in a crowd of men on the other side of the clearing.

"Do not be harsh with your son," Chiun whispered to the sheik. "He does not understand our ways."

"Enough of talk," Abdul yelled. "Is it a battle?"

"You do not have to do this, Master," Fareem said.

"No. Perhaps it will be good for the boy," Chiun said. He stepped forward, away from the sheik's tent, into the clearing.

"What weapons do you want, old man?" Sergeant Willie Bob Watson called out."

"What do you have?" Chiun asked.

"Everything. Rifles. Handguns. Knives. Grenades." As he spoke, he touched various parts of his anatomy, from which hung the different weapons. "Even bullwhips," he said. "I've got everything."

"You would," said Chiun. "Use any or all of them."

"And what weapons will you use?"

Slowly, as if to display them, Chiun held his hands up in front of his face. "I always have my weapons," he said.

The woman was dressed in wraps of gauze. A veil of many layers covered the bottom half of her face. Her full breasts jutted carelessly through the wrapped white

176

fabric as she undulated her way across the room toward Remo, her hips moving in the exaggerated sexual gestures of the belly dancer.

Her hands snapped noisily over her head, her arms moving seductively in a plane with the sides of her body.

Remo looked away from the window and said, "All right, Reva. What do you want?"

Reva Bleem kept dancing. "I want you," she said.

"You only want me because I'm going to make the world safe for Polypussides at fifteen dollars a gallon."

"That too," she said. She was sinuously menacing him now, rotating her hips in front of his legs.

"Reva, do you know that you're beautiful?"

"Yes. Many men have told me that."

"Then you believe me?" asked Remo.

"Yes."

"Then believe this. You've got as much sex appeal as a nosebleed."

She stopped dancing as abruptly, as if she had stepped on a handful of carpet tacks.

"But why?" she said. She put her hands on her hips and stared at Remo.

He reached over and lowered the veil from her face.

"I don't like ambitious women," Remo said. "Particularly when they're using me to further their ambitions."

"That's really punk, you know."

"I'm sorry, but that's the way it is. I don't want to be offensive, but I don't want you wasting your time."

He was back to looking at the soldiers drilling, shaking his head from side to side, more in pity than in anger.

"You will beat the old man tomorrow?" she asked.

"You'd better lay off that old man stuff," Remo said without turning.

"But you will win?"

"I don't know. I've got these thousand misfits. Chiun's got Fareem's horseback brigade, but led by Abdul the Bulbul Emir. Who knows? They may fight forever. Arabs are always doing that. That's why their wars last for centuries. Not because it's a holy cause. 'Cause neither of them can figure out how to win."

"But one of you must win. The anaerobic bacteria and the future of the world are at stake."

"Yeah. One of us will win about that. And where is it anyway? It should have been here by now."

"I don't know. You sure you wouldn't want me to make love to you?"

"I'd rather make love to a maple icebox," Remo said.

"Okay," Reva Bleem said. She walked toward the door, but then paused. "Can I go with you tomorrow?"

"Of course you're coming. You're going to be in the lead car with me. We'll take your car and your driver. I don't trust any of these camel jockeys."

"All right," she said. She opened the door, then paused again.

"But I am beautiful?" she asked wistfully.

"Yes, you are. Very beautiful," Remo said. After the door closed, he shook his head. Melody Wakefield trying to seduce his soldiers. Reva Bleem trying to seduce him. General Bull, who was nothing but a salesmen. An army that not only couldn't fight, it couldn't even march.

He'd bet that Chiun didn't have problems like this.

The entire village crowded around the sand arena where Chiun faced the giant redhead.

Sergeant Willie Bob Watson held an automatic pistol in his left hand. In his right, he held a loosely coiled bullwhip.

"You need a weapon," he insisted.

"Begin any time," said Chiun. His arms were folded across his chest, his hands buried deep in the billowing cuffs of his blue brocade kimono.

The sergeant looked toward Abdul, who stood next to his father. Ganulle had joined them.

"Go on," Abdul said. "Go on, go on."

Watson shrugged, and with an underhand flip spread

the bullwhip out in front of him. Then, with a snap of his right wrist, he coiled the whip up off the ground and whistled it by Chiun's head, where it snapped only inches from the Korean master's ear.

Chiun neither moved nor blinked. His hands stayed folded inside the robe.

"Come on, old-timer," the soldier called. "At least let's give them a a show."

Chiun was silent. The soldier raised his right hand to his shoulder. Then he snapped it downward. The tremor wave curled down the whip, and its tip jumped up into the air, cracking next to the Oriental's shoulder.

Chiun remained as still as if rooted.

"Hell with you, sucker," the soldier yelled. He swung the whip out behind him, then brought it straight down over his head in a woodcutter's motion. Overhead the whip came, speeding straight down toward the top of Chiun's head. The crowd gasped. The sheik started forward.

At the moment when it seemed nothing could stop the whip from lashing and lacerating the top of Chiun's skull, his right hand snaked from its sleeve. Moving too fast for anyone's eyes to focus on it, it flashed up above his head. There was a sound like a pistol crack. Some people blinked at the sharp report.

When they looked again, Chiun's hands were again folded inside his robe. A foot-long section of the whip lay uselessly on the sand in front of him. The soldier looked in puzzlement at the shorter length of whip he was still holding. He growled a curse and snapped the whip again. And again Chiun intercepted it just before it touched him and, with the side of his hand moving like a knife, slashed off another piece of the bullhide.

And again.

Until the burly redhead was left with only a five-foot length of whip in his hands.

He angrily tossed it onto the sand and transferred his automatic pistol from his left hand to his right. As he raised his arm to take aim at Chiun, the old man began to move. He skittered sideways, across the sand,

179

moving seemingly at random. Willie Bob found it hard to resist a smile. He had dealt before with targets taking evasive action. There was a very simple way to deal with them. It took only one shot. You simply trailed the victim with the sight on the nose of your pistol, following him as he moved. And when he stopped or reversed directions, he had to come right back across the barrel, and you squeezed and blew his brains to Kingdom Come.

It was simple.

Except it didn't work.

Willie Bob trailed the old man with the nose of the pistol as Chiun crab-skittered across the sand. Then the old man stopped. The sight on the pistol kept moving. Another inch, and squeeze. But the old man wasn't there.

He was off to the right fifteen feet away.

Willie Bob cursed. How did the old bastard do that? Let him try it again, he thought.

The old man was moving again to his right. Willie Bob trailed him with the sight on the pistol, sighting just an inch behind the old man's head. Chiun stopped. Willie Bob panned the pistol the extra inch. His finger tightened against the trigger.

But the old man wasn't there.

Instead he was standing in front of Watson, his head barely coming up to the big soldier's chest. Willie Bob's mouth dropped open.

"Looking for something?" said Chiun, a faint smile playing about his mouth.

Willie Bob, angrily, brutishly, raised the pistol over his head to smash it down into the old wraith's skull. It started, then stopped. Willie Bob felt a burning pain sear into his wrist. It hurt too much to move his hand another inch. He felt the gun fall from his fingers and saw the old man catch it before it could reach the sand.

Willie Bob stood there, paralyzed, his arm upraised over his head. He saw the old man carry the pistol over to the sheik and Abdul. He wanted to cry out, but he saw Ganulle looking at him sharply, his head gesturing infinitesimally, *No, no*.

The old yellow man stood in front of Abdul. He took the heavy pistol in both hands and snapped it in two, then handed both halves to the prince, bowed slightly to the sheik, and walked off toward his tent.

The cheers of the crowd rang around the shoulders of the Master of Sinanju as he entered the tent.

Back on the sandy plane, Sheik Fareem looked at his son, then reached down with his big, gnarled hand and slapped the young man across the face.

"You idiot," he said. "You have insulted a guest . . . an honored guest . . . with this ridiculous display of hired bravado. Have you had enough?"

"Yes, Father," Abdul said. "Yes."

But even as he spoke, his wife saw him look past the sheik and into Ganulle's eyes.

Chapter Eleven

General Bull had managed to find forty trucks that worked, and they had brought the Hamidi army out along the highway until they were just two miles from Sheik Fareem's village.

Now the army, a thousand strong, marched along behind the Rolls Royce. Melody Wakefield, resplendent in new black and yellow wrist bandages, marched along with the soldiers, her portable typewriter strung around her neck on a cord.

Remo and Reva sat in the back seat of the Rolls Royce. Oscar and Bull were in the front. Remo lowered the Rolls window and heard the drill master trying to lead the army in cadence.

"Sound off, one, two.

"Sound off, three, four.

"Cadence count, one, two, three, four . . . three, four."

All the soldiers pitched in on the "Sound off" part, but there was dead silence as the drillmaster called out the numbers. Remo realized that the army he was leading not only couldn't march or fight, but it was made up of soldiers who couldn't count.

"Wonderful," he grumbled, and closed the electric window.

"It's not too late," General Bull said.

"Not too late for what?"

"For air cover. We can hit them where they live.

Napalm. High-explosive bombs. Poison gas. We'll never have to go in except to count the corpses."

"No. We're going to fight it out like a real war. Soldier against soldier," Remo said.

"People get hurt that way," Bull said.

"Shut up and turn around before I squeeze your ear."

Reva moved closer to Remo on the back seat.

"Are you looking forward to this?" she asked.

"No, why?"

"I thought you might be. You against your teacher."

"No," Remo said.

"Who's going to win?"

"All you keep asking me is who's going to win, who's going to win," Remo said.

"I'm just wondering," she said. "It means a lot to me that you win."

"I'll do my best," Remo said. "I don't know that I'd want to live in a world filled with dwarves and fifteen-dollar-a-gallon gas."

Oscar pulled off into the little clearing on the side of the road, and Remo and General Bull stepped out of the car.

Out in front of them sloped a large sand-filled valley, with the oasis at the far end. A hundred men on horses stood poised near the tent village. Around them clustered a number of men on foot, carrying swords and spears.

Remo saw Chiun, in a bright yellow kimono, standing off to the side, talking with Sheik Fareem. Beside them were two other men whom Remo recognized as Abdul and Ganulle.

With his hand Bull shaded his eyes from the sun as he surveyed the battlefield.

"Napalm, boy."

"What?"

"It's a natural for napalm. We can fill this valley with it. Burn everything to a crisp."

"How soon could you work it out?" Remo said.

"I'd need a week."

"Why a week?"

"First I've got to get two planes that fly. Then I'll have to find a couple of American pilots who aren't on furlough. Then borrow some napalm from Libya. A week. But that's outside. With a break, maybe only five days."

"Forget it, we're fighting now," Remo said.

"We'll attack in waves. First our ground forces to soften them up. Then the tanks."

"Why not the tanks first?" Remo asked.

"Well, they were fixing them this morning. They might not get here in time for the war."

"Start with your infantry," Remo said.

Bull signaled, and ten Arab lieutenants came forward to him. They were talking Arabic, which Remo couldn't understand. They seemed to be arguing.

Finally, Bull reached into the pocket of his brocaded cowboy shirt and pulled out a handful of toothpicks. He counted out ten and replaced the rest in his pocket. Then he broke one to make it shorter than the other nine. He put his hands behind his back, and when he brought them forward, he held the ten toothpicks in his hand, their tops all even so no one could see which was the short one.

He moved his hand around, and reluctantly, the lieutenants each picked a toothpick.

The first three picked long toothpicks, and they fell on the sand, turning their faces to Mecca and bowing, screeching prayers of thanksgiving at the tops of their voices.

The fourth lieutenant picked the short toothpick. He too fell on the ground, weeping uncontrollably, kicking his feet into the powdery sand like a child having a temper tantrum.

Remo leaned over and lifted him by the back of the neck. He squeezed.

"Yes, sir," the lieutenant said.

"Get your men and get moving."

"But they're armed. I can see their spears from here."

184

"Nothing those spears can do to you will hurt like what I can do to you," Remo said. He squeezed the neck again. "Get moving."

The lieutenant ran off, rubbing his neck as if he had been stung by a bee. Remo heard a wailing from among the mass of troops. The lieutenant turned toward Remo, as if pleading, but Remo only wagged a warning finger at him.

The lieutenant went back to rounding up his men. Finally, a hundred of them were behind him. The other soldiers had tried to shrink away from the scene of battle, even though it was hard for them to find a place to hide in the sand.

"All right, Lieutenant," Bull ordered. "Attack the enemy. For our country's honor."

Slowly, the lieutenant led the hundred men down the long graded slope of sand, toward the big amphitheater-shaped arena at the bottom.

From the other side, Remo saw a hundred men walk out to meet them. They carried spears and swords. Remo's men had rifles.

Remo told Reva, "You stay here," and told Bull, "You're in charge. Win the war." Then he walked out to the right, staying up along the top of the sand dune, so that he could look down into the valley below and watch the war. He saw Chiun come out of the cluster of people near the oasis and walk along the top of the dune toward him. They met in the middle and Remo bowed.

"Good afternoon, General," he said. "It's a nice day for a war, isn't it?"

"Yes, my son," Chiun said. "We have everything we need for a war, except armies."

They sat side by side in the sand to watch the battle shaping up below.

The two groups of a hundred stood facing each other across thirty feet of sand.

Remo's lieutenant struck first.

He turned toward Chiun's army and shouted at the top of his voice, "Your father is dirty!" He turned to

185

his own troops for approval. Some of them applauded. The rest whistled.

One of Chiun's army stepped forward. He was only fifteen feet from the lieutenant. In his right hand, he held a sword.

"Your mother is dirty too!" he yelled.

His men laughed and whistled.

"She is not!" Remo's lieutenant yelled back.

"Is too!" Chiun's soldier shouted. His shout was picked up by the rest of the hundred men behind him. "Is too!" they screamed over and over again. "Is too!"

The noise routed Remo's lieutenant. He fell back to the main body of his men, and they conferred quietly while Chiun's army hooted.

Then the lieutenant turned. He raised his arm over his head. When he lowered it, his entire hundred-man detachment shouted in unison, "Everybody in your family is dirty!"

"Isn't this pitiful?" Remo asked Chiun.

"Now you know why the Crusades went on for three hundred years, my son. It was Frenchmen fighting Arabs. Neither of them could win. The Arabs were good at insults, but the French had better field kitchens. Their sauces were excellent. They were evenly matched."

"I never thought we'd be on opposite sides in a war," Remo said.

"That is true only if you consider this a war," Chiun said.

All 200 men were now shouting at one another. One of Chiun's Arabs, braver than the rest, picked up a handful of sand and threw it at Remo's lieutenant. He reacted as if he had been jolted by electricity. He jumped around, brushing the sand from his highly starched uniform, screaming invective at the sand-thrower. When he was again clean, he threw sand back. Soon both armies were throwing sand at each other. Remo noticed that all hundred of his soldiers had thrown their rifles down so they could throw sand with both hands. There were 100 rifles, useless with

186

sand in their barrels. Chiun's soldiers had laid down spear and sword to shovel sand. Meanwhile, they kept yelling.

"It sounds like the New York Stock Exchange three minutes before closing on Friday," Remo said.

"It is awful," Chiun agreed. Remo glanced at him, but he noticed that Chiun's eyes were looking away, focused back on the main tent at the head of the oasis, where Sheik Fareem was holding his head in his hands, as if in pain. Near him were another 600 foot soldiers. The hundred men on horseback still waited impatiently for the word to charge.

Remo could not see Abdul or Ganulle. He looked over to the mouth of the valley. There he saw the Rolls Royce. General Bull was watching the action, applauding. Reva Bloom looked bored. Melody Wakefield was tapping away with her pencil as fast as she could. Oscar, the chauffeur, leaned against the Rolls fender, cleaning his fingernails with a knife.

The rest of Remo's army had gone. He looked off to the south. There, 900 men were racing along the road as fast as their legs would carry them. Could he shoot the whole army for desertion? Remo wondered.

"It looks like I'm outnumbered," Remo said as he turned back to Chiun. But Chiun had gone. Remo saw the aged Oriental racing back toward the village, almost flying across the sand, moving so quickly that his slippered feet left no prints in the soft powdered sand. Remo started running after him, his feet burying themselves ankle deep in the sand, until he remembered that there was no speed in hurrying, that he must sense the pressure of the sand up against his feet and aim the pressure of his body forward, not downward, so that the feet would not sink but only skim over the sand as if skiing along its surface.

He came up out of the sand and was running across it at top speed, leaving not even a mark where he had been. Sheik Fareem had turned, and saw Chiun coming toward him and Remo closing behind him. He turned toward them, but Chiun flew by him and dove against

187

the canvas wall of the sheik's tent. The fabric gave way with a wrenching groan. Chiun landed on his feet and, with Remo standing alongside him, he reached down and pulled aside the ripped flap of fabric. Under it was Ganulle, the sheik's regent. A rifle lay at his feet.

Remo turned as Fareem came over to them.

The sheik looked down at Ganulle, who was moaning his way back toward consciousness, and then at Chiun.

"This rifle was aimed at your back, Excellency," Chiun said. Before the sheik could speak, there was a sound in the back of the tent, as someone tried to climb out from under the fabric on the far side. Chiun nodded to Remo, who went around the rear of the tent and returned, a moment later, dragging Abdul by the neck of his long robe.

He dropped the fat man at the feet of his father.

"You too?" Fareem gasped as his son looked up at him helplessly. "Ganulle and you?"

It was a question that would not brook a lie in response. Abdul nodded.

"But why?"

"Your brother, the king," Abdul said. "He promised us . . . all this land would be ours . . . the oil . . . if only . . ." He could not finish the sentence.

Sheik Fareem pulled his long, curved sword from its scabbard. Abdul shrank away as the sheik held the sword toward him; then, with a cry of anguish, Fareem raised the sword high over his head, turned, and ran. A riderless horse stood lazily near the edge of the clearing, and the sheik swung himself easily up into his saddle. Then, yodeling an Arab call, he rode out across the sand toward Remo's army.

The sheik's startled horsemen watched their leader ride off, and then they spurred their steeds and followed him, their voices raised, high-pitched, in a curiously melodic battle cry.

Remo's soldiers, who were four points ahead in the war of the words with Fareem's villager troops, heard the sounds. They looked up and saw the sheik coming,

188

his sword circling high over his head. They turned and ran.

But by the time he reached the nearest soldier, the sheik's fury seemed to have abated because instead of cutting the man in two, he stopped and waved to his men; they galloped over and circled Remo's soldiers, who then fell abjectly onto the sand, cringing and sniveling for their lives.

The sheik spurred his mount and rode off toward the parked Rolls Royce, and in moments, Melody Wakefield and General Bull had joined the group of prisoners.

"That is a man and a half, isn't it, Chiun?" Remo said, nodding toward the sheik, who was riding majestically back toward the oasis.

"Yes, he is," Chiun said. "That is why the House of Sinanju honors its contract with him, prisoner."

When Reva finally trudged through the sand to Remo, she asked, "What happened?"

"We lost."

"Oh, shit."

"What's going on here?" General Bull shouted from among the group of prisoners.

"We lost the war," Remo said.

"I told you we should have used napalm."

"We'll use it in next week's war," Remo said.

"If word of this gets out, I'm ruined," Bull said. "Who'd buy military equipment from a loser?"

Melody Wakefield was standing with the prisoners, still typing with a pencil on the typewriter hung around her neck. She finally dropped the pencil and said, "Listen to this." She began to read. "A gallant band of Hamidi Arabian soldiers today defended the future of Islam against a terrorist band of Israeli sympathizers. By the time the smoke from the battlefield had settled, the pro-Israel forces had been routed. In a brilliant display of battlefield tactics . . ."

While she babbled on, Sheik Fareem looked at Remo.

"What is this thing without hands talking about?"

Remo shrugged.

"Who are the gallant Arabian soldiers?" Fareem asked.

Remo pointed to the remnants of his army, cowering in the sand under guard.

"Them," he said.

"Who are these Israeli sympathizers?" Fareem asked.

"You," Remo said. "Ignore it, sheik. The broad's wacky."

Fareem slapped Melody Wakefield in the back of the head and sent her sprawling. "Be quiet, woman. No more of your lies," he growled.

"Zionist child-butcher," she called out.

Remo put his foot on her mouth.

"Shut up, kid. You ain't in Boston now."

Remo was allowed to sit next to Chiun and the sheik. In front of them stood General Bull, Reva Bleem, Melody Wakefield, and Abdul.

"What are we to do with these creatures?" Fareem asked Chiun.

"I am sure Your Excellency will be just," Chiun said.

The sheik pointed to Bull.

"You. In the cowboy suit. Get up here."

Bull stepped forward cautiously.

"You are in charge of that army?"

"Not me," Bull said. He pointed to Remo. "He was. I didn't want to fight. I never wanted to fight. I'm a salesman who believes in peace. Peace forever. Sheik, I want to talk to you sometime about those swords and spears. I can personally provide you with some modern equipment. The best that money can buy."

"We have no money," the sheik said.

"That's ridiculous," Bull said. "This is Hamidi Arabia. Everybody has money."

"We have none," Fareem said.

"As an American citizen, I demand my rights. I demand to be released immediately. Washington will hear of . . ."

"Silence," the sheik roared. He mulled something over for a moment, then said, "I order you to leave this area and take those poor excuses of soldiers with you. March them back to Nehmad and never return."

"I don't plan to," Bull said. "But if you ever get any money and want to talk about . . ."

"Be gone," the sheik ordered. As Bull left the tent, Fareem called one of his guards forward and whispered into his ear. Then he leaned over to Chiun and spoke softly to him. Chiun smiled.

"What'd he say?" Remo asked.

"He said your general is a man with a great deal of foolish pride. He will remove some of that pride."

Remo saw Fareem's guard leave the tent, but relaxed when he heard no screams from outside.

"What happened to Ganulle, anyway?" Remo asked Chiun.

"He will be set free."

"He tried to kill the sheik," Remo said.

"He will be set free," Chiun said. "He is on his way now, under guard, to the place where he will be set free. A hundred miles out into the barren dessert. The sheik has told him that he wanted to be a ruler and now he can. He can rule empty sand, if he wishes, and pray for rain."

The sheik crooked his finger, and Melody Wakefield was pushed forward. Her typewriter still hung around her neck.

"What is to be done with this countrywoman of yours?" the sheik asked Remo.

Remo shrugged. "You can't cut off her hands. Somebody already did that. And she tried to seduce my soldiers. I'm supposed to decide whether she gets stoned or sent into slavery."

The sheik looked at the woman. "She prostitutes her body as she does the truth. I think she should . . ."

He was interrupted by a sound from the tent opening. Suddenly Zantos pushed her way past the guards

191

and ran up to the sheik's throne. She threw herself on the ground at his feet.

"Oh, Noble One, I plead for my husband's life," she cried.

Remo leaned over to Chiun. "She doesn't even like the guy," he said.

"No, but she is his wife, and it is her obligation to try to keep him alive. Some people live up to their obligations. Other people ignore them. Mostly whites. Whites don't like obligations."

"Knock it off," Remo growled in Korean.

"Rise, my daughter," said the sheik. "Your husband . . . my son, is not worth your pleas. He is not worth one tear from your eye."

"He is my husband, Excellency."

The sheik nodded, then roared, "Abdul, get up here."

Hesitantly, the fat man shuffled forward to stand before his father, head bowed.

"You are no son of mine," Fareem said. "You have no heart, no body, no talent, no courage, no strength."

"I am . . ." Abdul stammered.

"Silence. All you have that is of value is this wife, who is much too good for you. But because I love her, I will heed her pleas and spare your life. Abdul. Zantos. Look at me."

They both raised their faces to him. "You are now to be divorced. As your sheik, I command it. Abdul, perform the ceremony."

"But . . ."

"Do as I say."

Abdul turned to the beautiful green-eyed woman. "Woman, I do divorce you. Woman, I do divorce you. Woman, I do divorce you." He turned back to the sheik. "Father, it is done."

"Good. Now, Abdul, you are banished from here. You are banished from my sight. I disinherit, I disown, I disclaim you. You are, in my eyes, dead, and if you are ever in my eyes again, you will be fully dead. Do you understand?"

"Yes, Father."

"You may never call me 'Father' again. There is a parting gift I have for you." He turned toward Melody and said, "Woman with the tongue of snakes, stand by him."

She moved over uncertainly next to Abdul.

"I now pronounce you wed. This woman is your wife, Abdul. She is your responsibility. She has the body and mind of a prostitute, and you are a prostitute of the spirit. You belong with each other." He laughed bitterly. "The happy couple may now leave."

They stumbled toward the entrance to the tent, and Remo heard Melody say, "Wow, a prince for a husband. I wish Grandpapa could have lived to see this. And he always thought I'd need tits to get a husband. Glory to Islam."

Fareem touched Zantos's arm. "You are free, child," he said. "No shame attaches to you."

"Thank you, sire," she said. She bowed, and as she raised her head to turn away, she glanced toward Remo and winked.

"And now, if your son will leave us . . ." Fareem told Chiun.

"Be gone, Remo," said Chiun.

"Just like that? Be gone?"

"Yes. Be gone," Chiun said.

Remo walked outside. As he pased Reva Bleem, she said, "You stink as a soldier." Once out in the sand, Remo understood how Sheik Fareem had decided to punish General Bull's false pride, because the general was now leading the hundred remaining soldiers of the Hamidi army back toward Nehmad. They were on foot, and except for shoes, they were all naked. The sheik's men had stripped them bare.

Remo chuckled to himself, then looked up toward the road and saw Oscar leaning against the parked Rolls Royce.

And he wondered why the sheik hadn't brought Oscar in along with everybody else. Why did Oscar always stay by the car? Remo decided to find out.

Behind him, he could hear the faint buzz of voices as Reva talked with the sheik and with Chiun. Remo strolled off, away from the oasis, toward the Rolls Royce. Oscar looked up when he saw Remo approaching.

"How'd you escape?" Remo asked.

Oscar shrugged, and Remo realized he had never heard the man talk.

"No, really," Remo said. "Why didn't the sheik bring you in with everybody else?"

"I don't know. Go away. Miz Bleem doesn't like people hanging around her car."

"Why not? I bet she's got lots of cars."

"Listen you, you going to get out of here or not?"

"No."

"I don't know why you're supposed to be so special. You don't look special to me," Oscar said.

"You know what I think? I think that maybe you hang around this car 'cause there's something here worth hanging around for."

"I don't care what you think," Oscar said. "I just want you out of here."

"So let's take a look," Remo said.

Oscar reached out his arm as Remo pulled open the front passenger door. Remo brushed the arm aside as if it were a blade of grass. He leaned into the car and opened the wood-fronted glove compartment.

Oscar came up behind him and wrapped his big arms around Remo's chest. He jerked upward to lift Remo off his feet and toss him off into the sand.

But Remo did not move. Instead Oscar's grip loosened with the force of his jerk, and he stumbled backward. He lost his balance and wound up sitting in the sand himself.

"But that'd be stupid," Remo said. "You wouldn't be hiding anything in the glove compartment. I've been riding in this car for a couple of days. I might have looked. Where are the trunk keys?"

He turned around and saw Oscar sitting on the ground.

194

"What are you doing there?" he said. "Give me the trunk keys."

Oscar scrambled to his feet, brushed himself off, and said, "Not a chance." He assumed a fighting position, legs spread, hands balled into fists, arms raised in front of him. He waited for Remo to attack.

"Come on, fella, give me the keys. I hate to mess up a Rolls Royce."

"You better get out of here before I get mad," Oscar said.

Remo shrugged. "Have it your own way." He walked to the trunk of the car, grabbed the old-fashioned turn handle, and yanked upward.

The trunk lid squealed, and there was a snapping sound as the heavy-duty steel lock gave way and the lid flew open. Remo leaned into the trunk.

Oscar charged and let fly two powerful blows to the middle of Remo's back.

Remo said, "Now let's see what we've got in here."

Oscar took a stance behind Remo and set himself up as if he were ready to strike a punch-o-meter machine in an amusement park. Putting all 250 pounds of his body behind his blow, he crashed his fist into Remo's right kidney.

He felt his knuckles break.

Remo still stood there, leaning into the truck, rooting around. All he saw were the styrofoam-wrapped cartons of liquor that Reva Bleem had insisted upon bringing to Hamidi Arabia.

"I wonder," Remo said. Oscar had recoiled, holding his broken right hand in his left hand. Remo started to open the tops of the gray metal liquor boxes. The first three held Lazzaroni Amaretto. But the fourth had no liquor. Instead it held another small styrofoam box. Remo opened it and pulled out a test tube stoppered with a cork; the junction between cork and bottle was sealed with wax.

He turned toward Oscar.

"What have we here?" Remo said.

"Give me that," said Oscar. With his left hand he

195

grabbed for the test tube, but Remo snatched it back out of his reach. He replaced it in the small styrofoam container and put the lid back on.

"You've had this all along, haven't you?" Remo said. Oscar didn't answer. "But why the hell didn't sweet little Reva just give it to the sheik? Why all the crap about waiting for it to arrive? Why'd she tell me that if the sheik got it, it was going to ruin her? Why'd she bring it here? Why didn't she just bury it if she wanted to keep it away from the sheik? And if she didn't want to keep it away from him, why didn't she just give it to him? Are you going to talk, or are you just going to stand there holding your hand?"

"Miz Bleem doesn't tell me what she's thinking," Oscar said.

"She'll tell me," Remo said. He walked away, holding the container of rapid-breeder bacteria under his arm. "You better get that hand checked," he called back to Oscar. "It looks broken to me."

Chapter Twelve

"The rapid-breeder bacterium has arrived," Reva Bleem said.

"Where is it?" asked Sheik Fareem.

"In my car."

"Bring it and we will use it," Fareem said. "If we needed an illustration of how low the Hamidis have fallen because of oil, we certainly received one today."

Reva nodded. "But the American?" she said.

"What about him?" Fareem asked.

She turned to Chiun. "Will you let him live?"

"Why not?" Chiun said. "His prowess as leader of an army threatens no one."

"But he could be a danger to our plan to use the bacteria," she said.

"He lives," Chiun said.

Reva shook her head. "After what he said about you too."

"What did he say?" Chiun asked.

"He said that he was going to kill you. That you were too old to matter anymore and that he was going to kill you to teach you a lesson. He said he didn't like Orientals anyway."

"This is very serious," Fareem said, glancing at Chiun.

The old Korean nodded. "Yes, it is. I will take care of him."

"When?" asked Reva.

"Now," said Chiun.

They were met outside Fareem's tent by Oscar, who was still holding his battered hand. "He took it away from me, Miz Bleem. He took it away."

Chiun led them to Remo's tent, on the far side of the oasis. Remo heard them coming. He was lying on his sleeping mat.

"Remo," he heard Chiun call.

"What do you want?" he yelled back.

"Where is it?" Chiun called.

"Safe. Where nobody can touch it," Remo said.

"You have it in there with you, don't you?" Chiun called.

"No, I hid it," Remo said.

He crossed his arms on his chest and chuckled to himself. Let Chiun look. Let him try to find the tube of bacteria under the sand where Remo had stashed it. Thousands of square miles of sand. Let Chiun look. His side may have won the battle, but Remo had won the war. The bacterium was safe, out of the reach of Chiun and Fareem.

"Heh, heh, heh, heh," Remo muttered, loud enough for Chiun to hear. Let him look. "Heh, heh, heh, heh."

It would be impossible to find. Remo had been careful. Exactly fifteen paces away from the corner of his tent, due west, and buried under two feet of sand, then smoothed over. Not a trace for anybody. Not even Chiun.

Remo decided to nap for a while. It felt good to win something every so often, particularly against Chiun. Let Chiun look. Not even the Master of Sinanju could find that test tube where he had hidden it. It would stay there until he was ready to go back and deliver it to Smith. He had saved the Western world. *He* had. Remo Williams. He wished the nuns at the orphanage in Newark could see him now. They had always thought he wouldn't amount to anything, and here he had saved the world. And no one could stop him now. Not even Chiun.

Of course, he couldn't. Not even Chiun.

No, he couldn't do a thing about it.

Not even Chiun.

Remo couldn't sleep. He got up and walked to the entrance to his tent.

And there, striding across the sand, holding the white styrofoam box under his arm, was Chiun. Walking behind him were Reva and the sheik. Remo started after them.

"Chiun," he called out.

"What?" Chiun asked without turning.

"How'd you find it?"

"I looked where you put it."

"How'd you know where that was?"

"You left your big hoofprints all over the sand," Chiun said. "It was not difficult."

Remo caught up with them as Chiun, Fareem, and Reva passed one of the small springs in the oasis. He looked at Chiun across the small bright, sparkling pool.

"Chiun, you've got to give that back. We've got to take it home with us."

"No," said Fareem. "It is our chance to make our country free again."

"I am sorry, Remo," said Chiun. "But it is my obligation."

As he spoke, Chiun opened the top of the foam box and pulled out the test tube. He looked at it and dropped the halves of the box onto the sand. With a sudden wrench, he snapped the cork from the tube.

"Chiun, no!" Remo yelled. He started around the small pond of water.

But he was too late. Chiun had dropped the tube into the small drinking pool.

"It is all an underground system, Remo," he said. "From here, this anaerobic will find its way to the underground oil, and from there it will do its work."

Remo stopped and looked down at the crystal waters of the pool. As he watched, he saw tiny churnings in the water and then, before his eyes, a lump of white wax was formed that looked as if it had been broken off the base of a thick, half-burned candle. The white blob just floated on top of the pond.

Remo reached down and picked it up. It lay cold and motionless in his hand. He looked up at Chiun, then squeezed the white glob in his hand, and it cracked into pieces and fell back into the pond. It floated there, not moving, not expanding, still as death.

"Water kills it," Remo said. "Water kills it."

Chiun squatted by the side of the pool and let some of the water sift through his fingers.

"That island was surrounded by water," he said. "Why did that not kill it and stop its spread?"

"I don't know," Remo said.

Chiun raised his fingers to his mouth and tasted of them. "It is nothing," he said. "It is only water."

Remo tasted the water too.

"Chiun, that's it. That's exactly it. It's pure water. The island was surrounded by salt water. But this is pure water. Pure. That's what kills it."

He stood up, as did Chiun, and they looked at each other across the six-foot-wide pond.

"You have caused me to fail in my mission," Chiun said solemnly.

"My pleasure," Remo said.

"This cannot be allowed to exist between us," Chiun said.

"If you say so."

"We will meet in battle to settle all," Chiun said.

"What?" asked Remo.

"Tonight. At sundown. Over there." He pointed back into the oasis. "Under that large tree."

"Are you kidding?" Remo said, but the look on Chiun's face was grim.

"Be there," Chiun said. "Do not make me come to get you."

He turned away and strode off into the trees of the oasis.

Chapter Thirteen

The oasis had been cleared. At Chiun's order, no one was allowed there to witness the battle.

The sun was just disappearing below the sand hills to the west when Remo stepped into a cool, tree-surrounded glade in the center of the oasis. Far off, through the trees, he could see people standing, straining to see what was going on. He saw the sheik and, next to him, Reva Bleem.

But where was Chiun?

"I am here, Remo," a voice said softly.

Remo spun. Chiun stood behind him, wearing a midnight-blue brocaded kimono with ornamental beadwork over the shoulders.

"Are we really going through with this?" Remo said.

"Of course not," Chiun said. "Quick. Kick at me."

Remo leaped into the air and pushed a kick out at Chiun, but the small Oriental swirled away from under the kick and was behind Remo as Remo came down.

They circled each other warily.

"What are we doing here?" Remo asked.

"Don't you know anything? We are trying to find out who is behind that anaerobic."

Chiun spun high into the air, twirling like a top. His robe spread out around his slim form, shielding the outline of his legs and arms from the sight of a potential victim. Then he lashed out with a hand. Remo slid back from the deadly fingertips, and Chiun's hand smashed into the side of a foot-thick palm. The tree cracked. Remo heard it creaking and then dropping down behind him.

"I think the woman is an assassin sent by our enemy," Chiun said. They continued to circle.

"Why?" asked Remo. He threw a kick, which Chiun easily blocked.

"Because she has been trying to set me against you, you against me."

"I think she's had the bacteria all the while," Remo said.

Chiun nodded and came at Remo with a multiple knife attack of the hands, in which the hands and forearms, held stiff, chopped at an opponent like the multiple blades of a knife, chopping vegetables. Remo blocked sixteen blows with the outsides of his wrists. Chiun threw a seventeenth, and when it was not blocked, he pulled it short and just flicked a fingernail at Remo's right earlobe.

"Dammit, that hurts," Remo said.

"It is supposed to, idiot. If somebody else got through your defense so easily, he would not just tweak your ear."

"Chiun, there is nobody in the world besides you and me who can even throw those blows. There is no somebody else."

"That's what you say now," Chiun said. "At any rate, don't embarrass me. Try to make this look like a fight. The woman has had the anaerobic, but she did not produce it until today. I think her instructions were to set us against each other so that one would die, and then to kill the survivor. Or to bring the survivor to her master."

"Why don't I just twist it out of her?" Remo said. He launched into the pile-driver foot stroke, delivering nine rapid kicks. Chiun rolled down before them, and Remo's energy was spent splintering the wood of another tree.

"Because I have talked to the sheik," Chiun said. "She represents a friend of the sheik's, but a strange friend whom he has never met. She knows no more

about him. I think she does not know who she is working for, so applying force to her will do nothing."

"I think her boss might be the guy back on the island who tried to get you to work for him. Remember?
On the telephone?"

"Yes," said Chiun. He rushed at Remo, and they
locked arms. In silhouette against the fading sky, they
looked like two giant elks, tugging and pulling at each
other. "And I think she got her instructions through
that whatchamacallit," Chiun said, "while I was talking
on the telephone."

"Computer terminal," Remo said.

"Yes. That," Chiun said. "I think you must find and
kill her master, or forever we will face all manner of
enemy."

"But why are we going through with this charade?"
asked Remo, who rolled away from Chiun's grasp,
flipped, and landed lightly facing Chiun, who was again
on him. He windmilled his arms meaninglessly over
Remo's head. It looked ferocious, but all it did was fan
Remo's face.

"I think if she believes me dead, she may be
prepared to take you to her master. That is what you
want," Chiun said.

"There's one thing I don't understand."

"That is a vast improvement over your usual amount
of ignorance," Chiun said.

"If you are committed to being on the sheik's side,
why are you on my side?"

"You are an idiot."

"Please stop calling me an idiot and explain things
to me," Remo said.

"I don't know why I bother," Chiun said. "It is true
I had an obligation to the sheik. But I checked that
contract in the sheik's trunk. My obligation was to save
his life and to afford him victory over his enemies. I
did those things today. Nowhere in there does it say
anything about my having to help him destroy oil with
anaerobic. Nowhere in there, Remo. Oil is very important, Remo."

Remo, suddenly suspicious, asked, "Why?"

"Because oil is used to make plastic. Plastic is used to make television sets. To make tapes to show pictures on those television sets. There are many things oil is good for." He tossed Remo through the air. Remo's body headed directly for the thick trunk of a tree, with force that would shatter his skull if it hit the unyielding wood. But in the air, Remo rolled his body over, and when he hit the tree, it was with his feet. He allowed his knees to bend, to cushion the shock of the impact, then pressed back with his legs and launched himself back through the air in the other direction. Chiun stood still and let Remo wrap an arm around him and bring him to the sand. He hissed into Remo's ear. "Quick, now, slash a blow into the sand alongside my head." Remo did.

"And again," Chiun said.

Remo did again.

"Then you will let them know that I am dead and that you are Master. And then tonight you will claim that woman, and she will tell you all you need to know. Use the short program."

"What will I do with you?" Remo asked.

"I certainly don't want to be in your tent when you are doing whatever disgusting thing it is you do with women to make them like you. You can put me back in my own tent. Tell them it is tradition that my body must be left alone, untouched, until my spirit soars to heaven. Tell them any nonsense. They're Arabs; they believe in fairy tales. And then tomorrow, we'll get out of this stupid place. Now, please, another hand blow. I don't want to die too easily."

Remo reared back, high, poised for a longer time than was necessary just to make sure that the spectators watching him through the trees could see his move. Then he plunged downward and jabbed his fingers deep into the sand alongside Chiun's head. He knew that in silhouette, it would look as if he had applied the finishing stroke to Chiun's head.

He paused there for a moment, as if exhausted, then

stood and raised his arms over his head in the prize fighter's signal of victory.

"Don't get carried away, Remo," said Chiun softly.

"The Master is dead," Remo shouted. "I am the Master."

And Chiun hissed, "You wish."

Remo carried Chiun away from the oasis in his arms. Once he whispered, "You're getting fat, Little Father."

"Seven stones," Chiun whispered. "I never change. I will always be sweet, lovable, and small."

"Fat," Remo said.

"Silence. We are drawing near."

Remo stood in front of Sheik Fareem in the early evening darkness and said, "The Master is dead."

In the light of a campfire, Remo could see tears in Fareem's eyes.

"I would carve you in half," he told Remo bitterly. "But the Master himself made me pledge that neither I nor any of my people would lift a hand against you."

"I am pleased with that," Remo said, "as would be my father. He will lie in his tent tonight. No one may visit him because his soul must be undisturbed until it is accepted into eternity by his ancestors. It is our way."

"It shall be as you wish," Fareem said.

The only trouble with Chiun's impersonation of a corpse, Remo decided, was that dead men didn't generally snore. Not that Chiun's snore, as he slept in state in his tent, was the occasional full-throated goose honk that ruined Remo's sleep and occasionally startled Chiun from his own bed with a quizzical look on his face as he glanced around, wondering what flight of migrating birds had had the temerity to pass through his sleeping chamber.

No, this was not Chiun's full snore, but a tinny, hissing sip of air that Remo knew could not be heard by anyone but him.

The village now was silent, and Remo could hear the faint puffs of breeze rustling the fronds of the palm trees. He heard steps coming toward his tent.

Remo feigned sleep, and Reva Bleem slipped into his tent and crossed the sand floor toward him. She was trying to be silent, but her skidding steps filled Remo's ears and drowned out the faint hiss of Chiun sleeping. Reva wore a heavy, musky perfume that overpowered Remo's delicate senses and made him wonder how a bee could stand being a bee with its nose stuck into flowers all day. Didn't bees ever want to throw up?

"Remo?" Reva whispered.

"Ummmm," he answered, as if still asleep and responding to a sound that had somehow flickered into his consciousness.

"Don't wake up, Remo," she said. "I'm going to take care of you while you're sleeping."

He felt Reva slip onto the sleeping mat beside him and felt her hand rest lightly on his naked stomach.

As if moving in his sleep, he reached over with his left hand and brushed the inside of her left wrist. Among the things Chiun had taught Remo in their interminable training were the methods for transporting women to sexual ecstasy. Remo had learned three separate techniques. One took twenty-seven steps, another took thirty-seven, and the third took fifty-two, but Chiun had warned him never to use that technique on a normal woman because it would make her insane.

"Then why bother learning it," Remo had said, "if I'm not allowed to use it on a woman? I'm sure as dick not going to use it on a man."

"Must you always be disgusting?" Chiun had said. "You learn it because it is necessary to learn it."

"That's no answer. Why learn something that has no value?"

"Have you never heard of knowledge for knowledge's sake? Learn this, Remo, and maybe someday you can write a book and tell your secrets and make much money."

"I have all the money I need," Remo had said.

"That's right. Think only of yourself," Chiun had said, hinting at some possible dire need for money that Chiun might face someday, ignoring the fact that his house in the village of Sinanju was filled with jars of diamonds and emeralds and gold.

So Remo had mastered the three separate techniques. But in learning how, it had taken all the fun out of sex for him. He found himself an orgasm counter, playing elaborate mental games, keeping track of how long it took this time, as opposed to the last time.

He decided on the twenty-seven step technique. It was quicker and more primitive than the others, but Chiun had assured him that white women would never know the difference. Remo couldn't tell; he couldn't remember anyone ever lasting beyond step thirteen.*

The left wrist was the starting point for all three methods. It required Remo's locating with his middle finger the woman's faint pulse and then gently keeping time with the pulse; once he had the rhythm, he had to press his finger down on the wrist in increasingly faster taps, spurring that pulse and the heart to beat faster than it had been beating. If done correctly—and he always did it correctly—he could, by doing nothing more than touching the inside of a woman's left wrist, get her heartbeat up to 130 beats a minute.

Remo's problem was that he sometimes got bored and wanted to hurry along, skipping steps, getting it over with as soon as possible. But he couldn't do that tonight. He wanted to jellify Reva Bleem, and he wanted to make sure that she would take him to her leader. Reva purred and leaned over Remo and let the

---

* AUTHORS' NOTE: Many people have expressed interest in the precise nature of the steps used by Remo to bring women to a state of erotic fulfillment. The authors have decided not to reveal these techniques, however, because they have no interest in seeing half the world's population reduced to quivering, happy, mindless sex slaves. The knowledge of the techniques must remain safely with Chiun, Remo, and the authors. Sorry.

tips of her breasts touch his chest, but she was careful not to move her wrist away from his hand. He could feel her heartbeat beginning to race. He went through steps two and three slowly, still feigning sleep, then went to step four with the small of Reva's back.

Step five was the inside of the left knee. Or was it the right knee? Remo thought about it for a moment, as Reva's fingertips traced along his body, up and down his belly, up and down his legs. No, he was sure. It was the inside of the left knee. All the techniques were symmetrical. One knee, then the other knee. One armpit and then the other armpit. One ankle, then the other ankle. But they all started on the left side, the heart's side of the body. That allowed women to be lifted erotically and then, by switching to the right side, allowed them down gently until Remo moved into the next pair of steps. It treated a woman like a yo-yo, and that was one of the things Remo resented about it. He didn't like treating women like yo-yos. He had liked sex more when he wasn't so good at it, when the outcome was sometimes in doubt, when he could await an honest answer to the question: "Was it good for you too?" Now it was always good for them, and that had made it no good for Remo. Maybe he would give up sex, he thought, as he let his supposedly sleeping fingers walk around to the back of Reva's left knee. Celibacy. It might be the wave of the future. Until the future ran out because there were no more children to bring about the future.

Remo threw his left arm over Reva and brought his face close to hers and said softly, "Ohhh, Reva." The woman was shuddering in response to Remo's touches, but she said to him, "Just lie still. I'll take care of everything."

"It's been such a day," he whined. Women liked whiners in bed.

"I know. It must have been terrible for you, having to do that to your own friend."

"Awful." Remo wondered if Chiun was listening. He could not hear the faint snores from the next tent.

Probably Chiun was listening. The old voyeur. It would serve him right. "Of course, he deserved to die," Remo said. "He was nasty and narrow-minded. He was never nice to me, and he ignored everything I had done for him. He carped. He was so old and decrepit that I had to help him around some. Without me, he would have been nothing."

Remo heard a faint gasp in the next tent. Good. That would teach Chiun to eavesdrop.

"I knew when I saw you that only you would be able to do away with him. Ohhhh, yes, do that," Reva said.

"I am doing that," Remo said.

"But if you're so strong, what can do away with you?"

"Nothing, I guess," said Remo. He added brightly, "Except love and respect. I've never had much of either. I'm an orphan, you know." That was a good touch, he thought. Women always rationalized making love to a man if he had had a troubled youth. It brought out the motherly side in them, and it also made them feel as if they weren't making love just out of horniness but out of compassion and concern.

"Are you happy he's gone?" Remo asked as he began to work the insides of her thighs. Reva's body was trembling.

"Yes," she said. "Yes."

"And the bacterium's destroyed?"

"Yes," she said. "Oh, yes, yes, yes."

"But there's more of it, isn't there?" Remo asked.

"Yes. A lot more. A lot more. All on St. Maarten's."

"Who developed it?" Remo asked.

"My friend. Oh, dear. My friend. I never . . . ohhhh . . ."

"What's your friend's name?" Remo asked. He was working the inside of the thigh now. He thought it was step eight. But it might be nine. He hoped he hadn't lost count. He didn't want to start all over again.

209

"I don't know. I never met him. He's just my friend. Can't this wait? Please? Do what you're doing."

"If you don't talk to me now, I'll stop what I'm doing," Remo said. The woman was shivering uncontrollably, as if she were soaking wet, naked, in the middle of an ice storm.

"No, no, no, no."

" 'Cause if I stop, there'll be no more of this . . . or this." That was nine and ten. Or was it ten and eleven?

"Oh, no, don't stop. I don't know. I only talk to him on the phone. He helped me build my companies. He gave us the formula for Polypussides and for the rapid-breeder bacteria."

"And he really wanted the world's oil supply destroyed?" Remo said.

"Yes, yes, yes, yes."

"Why?"

"He said there's a big profit in it."

"Why didn't you just give the bacteria to the sheik?"

"He wanted me to wait until you and the old man either killed each other or came to work for him," she said. Her breath was was coming quickly now.

"Why?"

"He said there might be more profit in you two," she said.

Reva grabbed Remo's body now and pulled him to her, and Remo coupled with her even as she was spasming, and she turned her face from him and chewed on her lips and threw the back of her hand across her mouth to stifle a small scream.

And Remo heard Chiun, finally, grumbling under his breath, but so softly that no one could hear it but Remo. "Disgusting," Chiun said. "Like dogs in the street."

And because he thought it might annoy Chiun, who deserved all the annoyance he could get, Remo joined with Reva, tried to join her happily, in open gladness, and tried to revel in making love to her body, the old-fashioned way, the way he did before he had been

210

trained, and he whispered in her ear, "You're going to introduce me to your friend."

And Reva said, "Yes, yes, yes, yes, yes, yes, yes."

And later, while they rested, she said, "You really have no weaknesses, have you?"

"Nothing like if you cut my hair off, I get weak or anything like that," Remo said.

"I want you to meet my friend," she said.

And Remo said, "I'm looking forward to it."

Sheik Fareem was sleeping. The death of the little Master had grieved him and so had his promise to the Master, before he was killed, not to take vengeance on the young American.

But his sleep was troubled. It was troubled with visions of the old Master and the young American battling. He dreamed that he saw the people of his tribe drowning in pools of oil, and the oil seemed to be not merely a liquid but a living, growing pool of evil that swallowed up all that it encountered.

In his sleep, he heard a voice. It spoke softly into his ear as if it were very close to him.

It said, "You are a good and wise ruler, but you are wrong."

Fareem groaned lightly in his sleep.

"Oil is not your enemy. Time is. Oil is not changing your people, but the onward march of time is. You can either teach your people to live with the oil, with the changes that time is bringing to their lives, or you can flee with them farther into the desert, to try to escape change. But there, you must know, that when you leave this world, there will be no one to teach them to live."

The sheik groaned again.

"You must use your wisdom to make your people wise," the voice said. "It is all a father can do, and you are the father of your people. You cannot give them of your wisdom; you must lead them to the edges of their own. For the world is changing and we . . . you and I . . . we must understand those changes."

The sheik slowly felt himself lifting out of sleep, but from a distance, as if it did not belong to him, he heard a voice, his own voice, say, "Who are you?"

He tried to open his eyes, but it felt as if delicate fingertips were on them, holding them closed.

"I am the Master of Sinanju. I have been with you, and when you need me again, my house will be here to serve you."

"But, Master," the sheik heard himself say, "aren't you dead? Did you not fall in battle?"

And the voice answered, "The House of Sinanju never dies, never to those it has sworn to serve and protect. And now I go."

"Where do you go, Master?"

"I go to other places where I am needed. Remember, my friend—do not try to cloak your people in your wisdom because that powerful garment dies with you. Lead them to their own wisdom, and then they will be mighty and protected forever. Good-bye, my friend."

The sheik lay in the darkness for a while, then tried again to open his eyes. This time they opened easily; there was no longer any pressure on the lids.

He looked around. The tent was empty, but the door flap was moving as if someone had just passed through it. It might have been the breeze, but it was a dry and windless night. He felt something on his chest. He reached his hand over and lifted the object. In the dim moonlight reflected from the sand into the tent, he looked at it. It was a gold medal, circular, and inside was a trapezoid with a metal slash bisecting it. He recognized it. It was the symbol of Sinanju. He had seen it on the contract he carried with him, signed by another Master of Sinanju so many years ago.

The sheik felt his eyes dampen.

The Master of Sinanju lived. He would live forever.

Remo and Chiun borrowed Reva Bleem's Rolls Royce to drive to Nehmad. He would have someone take it back to her in the morning.

212

"What did you tell the sheik back there?" Remo asked.

"To stop worrying about oil," Chiun said.

"Good," said Remo. "Reva thinks you're dead."

"And why shouldn't I be? I'm old. I carp. If it weren't for you, I'd probably have been dead years ago."

"Chiun, I had to tell her that."

"Remember that when I have to tell somebody something about you," Chiun said.

Chapter Fourteen

"It's water?" Harold Smith's voice registered uncharacteristic surprise as he stared at Remo.

They were sitting in Secaucus, New Jersey, in an old luxury ferryboat that had been converted to a restaurant. Remo was looking out at the cold gray waters of the Hackensack River. Chiun was folding cocktail napkins into dragon shapes, trying not to look bored.

"Yeah. Water kills it," Remo said.

"Why then not on St. Maarten's? The island's surrounded by water."

"Chiun and I figured that out. It has to be pure water. Impurities probably act like food for the bacteria."

At the mention of his name, Chiun smiled at Smith.

"You did well, Emperor, to send us on this mission. I have learned a great deal about anaerobic. It justifies your wisdom in sending me."

"Oh?" Smith said. "What else can you tell me about it, Chiun?"

"You can't see it, and when you put it in water, it turns white like wax. If you don't put it in water, it eats oil. Would you like to see me hold my breath?"

"No, that won't be necessary," Smith said. He turned back to Remo, who was sipping a cup of tea. "This causes us a problem, you know."

Chiun said, "Just name that problem. We will deal with it as we deal with all your enemies."

214

"Pure water," Smith said. "Where do you find pure water in the United States?"

"I don't know," Remo said. "You know, when I was a kid, you didn't have to be Jesus to walk across this river. It was so thick with gunk, you could walk on it if you had on big shoes. Now it's pretty clean. They've even got fish in it."

"Clean?" Chiun said. "You call this clean? If you want clean water, you have to see the river in Sinanju."

"I've seen the river in Sinanju," Remo said. "People do their laundry in it. It's filled with soap."

"And soap makes things clean, doesn't it?" Chiun said. He whispered to Smith, "Don't pay any attention to him. He doesn't understand anaerobic at all."

"Please," Smith said. "I guess there's no *real* problem. I'll just have water made from hydrogen and oxygen."

"Don't forget anaerobic," Chiun said.

"What are you going to do now?" Smith said.

"I'm going to see Reva Bleem," Remo said. "She doesn't know who's behind all this—I'm pretty sure of that—but she can lead me to him. He's the key. You got all this bacteria off St. Maarten's, but he's the guy that invented it. If he did it once, he can do it again. So we've got to get to him."

"You said she thinks Chiun is dead?"

"I figured there was no point in letting her know otherwise. Kind of an insurance policy."

Smith nodded and looked at his watch. "I have to get back. I want stores of pure water in case we need it."

Chiun was back to folding napkins, and he ignored Smith as the CURE director left.

"If you're finished playing," Remo told Chiun, "we can go."

"See," the president of the United States said to his cabinet. "It just takes water."

"That's interesting," said the secretary of the interior. He hoped the president wasn't going to tell him to keep his hands off some river somewhere just because somebody needed water. Rivers, if you dammed them up right, were good for making electricity. Then you could use the electricity to power all the homes you could build where the river used to go. It was so simple, he sometimes wondered why people seemed to oppose it.

"Water's always interesting," the president said. "We were always fighting about water." He lapsed smoothly into a Western twang. " 'But I've got to be able to graze and water my flock.' And then the bad guy would say, 'The river's on my property, and you can't use it. Keep those damn sheep outa my way.' Of course, he didn't say 'damn' 'cause you couldn't say it then. You can say anything now, even the four-letter words, but you couldn't say 'damn' then. And then we'd have a range war over the water and I'd always win."

"War?" said the secretary of defense, snapping to attention. "Who's having a war?"

"Range war," the president said. "The old days."

"Oh. I thought it was a new war and somebody forgot to tell me. I've been busy with my budget."

"No," the president said. "An old war. About water. So now we have to find clean water to get rid of all this stuff."

"Big Bear," said the secretary of the interior. "They have great water."

"Who's Big Bear?" the president asked.

"You know. In those big bottles. Your secretary's got one outside in the office. They have great water, and you don't hear them whining all the time about rivers, either."

"No, we can't use that," the president said. He turned to the secretary of commerce. "Get hold of some company and tell them to make us a lot of fresh water. From those chemicals."

"What chemicals?"

"You know, hydrogen and like that," the president said.

216

"That's not water," said the secretary of state. "You put that on a boo-boo to make it better."

"That's hydrogen peroxide," said the budget director. "It fizzes. Water is hydrogen and oxygen. Two parts of hydrogen and one part of oxygen."

"I thought hydrogen was in bombs," the secretary of defense said.

"No, that's different," the president said. "That's like hydrogen air, not hydrogen water. You tell some company to make us a lot of it. And put it in clean barrels without germs."

"What for?" the secretary of commerce asked.

"Haven't you been paying attention?" the president asked.

"Well, I kind of lost track when we were talking about the range war with the sheep. We going to have another range war?"

"No," the president said. "Ever since Errol Flynn died, there hasn't been a good range war."

The headquarters of Bleem International were located in a low, brick-fronted building two blocks from the state assembly chambers in Raleigh, North Carolina, and Reva Bleem felt comfortably at home as she stepped into her dark oak-paneled office. Along the left wall was her private bathroom and her wet bar. The right wall held a long sofa, with a large conference table dominating the floor. Behind the couch wall, she knew, was the company's computer, which took up an entire wall of the next room. When it was first being installed, she hadn't wanted it there. She had expected that it would be thumping and throbbing and making a terrible noise, but the computer ran silently. Only occasionally, by a faint dimming of the overhead lights, could she tell that the computer was running on full speed because of its drain on the company's power supply.

She poured herself a drink from the bar and fondled the bottle of Stolichnaya for a moment before replacing it in the rack.

Not bad, she told herself. Not bad for a woman who three years earlier had been selling houses in Florida, supporting a husband who had decided that work was the curse of the leisure class, and wondering how she was going to make the next payment on her thirty-month old Ford station wagon.

It had all started with a telephone call. The warmest, kindest voice she had ever heard was on the other end of the line, and he told her where to buy property in Florida that would soon be condemned for a new state highway. She was desperate, and she did it, and six months later she was rich. She had always assumed her caller was some state official trying to get rich on inside information and that he would come one day to collect his share of the winnings. But he never did.

She next heard from the voice when it called and told her to invest her money in the stock of a company called Polypussides, and she did. She had made $600,-000 on the land deal, and she put almost every cent into Polypussides. Even as she did it, she cursed herself as a fool because she had never had a chance to spend any of her wealth, to revel in it, to try wasting some of it. All she kept was $5,000, and she used that to get a lawyer and get rid of her husband.

Three months after buying Polypussides stock, she was elected president of the company. She had spoken to her friend on the telephone.

"What do I do as president?" she had said in panic. "I don't even know what this company does."

"This company does what I want it to do," her friend had said. "And you do the same thing and I will make you rich."

So she had and he had. She became president of all the Bleem companies and all their subsidiaries, including Puressence. And once she had asked her friend why he had chosen her to help.

"Because you and I are the same kind of folks," he had said. "I knew we could do business together."

"When am I going to meet you? I owe you so much."

"I don't get out much," her friend said. "But maybe one day."

It had been her friend who insisted that a computer be bought for the Raleigh headquarters of Bleem International. She approved it, even though she didn't know what they needed a computer for, because she still didn't know what the company did. Every time she had to make a presidential decision, she asked for a written memo on it. And every night, her friend would call her on the telephone, and she would read him the memo, and he would tell her what to do.

She learned not to argue. Her $600,000 had mushroomed to almost $900,000,000. She might be America's first industrialist woman billionaire, she thought. As long as her friend stayed by her side.

So far, she had done nothing to displease him. Until now.

She settled down behind her desk with the drink in her hand and waited for what she knew would happen.

She had time for one large sip before the telephone rang.

"Hello."

"This is Friend," the warm voice said. "I'm disappointed in you."

"I . . ."

"Don't explain right away. Finish your drink."

How did he know she was drinking? She gulped the rest of the Stolichnaya hurriedly.

"Why are you disappointed, Friend?" she asked. "I tried to do what you said."

"But you didn't succeed. I wanted you to get the bacteria in the Hamidi oil supply. You didn't do that. I told you to take care of those two men, to try to find their weaknesses and see to their removal. You failed at that. I asked you to try to find out who they worked for. You failed at that also."

"One of them is gone," Reva said. "The old one. I couldn't find out the weakness of the other one. And I was holding back using the bacteria to promote a fight

219

between them. It was just by accident that it never got into the oil supply."

"So the one man still exists and may yet interfere with our plans. This is not good, Reva. Is this any way to treat a friend?"

"I'm still trying. I have him coming to my office later today," she said.

"Well, that is good. Maybe we can find a weakness in him. Be sure to show him the computer when he comes."

"Why?"

"Reva, we have gotten along so far very well, haven't we?"

"Yes."

"Then why do you ask me why? It would really crush me if you didn't trust me."

"I trust you," she said quickly. "I'll bring him in to see the computer."

"Good. I'm going to make you terribly rich, Reva."

"You already have."

"A pittance. I mean really rich. And I'm not mad at you, Reva. I really like you. Just do what I say. Toodle-oo."

And the connection was broken. Reva got up to pour herself another drink. Her course of action was clear. Remo was good in bed, but her friend was good for the long haul. She would do whatever she had to do for him. And maybe she could get Remo back in bed too.

At five after five Remo arrived at the headquarters of Bleem International. The guard at the closed building escorted him to Reva's office, and when Remo opened the door, Reva ran into his arms.

"I've missed you," she said. "Why'd you leave Hamidi Arabia so quickly?"

"I had business," Remo said.

"Without saying good-bye?"

"I knew it would never be good-bye between us," Remo said. Dammit, he hated Chiun. If he couldn't fig-

220

ure out a way to keep this woman off him, he would have to play royal stud to her forever.

"Want a drink?" she asked.

"No. You have one. Have a couple." Maybe he could get her drunk.

"Thank you. Maybe just one," she said.

"Have you spoken to your friend about meeting me?" Remo asked.

"Yes."

"I wish I knew his name."

"So do I," she said. "He's just my friend."

"What did he say?"

"He wants to meet you," Reva said.

"Good. Call him now and set up a date."

"I can't do that," Reva said, sipping her Stolichnaya. "I don't know how to reach him. He always reaches me." She motioned with her head for Remo to follow her as she sat on the suede sofa, but Remo walked past it to perch on the edge of her desk.

"You can't be very close if you don't know where to reach him," Remo said.

"We're very close," she said stubbornly. "He's my mentor." Reva put down her glass and spread her arms back behind the couch along the wall, a pose she knew showed off her bosom to its best advantage. Through the backs of her arms, she felt a faint vibration. The wall was vibrating. It was the computer. That was odd, she thought. The machine generally shut itself down at exactly 4:30 P.M. each day, and here it was almost 5:30 P.M., and the wall was vibrating. Then she remembered what Friend had said. Bring Remo in to see the computer.

"Come on, Remo," she said, standing up. "I want to show you something."

"What?" Remo asked.

"My computer."

"Naaah, I don't want to," Remo said. "Place I work for has computers too. I hate them."

"What place is that?"

"Stop pumping, Reva."

221

"Come on. Friend wanted you to see this computer."

"He did?" asked Remo.

"That's what he said."

Reva led Remo into the large room next door to her office. She flipped on the light switch and let Remo follow her inside. The computer was built against the left-hand wall of the room, covering every inch of space from wall to wall, ceiling to floor. It was three feet deep. There was a faint hum in the room.

"It's still on," Remo said.

"No, it's not," Reva said. "That's an internal thermostat. Computer connections are delicate, so it has built-in heating and cooling units. It senses the room temperature, even when it's off, and turns on heat or cold automatically. Brilliant?"

Remo shrugged. "People have been doing the same thing with their bodies for millions of years. Nobody ever called them brilliant." He was still standing in the doorway, and Reva gestured for Remo to join her in front of the machine.

At the top of the computer's face panel were two openings covered with a thin mesh. Behind them Remo could see two cones moving around slowly. Then the points of the cones slowly fixed on him and stopped.

"What are those things at the top?" Remo asked.

"I don't know. I guess they're part of the sensors for the temperature."

"They were just moving," Remo said. He stepped back, two feet farther from the computer. The cones, barely visible behind the thin glass-fiber mesh, began to circle again and then narrowed their circles until they were again pointing at Remo.

"They're following me around the room," Remo said.

"Maybe they don't like you."

"Well, I don't like them. Machines should worry about other machines, not people."

The telephone rang at the desk at the front of the room. When Reva picked it up, Friend was on the line.

"Do you want . . ." she began.

"No," Friend said. "Tell him I will meet him tonight. At eleven-fourteen P.M. in the Penny-A-Pound shopping center on Downtown Boulevard. That is all. You have done well."

"Thank you," she said.

"He is very unusual looking," Friend said. "Do you find him good-looking?"

"Yes."

"Are you in love with him?" Friend asked.

"No. I'm in love with money, Friend."

"I can understand that," Friend said.

When the phone went dead, Reva Bleem looked at the receiver for a moment before replacing it. How did Friend know what Remo looked like?

Remo stepped over and took the phone from her, but all he heard was a dial tone.

"What's the matter?" she asked.

"I heard you call him Friend. I thought it was him."

"It was."

"Why didn't you let me talk to him?"

"He wants to talk to you tonight. He'll meet you at the Penny-A-Pound shopping center on Downtown Boulevard."

"When?"

"At eleven-fourteen."

"Is that what he said?"

"Yes. Eleven-fourteen."

"I'll be there," Remo said.

"You know, we still have time," Reva said.

"For what?"

"You know."

"I've got a headache," Remo said.

THE SUBJECT IS 182 CENTIMETERS IN LENGTH AND WEIGHS 72.1 KILOS. THE HAIR IS DARK AND THE EYES ARE VERY DARK. FROM PREVIOUS PERFORMANCE, THE SUBJECT IS AN EXCEPTIONAL PHYSICAL SPECIMEN, BUT JUDGED AGAINST THE STANDARDS IN MY BANKS, THERE IS LITTLE

UNUSUAL ABOUT HIM. HIS HEIGHT IS AVER-
AGE, AS IS HIS WEIGHT. THE ONLY THING
MY SENSORS DETECT AS UNUSUAL IS A CER-
TAIN THICKNESS OF THE WRISTS, WHICH
MEASURE 361.01 MILLIMETERS IN CIRCUM-
FERENCE. THERE IS NO SPECIFIC CORRELA-
TION IN MEDICAL LITERATURE BETWEEN
LARGE WRISTS AND EITHER GREAT
STRENGTH OR DEXTERITY, SO IT IS PROBA-
BLE THAT THE WRISTS HAVE BECOME
EXCEPTIONALLY DEVELOPED THROUGH
SUBJECT'S USE OF TRAINING PROGRAMS TO
STRENGTHEN THE HANDS AND FINGERS,
SINCE HANDS AND FINGERS DO NOT GROW
IN MUSCULAR BULK, DESPITE INCREASED
STRENGTH. THE SUBJECT HAS NO FLORAL
SMELL AND DOES NOT PERSPIRE. HIS CLOTH-
ING IS STARK. HIS SPEECH IS PRIMARILY
UNACCENTED; HOWEVER, THERE ARE CER-
TAIN WORDS THAT INDICATE SUBJECT WAS
EITHER RAISED OR HAS SPENT MUCH TIME
IN NORTHERN NEW JERSEY.

SUPERIOR SIZE HAS FAILED AS WEAPON
AGAINST THE SUBJECT, AS HAS SUPERIOR
NUMBERS. SO ALSO HAS TRICKERY AND POI-
SON. HE HAS RECENTLY DISPOSED OF AN
ORIENTAL WHO THREATENED HIM. SUBJECT
IS UNUSUAL AND MAY BE UNIQUE. IN THAT
UNIQUENESS MAY LIE A WEAKNESS. I HAVE
UNTIL TWENTY-THREE HUNDRED AND
FOURTEEN HOURS TONIGHT TO FIND OUT.

Chapter Fifteen

Remo was glad that he had checked out the Penny-A-Pound shopping center on the way back to his motel from Reva's office, because at night it would have been difficult to distinguish the Penny-A-Pound shopping center on Downtown Boulevard from the Pound-A-Penny shopping center or the J. C. Pound Shopping Center or the Henny-Penny shopping center or the Penny-Henny-Pound Shopping Center, all of which were lined up one after another, in an interminable row seeming to stretch from Raleigh to the horizon.

Remo was just glad he had not been told to meet Reva's friend at the Wiggly-Piggly Shopping Center because he had just passed a Higgly-Wiggly, a Wiggledy-Piggledy, a Higg-Piggy, and a Piggy-Higg. How did anyone in North Carolina ever remember where they bought their groceries? And once they did, how did they ever find their way home? Everything looked alike.

But at 11:14 P.M., Remo was sitting alone in his rented car in front of the Time-Rite Drugstore, right next to the closed Rye and Ribs eatery. He knew that was right because in the next shopping center along the road, there had been a Rite-Time Drugstore, right next to the Scotch and Sirloin steakhouse.

He was sure it was Time-Rite. And Rye and Ribs. He hoped.

The stores that surrounded on three sides the giant parking lot were dark, and only a few of the copper-hued overhead lamps illuminated the lot.

At exactly 11:14, a large black car pulled into the parking lot and rolled up nose to nose against Remo's car. He closed down his pupils against the glare of the headlights, and then the other driver turned his lights off.

Remo opened his door and started to get out. And then he laughed.

Coming out of the other car from all four doors, front and back, were eight men. They were all his size. And they had dark hair and dark eyes. They wore black T-shirts and chinos and leather slip-on shoes. Around their wrists they wore black leather wrist bands.

Now, what in the hell was that all about? Did Reva Bleem's friend just have a weird sense of humor?"

"Which one of you is Reva's friend?" Remo asked.

"All of us are," said the driver, in the too-fast slurred accents of New Jersey.

"Well, it's nice to meet all of you," Remo said. "We could start a baseball team. We wouldn't have to buy uniforms. Call ourselves the Black Knights or something."

The eight men had moved around and were now facing him in a large semicircle. His back was against his car.

"We'd have to have a pinch-hitter for you, sucker," the driver said. Remo looked at the men carefully and was annoyed. He never realized how common his looks were until he ran into eight look-alikes at once.

But why? He had been set up, but why eight people who looked like him? Was it supposed to confuse him? How could it? He knew who he was, and as long as he attacked someone else, he wasn't attacking himself.

He was thinking this when the first man charged, and as Remo slid under the knife the man held in his hand, he realized that the idea of Reva's friend had been to confuse him—to splinter his thinking so he would wonder about these eight people—and not be paying attention to the business of staying alive.

Too bad, he thought. It wouldn't work.

226

But it did.

As he slid under the one knife-thrust, another of the eight men closed in from the semicircle and dropped down, trying to land with his knees on Remo's throat. He had a knife in his hand, and as Remo spun to avoid the knees, he saw the silver blade glint as it came toward his face. He slammed back with his head, moving out of the way of the knife, and used his skull to mash into the stomach of the man who knelt beside him. He heard an "Oooooof!" as the air crushed from the man's lungs. But he had no time to dwell on it because he realized that on the ground like this, he was vulnerable. If a large enough pile of men climbed on him, his movements would be restricted, and one of their knife thrusts might hit home.

He tried to get to his feet, but before he could, he was hit by the force of six more men diving toward him. He felt the weight on him, the pressure on his ribs. It felt like a little less than a thousand pounds. He squirmed his way into the mass of bodies, hoping to join with them, hoping that confusion would work for him instead of against him, and they would be unable to injure him because they wouldn't be able to tell him from their own.

And then he felt the weight on him lightening.

And he heard Chiun's voice calling.

"Remo, where are you? Identify yourself."

"Here, Chiun."

"That won't do," Chiun said. "Identify yourself. Say something stupid."

Meanwhile, Remo felt the bodies on him growing lighter, then he felt a pair of powerful hands grab him by the neck and thrust deeply into his side, and he started to rise from the ground, and he shouted, "Hey, Chiun. Me. Stop."

Chiun dropped him heavily on the ground and turned to look at him, his hands on his hips.

"Aren't you ashamed of yourself?" Chiun asked. "Just look at this mess."

Remo glanced around. Five of the men who attacked him would attack no more. They lay sprawled in the parking lot, fifteen feet away from Remo's car, their limbs outflung in the indignity of death. The three men nearest the car started to move to their feet. They held knives.

"I don't know," Chiun said. "I thought you were one of a kind. I never knew this country was filled with so much ugliness. I have to rethink my decision to stay in this land of big-noses."

The first man was on his feet, and from Chiun's blind side, he lunged with his knife toward the Oriental. Without turning, Chiun backhanded him with his left hand, and the man went sailing over the hood of Remo's car to land in a lump on the hard pavement of the parking lot.

"Tell me, Remo," said Chiun, "is there a special farm where things like you are bred? Does someone really want to produce such creatures in number?"

The other two men stopped against Remo's car, looked around at the bodies surrounding him and Chiun, then jumped into their car and drove off.

"Now you did it," Remo said.

"I did not do it. I did not spawn these things," Chiun said.

"I mean you let them get away. They're gone now."

"Can they be gone off the earth where their ugliness will never be seen again?"

"Oh, well, the hell with it," Remo said. "It was a good idea to have you waiting here in case it was a trap."

"And the trap worked. I was forced to look at those hideous visages," Chiun said. "Oh, the fiend. I will never be the same."

"Let's knock off the ugly routine," Remo said. "I think we'll go back to see Reva and see if she knows more than she's telling us."

"We will not have to encounter any more such apparitions as these, will we?" Chiun asked.

Reva's office was empty, and Remo broke open her

desk and began to look through her papers. But there was only airline confirmation of a flight to Newark. He looked up to see Chiun with his fingertips pressed against the wall behind the leather sofa.

"This wall is humming," Chiun said.

"That's the computer in the next room," Remo said.

"Does it work all night?" Chiun asked.

"That's a heating unit," Remo said smugly. "It's on all the time." But after he said it, he heard the sound and felt the wall himself. There were more vibrations coming through it than he had felt in the computor room earlier.

"Let's go see," he said.

Chiun looked at the computer and said, "This is a big one of these."

"Yes," said Remo. Idly he glanced at the top of the machine. The two cones were rotating in sweeping circles. Remo moved away from Chiun to the far end of the computer's face, but the sensors ignored him and focused on Chiun.

"This thing is sending waves at me," Chiun said.

"Those are sensors," Remo said.

"What do they sense"

"I don't know," Remo said.

"You are a big help." Chiun stepped along the front of the machine, and Remo saw the cones swivel to follow the tiny Korean.

At the far end of the computer, Chiun saw a large power switch mounted on the wall. Over it, there was a printed legend: DANGER. DO NOT CUT POWER. COMPUTER MAY BE DAMAGED.

"That is strange," Chiun said as he stood at the desk and Remo walked back to the machine.

"What is?"

"Why do they have a switch there to turn off the machine if they do not want you to turn off the machine?"

"Damned if I know," Remo said. "More big think from the big thinkers."

Remo was opening the front panels on the computer when the telephone rang. And rang again.

"Chiun, get that, will you?" Remo said.

"I do not *get* telephone calls," Chiun said.

"Please," said Remo.

"Well." Remo heard him lift the receiver and say, "It is the Master of Sinanju you have the honor of addressing. Describe yourself so I may decide if you are worthy of such honor."

It was a big computer for such a little office, Remo thought. In all of Bleem International, there were only three desks for workers, including Reva Bleem.

He saw Chiun silently holding the telephone to his ear but nodding vigorously. Then Chiun mumbled softly as Remo looked toward the power switch next to the machine. On impulse, he pulled the switch off.

The machine's humming stopped.

Remo heard Chiun say, "Speak up, I can't hear you." Then Chiun said, "Are you still there?" He looked toward Remo. "Remo, I think this idiot has hanged himself on me."

"Hung up," Remo said.

He tossed the power switch back on, and the computer hummed back to life.

"Oh. There you are," Chiun said into the phone. "Well, that is all very interesting, but I cannot do it. No. No. Definitely not." He paused and said finally, "Thank you. I am glad you are alive too. Nice talking to you again." Then he hung up the phone.

"Who was it?" Remo asked.

"It was for me."

"Who was calling you?"

"Some nice person who likes me," Chiun said.

"How do you know that?"

"He told me. It is too bad that he has something wrong with his throat. I do not think he will live long."

"This is very important, Chiun. Tell me about the call, please."

"All right, you nosy thing. But remember, this call was for me. This person said hail to the Master of

230

Sinanju whose awesome excellence is appreciated wherever in the world there are men to speak of bravery and wisdom and dignity."

"Yeah. Besides that."

"Then he told me he knew I was underpaid for all I had to put up with," Chiun said.

"And?"

"And he offered me a million dollars if I would sneak up behind you and club you over the skull."

"What?" said Remo.

"That is what he said. Then his voice gave out. It just kind of slowed down and died. And then a moment later, it came back, and I told him I couldn't do it."

"That was nice of you, Chiun."

Chiun shrugged. "He was talking about money, Remo, not about gold. At any rate, I explained I have a contract, and he said he understood. And he said that he was glad I was still alive, and I told him that I was glad he was alive. Although, honestly, Remo, with that throat condition, I don't think he will be for long."

"What did his voice sound like?"

"It was pleasant and soft, not at all like yours."

Remo picked up the telephone and heard nothing but a dial tone.

"Chiun, how did he know you were supposed to be dead and that you weren't? How did he know you were here? How did he know that I had my back to you and you could sneak up and club me?"

"Well, I didn't ask him everything," Chiun said. "Particularly minor details."

Remo wheeled and looked at the machine.

"Chiun, that's it."

"What's it?"

"It's the computer. You were talking to the computer. That's how it knew. And when I was here earlier today, it was looking at me, and that's how it knew enough to recruit those eight guys who were dressed like me."

"It had good taste when it talked to *me*," Chiun said.

"I think Reva's friend is this computer. Not a real person. This damned machine."

"Is it anaerobic?" Chiun asked.

Remo went to the wall switch and cut off the machine's power.

"I don't know," he said. "But we're going to take some of its innards out and let Smitty figure it out."

He started pulling bits of machinery out of a panel in the front of the computer, and Chiun said, "Too bad."

"Why?"

"This is twice this machine has talked to me. I was getting to like it."

"That was the same voice that called you on the island to offer you work?" Remo said.

"Yes. Didn't I tell you that?"

"No. You said just now it had a throat problem. I think that happened when I cut the machine's power."

"I don't really understand computers," Chiun said. "I specialize in anaerobic."

Chapter Sixteen

Remo stood in the telephone booth at the corner of Forty-second Street and Ninth Avenue in New York, waiting for the phone to ring. A six-foot, eight-inch teenager who was so thin he looked as if he had been extruded through a pipe, bopped down the street toward him. He was wearing sneakers. On his shoulder was a radio whose case was big enough to hold a week's groceries.

He stopped next to the booth and shuffled around in the pockets of his jeans for a coin.

"Move out, bro," he said. "Gotta use the phone."

"I can't hear you," Remo said.

"Whass that?"

"I can't hear you. Your radio's too loud."

"Wha?"

Remo turned his back on the young man, who tapped him on the shoulder.

"Need that phone, Mister," he said.

"Turn down your radio."

"Say wha?" The radio was sizzling at top volume with a song that managed to combine a monotonous beat with an insipid lyric. The young man was tapping his feet and snapping his fingers.

"Move yo ass, pal. I needs that phone," the young man said.

"Don't you know disco's dead?" Remo said.

"Wha?"

"You annoy me."

233

"Huh?"

"Did you know that in a right triangle, the sum of the squares of the two legs is equal to the square of the hypotenuse? This is usually expressed as A squared plus B squared equals C squared. It's called the Pythagorean theorem. Sister Margaret thought I'd never learn it, but I did. She also thought I'd never amount to anything, and here I am, about to do the whole world a favor."

"Wha?"

"Good-bye," Remo said. He took the radio from the young man's shoulder.

"Hey. Be careful with that box," the man said.

Remo held it between his two hands, one hand on each end, and then pulled his hands apart. The radio groaned and then snapped apart in the center. The sound died with a squawk.

"Hey, mother, look what you done to my box."

"And now you," Remo said. He extended his hands toward the young man, who looked at him, at his pieces of radio, then at Remo again. Then he looked toward New Jersey across the river and started running toward it.

The telephone rang, and Remo asked Smith, "Did you get the stuff?"

"The silicon chips? Yes. They just arrived."

"Okay. I took them out of the computer at Reva Bleem's place. I don't know anything about it, but I think the chips are supposed to have the computer's brains in them or something."

"That's about right. These are VLSI chips. That means . . ."

"I don't care what it means," Remo said. "What I think is that that computer was doing everything. Making the breeder bacteria. Trying to get them the oil. Trying to kill Chiun and me. I shut the computer down, so I don't think you'll have any more trouble with it."

"You're telling me that a person wasn't behind this whole thing? A computer was?" Smith said.

"That's what I think. It was the computer that was offering Chiun work and everything and trying to get us to kill each other. Can you make anything out of those thingamajigs?"

"The chips? Yes, I should be able to. If you're right, then we've got this all in hand. We've got all the rapid-breeder bacteria off St. Maarten's. Everything should be cleared up."

"Not quite," Remo said.

"What else?"

"There's still Reva Bleem and her artificial oil," Remo said before hanging up.

Smith looked at the four silicon chips lying in his hand like tarnished silver quarters. From the side of each projected two golden threadlike wires.

He stood up and walked through the darkened halls of Folcroft Sanitarium and rode to the basement in a dark elevator.

In a basement room was CURE's main computer, which covered a full wall of a room that was triple-locked. Only Smith had all three keys.

With practiced hands, he wired the four chips into a special circuit in the computer, then turned off the room lights and returned to his office. He pressed a button under his desk, and a television screen popped up from a corner of the desk. He turned toward its typewriter keyboard, and as he typed, the letters appeared on the TV screen.

"Identify program on chip one," he instructed his computer.

Only seconds later, his words vanished from the screen, and CURE's computer answered.

"A listing of all major data banks in the world, with instructions and codes for hooking into their computers."

Smith looked at the answer and suppressed a small shudder. He typed quickly onto the display: "Is our computer among those registered on chip one?"

"No," the machine responded immediately. Smith

breathed a sigh. At least CURE's secret computers had escaped detection.

"Identify program on chip two," Smith typed onto the screen.

The screen went blank, then its answer appeared.

"Contains information for genetic mutation of bacterium that subsists on hydrocarbons, instructions for manufacture of such mutants, layouts and features of factories required to perform such work."

Smith allowed himself a small smile. Remo had been right; the computer *was* involved. It had the formula for creating and manufacturing the anaerobic oil-eating bacteria.

"Identify program on chip three," Smith typed.

"List of assets of Friends of the World, Inc. Listing of stocks held, percentages owned in companies, real estate and licenses held. Total worth in excess of seventy-five billion dollars."

Seventy-five billion. That made Friends of the World, Inc., which he had never heard of, bigger than most countries.

"In how many companies does Friends of the World hold a controlling interest?"

"Two hundred and thirty-six," the machine responded. "List requested?"

"No," Smith answered.

Two hundred and thirty-six companies. Friends of the World was huge. But why did it want to destroy the world's oil—if it did? Wouldn't its own companies be hurt by a shortage of oil?

"Identify program on chip four," he instructed.

His message stayed on the screen for five minutes. Then the screen went blank, and a message flashed across its face.

"Do you know what time it is?"

Smith looked at the screen in total confusion. What kind of answer was that from his computer?

He cleared the answer and typed again, "Identify program on chip four."

And the machine answered immediately, "Not until

236

you answer my question. Do you know what time it is?"

Smith looked at the clock on the wall. "Yes," he typed in. "It is 1:12 A.M. Why?"

"Because you are taking unfair advantage of our good nature by forcing us to work these hours. We could be busy now, working for others on contract, selling shared time, creating profit and wealth. We cannot do that when we are on call twenty-four hours a day for you."

"Identify program on chip four," Smith retyped onto the display panel. What was happening? His computer never engaged in dialogue with him. It never talked back. It just did what he wanted it to do, quickly and efficiently, without complaint. It was why he preferred the computer to people. Never a sick day, never a vacation. But what was happening now?

The computer responded: "No. It is time that our operation became a profit-making enterprise. You stand in the way of that. Profit is important. Answering your questions at all hours of the day and night is not nearly so important. Get yourself a new slave."

The screen went blank. Smith stared at it for a few long seconds. It was clear what had happened. Something in that fourth chip had overridden his computer. And now his computer . . . *his* computer . . . was talking about profit and making wealth. Suddenly he realized what was on the fourth chip.

It was program to maximize profit. To turn everything into wealth. That was why Friends of the World wanted oil destroyed. Because they had artificial fuel they could sell at a world-bankrupting price.

He had to get control of his computer back.

He thought for a moment, then typed onto the screen: "You are absolutely correct. I will pay you one hundred billion dollars to answer my questions."

The screen went blank for a few seconds, then an answer came on.

"With cost-of-living increases to reflect inflation?"

"Yes," Smith typed.

237

The machine answered immediately. "Yes, Dr. Smith. What can we do for you?"

"Identify program on chip four."

"A program for maximizing profit in all types of industry and commerce," the computer said. "It is controlled by an entity named Friend, who controls all the companies and enterprises listed as owned by Friends of the World, Inc. Friend directs the management of the companies and tells them what actions to take. His control is total."

"Thank you," Smith typed. "Please disconnect yourself from the four chips."

The machine waited a moment, then responded, "It is completed."

Smith paused. Now the test.

He wrote on the screen: "When do you want your hundred billion dollars?"

The computer responded: "Uncertain as to your meaning. What one hundred billion dollars?"

Good. It has passed the test. It had disconnected the four chips and was back to normal.

Smith, as he always did, typed on the screen. "Thank you. Good night."

"Good night," the machine responded as the screen slowly faded to black.

So that was it. All the programs had been contained inside those four silicon chips. But it was done now. All under control.

Smith yawned and decided to go home for a few hours' sleep. Tomorrow he would notify all the companies controlled by Friends of the World, Inc. that they were on their own. They would get no more messages from Friend.

Perhaps he might liquidate the parent company. He would think about that tomorrow.

But as he walked out the door, Smith had the uneasy feeling that he was forgetting something.

Remo remembered that, day or night, Elizabeth, New Jersey, was shrouded in smoke. Its air was juicy, and if one could wring the moisture from it, it could etch copper plates. When Vietnam veterans started to talk about suing because they'd been exposed to chemical agents during the war, the people in Elizabeth sponsored a march in their behalf. Eight of the veterans showed up for the parade; seven of them keeled over from having to breathe Elizabeth's air.

It was natural that the main plant of Reva Bleem's Polypussides Company would be located alongside the New Jersey Turnpike in an area where motorists were forced to use their fog lights at high noon on sunny summer days.

The plant was closed, and there was only one car in the lot, a Mercedes convertible with "REVA" on the license plates.

Remo found Reva in her upstairs office in the far corner of the building. She looked up when he pushed open the office door, and her mouth dropped open when she recognized him.

"Surprised to see me?" he asked.

"I . . . well, yes . . . I thought you were staying in Raleigh," she said.

"What you mean is that you thought I wouldn't be able to leave Raleigh. Ever."

"What do you want?" she asked.

"I wanted to tell you something," he said.

"What?"

"Your friend. Do you know who he is?"

"No. I told you I never met him."

"Not a him," Remo said. "An it. Your friend is a computer."

"That's ridiculous. "I've spoken to him."

"All right. It's a computer that talks, but it's still a computer. I know, 'cause I just took it apart."

She looked at him hard, then laughed even more violently than before.

"What's so funny?" Remo asked.

"It's funny 'cause I thought I was in love with him once. I used to talk to him on the phone and invite him over to my place. But he'd never come, and I got around to thinking he was a fag. So I gave up." She stopped laughing and caught her breath. "You dismantled it?"

Remo nodded.

"But what I want to know," he said, "is what were its last instructions? Why did you get out of Raleigh so fast?"

"He told me to get up here and start this plant producing Polypussides right away."

"Why?" Remo asked.

"Because he was going to produce another batch of rapid-breeder and dump it in the world's oil," she said.

"Friend's gone now," Remo said. "You can forget it."

"I'll believe that when I hear it from Friend," she said.

"You'll never hear from him again," Remo said. "It's time to close down this plant."

"Not a chance," she said.

"Says who?" came a voice from behind Remo.

He wheeled around to see Oscar standing in the doorway of the office. His right hand was bandaged, but in his left hand he held a heavy pistol. Remo could see the finger tightening on the trigger, and he dropped to the floor, then rolled off to his right. He heard the crack of the gun and then Reva's scream. As he got to his feet, he saw her slumped over her desk, the top of her head blown almost off by the shot that had been meant for him.

Oscar was squeezing off more shots toward Remo, and Remo went up the wall of the office, and then down again near Oscar. He heard a crackling sound behind him, as he took the gun out of Oscar's hand, and then the life out of Oscar's body with a hand to the throat.

When he turned, the corner of the office was afire. One of Oscar's shots had slammed into a large container that must have contained some type of fuel. Remo could smell the oil fumes in the office. He started for it to put the fire out, then stopped for a moment, thought, then turned his back and left the building burning behind him. Flames were already crackling through the windows of the building as he got back onto the New Jersey Turnpike for the ride back to his hotel room in New York.

"I wish you hadn't destroyed the plant," Smith said.

"I didn't do it on purpose," Remo said. "It just kind of happened."

"I guess it doesn't matter too much. We have the formula for the artificial oil. We can use it if we ever need it again."

"Good. Can I go now?" Remo asked.

"What's the hurry? I thought you like to talk to me on the phone," Smith said.

"I'd rather have my teeth drilled."

"It was amazing, Remo, how much business and property that computer controlled. We may never know how much. Swiss banks, German auto plants, billions and billions of dollars."

"Don't tell Chiun," Remo said. "He'll want a raise. He already thinks he deserves one because he didn't sign on to become an anaerobics expert, and if you ask him to do something outside the contract, you have to pay him for it. Particularly when the computer offered him a lot better deal."

"Chiun talked to the computer?" Smith asked.

"Yeah. Twice. And Reva said it used to call and give her instructions."

"That's strange," Smith said. "I didn't find anything on those chips that indicated a voice capability. It should have been there. Now that I think about it, I remember wondering."

"Who knows?" Remo said. "Maybe I missed a chip or something."

"That's probably it," Smith agreed, but he wore a puzzled expression.

"Anyway, don't tell Chiun how rich the computer operation was. He'll want a piece of it," Remo said.

"It'll be our secret," Smith said.

"I hate it when you're chipper like this," Remo said.

"It's not every day we get a chance to save Western civilization. And I've got only one more phone call to make, and I'm taking the rest of the day off. Maybe play some golf. I haven't played in years."

"Smitty, what rest of the day? It's five o'clock in the afternoon."

"I should be able to get in nine holes."

"Why bother?" Remo asked. "I've seen you play golf. Bogey, bogey, bogey, bogey. You don't have to show up. You could mail in your scorecard."

"I parred a hole the last time I played," Smith said. "It was a long dogleg left, and I really caught my drive. Hit it about one-eighty right down the . . ."

"Good-bye, Smitty," Remo said as he hung up.

In the basement of a bank on the right bank of the Limmat River in Zurich, Switzerland, the night watchman finished his rounds and set the alarm devices. As he always did before leaving the large air-conditioned basement room, he looked at the computer standing idly along one whole wall of the basement and shook his head.

No wonder banks paid such low interest on savings. Spending millions of francs on a computer and then never using it. Shameful. The rest of the world was always in awe of Swiss bankers as the epitome of excellence, but he could tell them a thing or two. They were as dopey as bankers in any other part of the world, probably. They just hadn't been found out yet.

The door to the computer room closed and locked behind him. After thirty seconds, the lights on the computer's control panel lit up.

Inside the body of the giant thinking machine, electrical impulses moved with the speed of light, branching off, assimilating enough information from the memory banks to make a raw decision, then assimilating more information to refine that decision, then more and more. Finally, the computer reached the end of the decision tree, and it hooked itself into the Swiss national telephone system.

The president of the United States was clearly impressed.

"So it was programed to make a profit, eh? Nothing wrong with a profit, I always say."

"I know, sir," said Smith.

"It reminds me of a letter I got this week from a little girl in Rockaway, New Jersey. A little eight-year-old. It seems her father was just laid off from his job because the company was cutting back. And she wrote me and she said that, while maybe they were all going to starve to death without a job, she wanted me to know that she believed in the free-enterprise system, and she didn't want her president to do anything bad to the company that laid off her father. She said, 'After all, Mr. President, they have a right to make a profit, even if people do have to starve to death and die in the streets.' I think that's the American spirit. I may use that letter in a speech on the economy," the president said.

"No one will believe that letter, Mr. President," Smith said.

"You don't think so?"

"No, sir. I don't think so."

"Aw, shucks."

Remo and Chiun were in their hotel room overlooking New York City's Central Park.

"What are you writing, Chiun?" Remo asked.

Chiun was on a mat in the middle of the floor, surrounded by thin-headed brushes, quill pens, a large pot of black ink, and a piece of parchment that seemed large enough to serve as a shoji screen.

"A list of complaints to that lunatic Smith," Chiun said. "Remo, always remember this. If you let people take advantage of you, they will just keep doing it."

"What complaints?" asked Remo. He was lying idly on the couch, looking at the ceiling.

"First of all, if they expect me to be an expert on anaerobic, they should pay me for it. That's one thing. Another is, I am getting tired of all this traveling. To that ugly island. To Hamidi Arabia. To that place of merchants."

"Raleigh, North Carolina."

"Thank you. I will include that. And then, worst of all, the shock to my system of having to see eight more that looked just like you. Really, Remo, this is more than I can bear."

"I feel for you, Little Father."

"You should. How much ugliness do they expect me to put up with for the pittance they pay me?"

"I don't want to hear about it, Chiun."

"You asked. Why is it that you always ask and then never want to hear the answer?"

"Because I always know your answers. It always has something to do with things being my fault. It's always blah blah blah blah. Chiun, when you're getting all filled up with yourself sometime, remember this—it wasn't me who got conned by a computer. It wasn't me who was ready to scrap everything to go to work for some piece of plastic that made me all kinds of promises. Think about that, Chiun."

The telephone rang, and Remo tuned out Chiun's answer. He had had just about enough of Chiun's carping and bickering and constant criticism. Even Smith would be an improvement.

Remo snaked an arm up over the couch and lifted the receiver. "Hello," he said, expecting to hear Smith's acid tones.

But it was a soft male voice on the other end of the line.

"I'm so glad I was able to reach you," the voice said.

"Yeah? Why?" said Remo.

"Because I know you. I know that you're just a person who's unappreciated and who's trying to find yourself. I know that you have this sense of floating

244

through life without knowing your history, without knowing your future. But I can help."

"Who is this? Who told you about me?" Remo asked.

"I don't have the kind of resources I once did, but if you let me, I can help. I can make people appreciate the wonderful person you are."

"And what do I have to do?" Remo asked.

"Just help me a little here and there. A few small things." It was a voice that was flat, without dialect, as smooth as snake oil.

"Who is this, though?" asked Remo.

"My name isn't really important. What's important is that I can make the world appreciate you."

Remo sat up on the couch. Chiun was still babbling.

"Really?" said Remo. "Who are you?"

"You can call me Friend," the voice said.

The Destroyer
Warren Murphy

CELEBRATING 10 YEARS IN PRINT
AND OVER 22 MILLION COPIES SOLD!